BLACKSTONE AND THE HEART OF DARKNESS

The new Sam Blackstone adventure

It is a worried letter from Tom Yardley, an old army comrade who once saved his life, that takes Inspector Sam Blackstone to the salt mining village of Marston. But by the time he arrives there, Yardley is already dead – blown to pieces in what was apparently a freak accident. Acting strictly unofficially, Blackstone begins to investigate Yardley's convenient death. It does not take him long to realize that there is true evil lurking in – and under – the village...

BLACKSTONE AND THE HEART OF DARKNESS

Sally Spencer

Severn House Large Print
London & New York

This first large print edition published 2009
in Great Britain and the USA by
SEVERN HOUSE PUBLISHERS LTD of
9-15 High Street, Sutton, Surrey, SM1 1DF.
First world regular print edition published 2007 by
Severn House Publishers Ltd., London and New York.

British Library Cataloguing in Publication Data

Rustage, Alan.
  Blackstone and the heart of darkness.
  1. Blackstone, Sam (Fictitious character)--Fiction.
  2. Police--England--Fiction. 3. Detective and mystery
  stories. 4. Large type books.
  I. Title II. Spencer, Sally.
  823.9'14-dc22

  ISBN-13: 978-0-7278-7814-4

Printed and bound in Great Britain by
MPG Books Ltd, Bodmin, Cornwall.

Prologue

February–August 1900

Emma Walsingholme had been missing for two days when Giles Yarrow, an agricultural labourer, came across the body.

It was a misty, early-August morning, and he was on his way to work. He would say later that it was purely by chance that he glanced into the drainage ditch – and usually add, with a shudder, that he would never stop wishing he hadn't.

The girl was lying on her back, and the first thing Yarrow noticed about her was her face – or rather, the lack of it.

She had been a pretty girl in life, with a slightly upturned nose and well-defined cheekbones. Now – from her hairline to what was left of her chin – there was nothing but a morass of splintered bone and gristle.

Yarrow lowered his eyes from the horror that had once been a face to the throat, which was ringed with dark bruises, almost as if the girl were wearing a black pearl necklace.

He lowered them even further, on to the girl's dress. It was made of a rich velvet, and was a finer piece of clothing than his own children could ever have even dreamed of owning. The

5

police had said it was green, and small patches of that colour still survived, floating like small lonely islands in a dirty brown sea of dried blood.

It was then that he noticed that, although both the girl's shoes and her gloves were clearly in evidence, the hands and feet that had once filled them were not.

Yarrow climbed down the steep embankment, and began to search around close to the body.

'Lookin'' for 'er 'ands – that's what I were doin',' he would later explain to his cronies in the pub. 'Daft thing to do, thinkin' about it now, but at the time it seemed important to find 'em an' give 'em back to the poor little mite.'

But the hands were not there to be found!

And neither were the feet!

The first girl to be butchered in this way had lived in Yorkshire and had disappeared six months earlier. Her name was Sarah Cavendish, and, like Emma Walsingholme, she had been the daughter of a minor local aristocrat. She had vanished somewhere between her family's country estate and the nearest village, where she had been planning to carry out a few basic errands.

Search parties had been organized, but it was not until two days later that her handless, foot-less, faceless and badly lacerated body had been discovered lying in the middle of a copse of trees.

A murder of so sensational a nature had

naturally enough dominated the newspapers for several days.

But though thousands of words were written on the subject, none of those writing them – or none of those who drew the gruesome pictures that accompanied the text – considered for a moment the possibility that this was anything more than a random killing by a local madman.

And then the second girl of good family had disappeared in Derbyshire – a place some fifty miles away from Sarah's murder. And when her body turned up – and was found to be mutilated in exactly the same way – the newspapers lost even the small measure of self-control that they had previously been exhibiting.

A wandering maniac was on the loose, they screamed.

A vicious, heartless killer had set out on a rampage of killing!

And who *knew* when – or where – he would strike next?

The moment that the Prime Minister saw the articles – ringed in red – sitting on his desk, he personally rang up the Metropolitan Commissioner of Police at Scotland Yard.

'But it's not the Yard's policy to investigate provincial murders, sir,' the Commissioner pointed out.

'And it's not *my* policy to stand by and do nothing while the children of England's ruling class are slaughtered like game birds in season,' the Prime Minister replied tartly.

'Of course not, sir,' the Commissioner of

Police agreed hastily. 'But we still have to consider—'

'I want your best man on the case,' the Prime Minister interrupted.

'Perhaps if you discussed the matter with the Home Secretary, sir, he might be able to explain to you the—'

'The best officer you have – and I want him on it *now*. Is that clearly understood?'

'Yes, sir,' the Commissioner said. 'It's clearly understood.'

The man entrusted with the task of tracking down the fiend behind the killings was Superintendent Ernest Bullock, a sound officer with a great deal of experience and a strong record of convictions. He arrived in Derbyshire reasonably confident that he would have the case safely sewn up within a few days. Two weeks later – after working round the clock, and still having failed to come up with a single significant lead – that confidence had taken something of a battering.

And then a third girl's body was found.

... And a fourth.

... And a fifth.

Emma Walsingholme was the ninth girl to have suffered the same grisly fate, and had Superintendent Bullock not been stricken with a severe case of influenza, this would have been the eighth murder he had fruitlessly attempted to solve. But the flu was undoubtedly what he had, and so it fell to others to pick up the burden.

Saturday–Monday: Lost Weekend

The sun was already setting when the two men who had inherited the Emma Walsingholme case from the indisposed Superintendent Bullock climbed out of the pony cart and walked over to the ditch where the girl's body had been discovered.

The first of the men – the elder – was in his middle thirties, nearly six feet tall and without an excess ounce of fat on his spare frame. He had penetrating green eyes, a large nose that was almost a hook, a wide mouth and a square jaw.

The other man was younger, shorter and fatter. In a few years he would no doubt come to be regarded as avuncular, but at that moment he merely looked a little overweight.

The taller man – Inspector Sam Blackstone – surveyed the miles of flat, open countryside that surrounded the ditch.

'Looking around me, I don't see a lot of potential witnesses to the crime, Archie,' he said.

'Neither do I, but someone's bound to have seen something – even in a place like this,' Sergeant Archie Patterson replied, optimistically.

'You think so, do you?' Blackstone asked. 'You'd have thought there'd have been witnesses to Jack the Ripper's murders, too, considering they all took place in the heart of

11

London. But there weren't. And if it was that easy for Jack to go undetected, it must have been a bloody doddle for this bastard.'

'At least there's a pattern,' said Patterson, who was not willing to abandon his usual cheerfulness quite yet.

'Oh, there's a pattern, all right,' Blackstone said dourly. 'In fact, there are two or three patterns, when you come to think about it. The problem is that none of them make any sense, do they?'

'No, I suppose they don't,' Patterson agreed, reluctantly.

'Why would the killer have mutilated the girls in the way that he did?' Blackstone asked.

'Some men get pleasure from inflicting pain on women.'

'True. But they like the women to be conscious enough to really *appreciate* the pain – to *scream* with the pain. That's why the whip's the preferred instrument for inflicting that kind of damage. But cutting off the hands and feet is as likely as not to send the victim into deep shock and unconsciousness. It's too *crude* a torture for a man who enjoys seeing his victims suffering. And why take the hands and feet away with him?'

'Maybe he wanted to keep them as a memento.'

'Surely *one* hand or *one* foot would have served that purpose.'

'More than served it,' Patterson said, and though it was still quite warm, he shuddered.

'Then there are the deep lacerations to the body. The dress was soaked in blood, but the material wasn't damaged, which means that the killer took the girl's dress off before he slashed her. Now, I can see why he might have decided he wanted to do that.'

'You *can*, sir?'

'Certainly. He'd have wanted to see the wounds opening up as he was inflicting them. But why go to the trouble of putting the dress back on when he was finished?'

'I don't know,' Patterson admitted. 'I can't even begin to understand what must have gone through his mind.'

'And why are all his victims from wealthy families? If there was a ransom demand, that would make sense – even if he *did* then kill the girls for his own twisted pleasure after the ransom had been paid. But there's *been* no such demand, so why is he focusing on the rich?'

'Maybe when we catch him...'

'We won't catch him,' Blackstone said dismissively. 'I know Superintendent Ernie Bullock. He's a bloody good copper, by any standards...'

'Even so...'

'...and if he's come up with nothing from the previous *seven* murders, we've absolutely no chance of coming up with anything on this *one*.'

'But we'll try,' Patterson said.

'Of course we'll try,' Blackstone confirmed. 'We'll bust our guts on it – just as Ernie Bullock has been doing – but it won't do us any bloody good.'

* * *

It was on the Monday morning following the discovery of Emma Walsingholme's body that the Honourable Jack Hobsbourne, MP, made the decision to use the series of murders as a convenient peg on which to hang a cause very close to his own heart. And it was in the Monday afternoon session of the House of Commons that he caught the Speaker's eye and was given the opportunity to do just that.

There were the inevitable loud groans from the government benches when Hobsbourne stood up to speak – and even a few, more muted ones, from his own side of the House.

It was not his comparative youth that engendered such hostility whenever he chose to make a speech, though that clearly was to be held against him to some degree. It was not even the fact that he was a radical – although many of the more established members believed that any sentence containing the word 'radical' should also include the phrase 'given a sound whipping'. What raised most hostility was that Hobsbourne was clearly – and worse, *unapologetically* – from a working-class background, and thus had no place in the hallowed halls of government at all.

'We live in an unequal and unjust society, Mr Speaker,' Hobsbourne said, 'and if proof of that is needed, we have only to examine recent events. Look what happens when a girl from a stuck-up country family is found murdered. The police are immediately mobilized, and Superintendent Bullock – one of Scotland Yard's most experienced and senior officers – is dispatched with haste to investigate that murder.'

'Shame on you!' bayed a back-bench member opposite. 'Have you no pity for the poor child who died?'

'Indeed I do have pity for her,' Hobsbourne countered. 'But my pity is not solely reserved for young women born into privilege – young women who have never shivered in the cold of winter, nor wondered where their next meal is coming from. My pity is wide enough to include those without the rich and influential parents who are able to see that justice is done by them. My pity also encompasses the weak and the powerless.'

'Oh God, he's about to mount his hobby horse,' said one of the government front bench wearily to his colleague next to him, and though he spoke in a whisper – as was normal on such occasions – it was a *stage* whisper that half the House could hear.

'The Right Honourable Gentleman opposite is quite correct in his assumption that I am about to address – yet again – the subject of child prostitution,' Hobsbourne agreed angrily. 'But if I were a mere rider of hobby horses, I would sit on his side of the House, where "special" interest is the *only* interest.'

There were cries of 'Shame!' and 'Withdraw,' but Jack Hobsbourne chose to ignore them.

'What I'm talking about here is a matter of both vital moral importance and national dis-

15

grace,' the radical MP continued. 'Girls as young as ten or eleven are being bought – or kidnapped – on our streets, even as we speak. But this so-called government does nothing about it. And why? Because these young girls, drawn from the poorer levels of society, don't matter to it. Well, they matter to me! And they matter to my electors! And if this government won't take action, then it's time we voted in a government that will!'

The Home Secretary had been listening to the speech with a sense of growing disquiet, and now he made a mental note to have a word with his parliamentary secretary the moment he left the chamber. There was no doubt in his mind that Hobsbourne was right about the extent of child prostitution on the streets of London, but he really wished the brash young MP would not make such an issue out of it. Still, since an issue *had* been made, he supposed he would have to take some kind of action. A couple of arrests would probably be all it would take to pacify the bloody man for the moment, he decided, and he was sure the Metropolitan Police could arrange for that to happen without rocking the boat too much.

Superintendent Bullock arrived in Staffordshire on Monday afternoon, shortly after Hobsbourne had finished his speech in the House of Commons, and made his way immediately to the police station that Blackstone and Patterson had been using as their base.

He looked rough, Blackstone thought. 'You should have stayed in bed, sir,' he said sympathetically.

Bullock coughed violently. 'You're spot on, Sam; that's *exactly* where I should be,' he agreed. 'But I couldn't just lie there, not while this madman was still running around. Besides, Sir Humphrey Todd called me, and said my immediate presence was required here.'

'I thought he was on a fishing holiday, somewhere in Scotland,' Blackstone said.

'So he is. But when he read in the newspapers that you'd been assigned to the case, he ... well, he...'

'Hit the roof?' Blackstone supplied.

'Not to put too fine a point on it, yes,' Bullock agreed.

That the Assistant Commissioner had reacted in such a way was hardly surprising, Blackstone thought. The two of them had had a stormy relationship, and it was well known at the Yard that one of Sir Humphrey's greatest ambitions was to see Blackstone kicked off the force.

'And it ... er ... doesn't end there,' Bullock continued awkwardly. 'Not only does Todd not want you to be in charge of this investigation, he doesn't even want you anywhere near it. So while I personally would be more than happy to have you working with me, I've not really been given any choice in the matter.'

Blackstone nodded. 'I quite understand the position you find yourself in, sir. I'll go and pack my bag.'

'You're taking this very well,' Bullock said, slightly suspiciously.

'Orders are orders,' Blackstone said flatly.

'And you've always been one to ignore them when they didn't suit you,' Bullock replied. 'I know you of old, Sam, and once you've got your teeth into a case, it'd take a team of wild horses to drag you away from it. So why don't you tell me what's really going on in that head of yours?'

Blackstone reached into his jacket pocket and fingered the rough envelope it contained.

'The truth is, sir, that walking away from this investigation is going to be one of the hardest things I've ever done.'

'But ...?'

'But there's a pressing personal matter that I need to deal with.'

Bullock raised a quizzical eyebrow. 'And what might this "pressing personal matter" concern?'

'This morning I got a letter from an old army comrade who's a salt miner now. He's in trouble, and he's asked for my help. So I intend to take a leave of absence and do what I can for him.'

Bullock grew thoughtful. 'Since you seem willing to drop everything and rush to his side, he must be a very good friend indeed,' he said.

'I said he was an old *comrade*, not an old *friend*,' Blackstone pointed out. 'I was a sergeant and he was a private. He had his pals, and I had mine.'

'Ah, so if it's not a question of friendship, you

18

must feel indebted to the man,' Bullock guessed. 'Is that what it is – a debt of honour?'

'More or less,' Blackstone agreed.

Bullock nodded. 'Then you have as little choice over going as I had over keeping you. But before you leave, I'd appreciate it if you'd brief me on the progress you've made.'

Blackstone sighed. 'We've made no progress at all, sir. There are a few things we *know* – like the fact that the killer's not a local man...'

'*Do* we know he's not a local man?'

'I think so, sir. He's killed in four counties. It's possible that he might be based in one of them – though that's unlikely, since he seems too careful to go shitting on his own doorstep – but he can't be local *everywhere* he strikes, and so there's no reason to assume he's local here.' Blackstone paused for a moment. 'You must surely have worked all this out for yourself, sir.'

'I have,' Bullock agreed. 'I was checking to see if you were thinking along the same lines. Carry on.'

'He's not a local man,' Blackstone continued, 'so you'd have thought that in a rural area like this, someone would have spotted him. But the Staffordshire police have questioned hundreds of people – and not one of them has reported seeing any strangers around at the time the girl disappeared.'

Bullock put his hands to his head. 'It's a bloody nightmare,' he groaned. 'It's as if the man was invisible. Every killing is a carbon copy of the ones that preceded it, and no killing moves us any closer to catching the murderer. I'm never going to collar this bastard, Sam. He's going to kill again and again and again – and there's absolutely nothing I can do about it.'

'You might think of bringing in Ellie Carr,' Blackstone suggested, tentatively.

'Who?'

'Ellie Carr. She's a doctor, and she works at University College Hospital, London. She specializes in forensic pathology.'

'Forensic pathology?' Superintendent Bullock repeated, saying the words carefully, as if they came from an alien tongue. 'What – in God's name – is that, Sam?'

'It's a way of applying science in criminal investigations,' Blackstone explained.

'Then why haven't I heard about it?'

'Because it's a very *new* science – so new that a lot of people don't believe it's a true science at all.'

'Then if it's—'

'But true science or not, I've seen it produce some remarkable results.'

'For example?' Bullock asked, unconvinced.

'Coppers like us can often learn something from looking at corpses – but nothing like as much as Ellie can. She's helped me solve two cases that I'd never have cracked if I'd been working alone.'

Bullock smiled. 'You keep calling her "Ellie",' he said. 'She's not your bit of tottie, is she?'

'No, sir,' Blackstone said – though there'd been a time when he'd hoped she might be. 'But

20

even if she was, it wouldn't alter the facts. Ellie's bloody good at what she does – and one day they'll be writing books about her.'

'They'll be writing books about me, if I don't solve this case,' Bullock said, dispiritedly. '"Superintendent Ernie Bullock – The Man Who Failed to Catch The Northern Slasher".' He paused for a moment. 'All right, if you're prepared to vouch for her, then I suppose I could send her a telegram.'

'I'm not promising she'll definitely get you a result,' Blackstone said cautiously.

'Of course you're not,' Bullock replied. 'How could you? But after all, what do I stand to lose? Even if she turns out to be no more use than a broken umbrella in a thunderstorm, she can't do any harm to an investigation that's already in the doldrums.'

Blackstone ran his fingernail along the edge of the cheap envelope in his pocket again. It almost seemed to him to be vibrating with its writer's urgency and desperation.

'If there's nothing more I can do here, sir, I'd like to go and book my ticket for the early-morning train to Cheshire now,' he said.

'Go ahead,' Bullock replied, waving his hand in a gesture of abstracted dismissal.

It was only when Blackstone had reached the door that the Superintendent recalled himself enough to say, 'Good luck with whatever it is you have to deal with, Sam.'

'Thank you, sir,' Blackstone said, over his shoulder.

And good luck was just what he was going to need, he thought. Because a man like Tom Yardley would never have thought of asking for help unless the situation he found himself facing had turned very nasty indeed.

Tuesday: Dead on Arrival

One

As the train began to slow for its approach to the station, Blackstone took the letter out of his pocket and re-read it for perhaps the twelfth or thirteenth time.

Dear Sergeant Blackstone (or perhaps I may be permitted to call you Sam), the letter began.

That sounded just like the old Tom Yardley, Blackstone told himself. The man was modest to the point of diffidence, but in a tight situation there was no one better to have covering your back.

Through the newspapers, I have been following your career with interest. You seem to have done very well for yourself.

Possibly I have, Blackstone conceded. But only as long as you're willing to believe that owning two good second-hand suits, a few books – and very little else – was doing well.

In fact, you are quickly becoming one of the most famous men our regiment has ever produced.

There was no need to butter me up like that, old chap, Blackstone told the writer mentally. I'm in your debt already – and I always will be.

There is something very unpleasant happening

25

in Marston, the village where I live. I don't want to say too much about it in a letter, but I'm sure you remember Fuzzy Dustman, and will quite understand what I mean when I tell you he would have felt quite at home here.

Blackstone nodded to himself. Yes, he *did* remember Faisal Dostam – or Fuzzy Dustman, as the enlisted men had called him. In the days when he and Tom Yardley had soldiered under General Roberts, Dostam had been responsible for running the biggest criminal network in Afghanistan. He had had his finger in a great many pies, but the most important one – the one that made him rich – had involved the smuggling of precious stones.

You're probably wondering why I don't go to the local police, instead of writing to you, the letter continued. *Well, the simple fact is that there's so much money involved that they've probably been bought off, and once they know that I know what's going on, my life won't be worth a brass farthing. But for the sake of everything you and I believe in, something <u>has to be done</u>, Sam. With you by my side, I know we can beat them, but if you can't come, then I don't see I have any choice but to take the risk and go it alone. Please reply with all haste, old comrade. Your obedient servant, Tom Yardley*

It must have been hard for a proud man like Tom to have written that letter, Blackstone thought. It must have taken almost as much courage as he had shown in the cave back in Afghanistan. And never once in the letter had he

26

mentioned the debt he was owed – never once resorted to the sort of emotional blackmail that most men in his position would have drawn on.

It was an honest letter – an honourable letter – which asked an old comrade to do no more than guard his back. And that was just what Blackstone intended to do.

Archie Patterson stood in an unfamiliar office in Scotland Yard, looking across a desk at Inspector Maddox, whom he didn't know – except by reputation – and was already deciding that he didn't quite like.

'You might do yourself a bit of good on this new case that we've been handed,' Maddox told him.

'Might I, sir?' Patterson asked. 'What does it involve?'

'Prostitution,' Maddox said, with some relish.

'But that's not illegal.'

'Not in most cases, no. Tell me, Sergeant, have you ever heard of a Member of Parliament called Jack Hobsbourne?'

Sam Blackstone would never even have bothered to ask him that question, Patterson thought. What Blackstone *would* actually have said was something like, 'Tell me all you can about Jack Hobsbourne, MP, Archie. And don't hold back on any of the juicy titbits.' Because Sam knew that his sergeant had an almost encyclopedic knowledge of people – both famous and obscure – and would have taken the opportunity to draw on it.

'Well?' Maddox asked impatiently.

'Yes, I have heard of him,' Patterson began. 'As a matter of fact, Jack Hobsbourne's a...' He saw a look of displeasure starting to fill Maddox's face, and he abruptly shut up.

He had the man's measure now, he thought. This inspector didn't *want* him to know things. *This* inspector – with his cardboard files stacked neatly on his desk in front of him – liked to be regarded as the fount of all wisdom.

'Jack Hobsbourne's a what?' Maddox asked.

'I don't know,' Patterson confessed. 'I thought I'd heard of him, but it turns out that I haven't.'

Maddox looked a lot happier now. 'Then it's a good thing that I *do* know something,' he said. 'It turns out that Hobsbourne is not Church of England, as any decent man would normally be. Oh no, the established church isn't good enough for Master Jack, and he's decided to be a Quaker instead.'

'A Methodist,' Patterson corrected him silently. 'The man's a strict Methodist.'

'And this Quakerism,' Maddox continued, making the word sound even more like an insult, 'has given him some rather strange ideas. Now normally, that wouldn't matter – he's only one out of hundreds of MPs, and half of them are deranged, anyway.' He paused, and a look of panic came to his face. 'You're not to quote me on that.'

'I won't,' Patterson promised.

'At any rate, for some strange reason, what this Hobsbourne chooses to say and do seems to

28

worry the Home Secretary.'

Well, of course it does, Patterson thought. Every time he gives an open air speech, thousands of ordinary people flock to hear it.

'And so if Hobsbourne happens to have a bee in his bonnet, it starts to acquire significance,' Maddox continued. 'And his particular "bee" at the moment is the "so-called" age of consent. What do you know about *that*, Sergeant?'

'Very little, sir,' Patterson said wisely.

'Then I'll instruct you in that, as well. When the Queen came to the throne, in 1837, the age at which a girl could consent to have sexual relations with a man was twelve, which, I must admit, seems like a pretty sensible age to me.'

You wouldn't think that if it was your sister or your own daughter you were talking about, Patterson thought.

'But throughout the Queen's reign there have been no end of do-gooders whining that twelve was too young for a girl to make that kind of decision,' Maddox continued, 'and about fifteen years ago Parliament gave in to the baying of the self-righteous rabble, and set the age of consent at sixteen. Now, as you can well understand, this made life very difficult for brothels that cater for clients who have a preference for very young girls.'

'Yes, it must have done,' Patterson agreed, deadpan.

'By and large, it's been the policy of the Metropolitan Police to look the other way when that particular law's been broken,' Maddox said.

'And quite right, too, in my personal opinion. Strict enforcement does no more than punish the girls themselves.'

'I beg your pardon, sir?' Patterson said.

Maddox looked at him as if he were an idiot. 'A pretty girl from the slums can earn twenty-five pounds for surrendering her virginity, which is three or four times what a housemaid can earn in a whole year,' he explained. 'So doesn't it seem right that she should be allowed to dispose of whatever assets she has, in whatever way she chooses?'

'Always assuming that she's willing to,' Patterson said.

'And why *shouldn't* she be willing to? The lower orders attach far less value to virtue than we at the higher levels of society do.'

'I didn't know that.'

Maddox frowned. 'Then you are a very poor student of human nature,' he said censoriously. 'In matters of morality, the lower orders are rather like the beasts of the fields.'

'But having disposed of her "asset", she doesn't get her fair payment, does she?' Patterson asked.

'Well...'

'It's the brothel-keeper who takes the bulk of it, and all she's left with is a few shillings.'

'Which it would take her quite a while to earn in any other line of business,' Maddox said, treating the collapse of the central pillar of his argument on assets and rewards as if it were still standing as solid as ever. 'But that's neither here nor there, from the point of view of this discussion. The simple fact of the matter is that the Home Secretary has asked us to investigate what our Quaker friend chooses to call – for some strange reason of his own – "child prostitution". And whatever our personal feelings, it certainly won't damage our prospects of promotion if we come up with the result he desires.'

I wish Sam Blackstone was back, Patterson thought. I wish he was the one I was working on this case with.

Two

The route from Northwich railway station to the village of Marston lay along a raised road between two stretches of water which could have been regarded either as very large ponds or very small lakes.

The road itself seemed to be mainly constructed of ash and clinker, and crunched under Blackstone's boot with every step he took, yet the porter at the railway station had assured him this was the *main* road.

It was a strange landscape he found himself walking through, the Inspector thought.

He was used to seeing manufactories – London had thousands and thousands of them – but

31

in the capital they tended to be well dispersed, so that, for example, there was a leather-curing factory and a bottling plant on Lant Street, Southwark, but there were also rows of terraced houses where the less prosperous workers lived.

Here there was a concentration of industry that was quite new to him, for on the fringes of the small lakes or large ponds (which he would soon learn to call 'flashes') were a number of small salt-extraction works and salt mines, their winding sheds standing starkly and skeletally against the grey sky, their squat brick chimneys belching out clouds of thick black smoke.

It must have been a shock for Tom Yardley to return to this industrial hell-hole after breathing the pure fresh air of Afghanistan, Blackstone thought. But there were compensations to returning home, too. At least here, he could be assured that half the male population were not wild-eyed tribesmen who would attempt to kill him on an almost daily basis.

He walked on, and discovered that merely thinking the word 'Afghanistan' had been enough to turn his mind back to the past – that he was becoming wrapped up once more in the time when he had been *Sergeant* Blackstone and Tom had been *Private* Yardley.

The cave is a dark gaping mouth in the face of the mountain. It is just the sort of place the Pathan warriors would chose to retreat to once they had finished harassing General Robert's column, but there is absolutely no way of telling if there are any of them inside it now.

'Are we going inside, Sarge?' Corporal Jones asks.

Perhaps there are no Pathans hiding in the cave at all, Blackstone thinks. Or perhaps there are only one or two. But there is also the possibility that there are a dozen or more – and he has only three men under his command.

He weighs his options. He has a responsibility to his own men, but he also has a responsibility to the rest of the column, which has been taking heavy losses as a result of the Afghans' hit-and-run tactics.

'Why don't you take out that gold watch of yours, Sarge?' Jones suggests, with a grin on his face.

'Why should I do that?' Blackstone wonders. 'I've only to look at the sun to see what time it is.'

Jones's grin widens. 'That's true enough, I suppose. But you always look at your watch when you've got a difficult decision to make.'

Blackstone returns the grin, acknowledging that though he himself has never noticed it before, what Jones has just said is perfectly true.

He takes the watch out of his pocket, and suddenly understands why he always does this at times of danger. It is not for his own benefit, but for that of his men. They admire this watch, which likely cost as much as they would be paid for half a lifetime's work. And more than that, they have come to regard it as a good luck charm. It is almost as if they have persuaded

33

themselves to believe that anyone who owns such a watch could never come to real harm himself – or bring harm down on the heads of those who follow him.

'You never did tell us where you got that watch from, Sarge,' Private Wicker says.

'No, I didn't, did I?' Blackstone agrees.

Nor will he ever tell them. The truth is that the watch was presented to him by General Roberts himself, as a reward for saving the general's life. But the men must never know that Roberts' life ever hung in the balance, because if the watch is a magic charm *for these particular men, then General Roberts is* the magic charm *for the whole army.*

Blackstone puts the watch back in his pocket.

'We're going in,' he says. 'I'll lead. Jones, you'll follow me. Wicker and Yardley will bring up the rear.'

He had taken a few steps inside, then paused to let his eyes adjust to the darkness. He could see right through to the very back of the cave, but noted that there was a narrow passageway leading off it at an angle.

Retreating at that point would have been easy, enacting the same manoeuvre once he was in the passage, much more difficult. If he had had some of his old comrades with him, he would have gone in without hesitation, but his old comrades were now all dead, and he was leading a group of men who had very little experience of battle.

34

A picture came into his mind of a small Hindu woman who had been one of the camp-followers – and who he himself had discovered just after dawn, strangled and with her dead baby lying by her side.

He signalled to his men to move forward.

The passage is even narrower than he had thought it would be, but he can see a further cavern – an illuminated cavern – at the end of it. Speed will be of the essence, he tells himself. Catch the bastards unawares, and they'll be dead before they even know what's happening.

He treads as softly as he can, all the while thinking of what tactic to employ. He must enter the second cavern, he decides – expose himself to whoever is there. It is a dangerous move, but there is really no choice, because his men cannot deploy themselves while he is blocking the entrance.

He can hear the Afghans talking now. He does not understand a word of what they're saying, but he can tell from the easy tone of their exchange that they are relaxed and unsuspecting.

Now, years later, walking along a cinder road and looking at the smoking chimneys, he found himself still wondering if he had made a mistake that day at the caves. But he also recognized that there was no clear answer to that question. Soldiers take risks. It's their job – what they've signed up to do. And if they lose their lives because of it, they can have no complaint.

He takes a deep breath and thrusts himself into the second cave. By the light of the oil lamp, he can see that there are five Pathans there, sitting cross-legged around a samovar, making tea. He aims his rifle and shoots one of them in the chest. The others start to rise immediately, but he calculates that he can bayonet at least one of them before they are in any position to fight back. Then he feels a crushing blow to the side of his head, and realizes that there were not five Afghans there at all – but six.

'Not five, but six,' Blackstone repeated to himself, as he walked along the cinder track.

He was still not sure whether it had been an ambush – whether they had been willing to sacrifice one of their own men to lure him in. Or whether the sixth man had simply been completing some task at the other end of the cavern. But whatever it had been, it had put him out of action.

He feels as if his head is lying on an anvil, and the blacksmith is attempting to fashion it into a horseshoe. Though the pain is mostly above the neck, it hurts his whole body to move. But he moves anyway, first getting into a crouch and then forcing himself painfully to his feet.

The cavern has become a charnel-house while he has been unconscious, with blood staining both the floor and the walls.

He counts the bodies: seven.

Corporal Jones has half his face missing, and

36

is undoubtedly dead. Private Wicker has had his throat slashed. But the other dead men are all Pathans.

He hears footfalls in the passageway, and gropes for his rifle. The noise alerts whoever is approaching, and a voice calls out, 'Who's there?'

'It's me,' he croaks.

Yardley enters the chamber. His uniform is soaked with blood, and his face is as grim as death.

'What happened?' Blackstone asks.

Yardley shrugs, as if he's not entirely sure himself.

'After you went down, they shot Corporal Jones,' he says, in a dull, exhausted voice. 'Wicker managed to get two of them, before he got his throat slashed. I finished off the other three. I don't quite know how I did it.'

'There were six of them, but there's only five here!' Blackstone says urgently.

Yardley nods. 'The other one ran. I was worried he might have some other mates nearby, so I followed him. I caught up with him just outside the cave.'

'He's dead?'

'Yes.'

'You're sure of that?'

'I blew a bloody big hole in his chest, so he'd better be dead.'

'We'd better check anyway,' Blackstone says.

He makes his way down the dark passage, into the first cave, and then out into the blinding

*light of an Afghan August afternoon. The Path-
an is lying on the ground, and Yardley had been
right – there is a* bloody *big hole in his chest.*

*'He was out here waiting for me when I came
out of the cave,' Tom Yardley says. 'He got off
the first shot, and I'd have been dead myself if
his rifle hadn't jammed.'*

'You're a real hero,' Blackstone says.

*Yardley looks uncomfortable. 'I only did what
anybody else would have done in my place,' he
says.*

'You saved my life.'

*'I didn't do it for you, Sarge,' Yardley says, his
discomfort increasing by the second.*

'No?'

'No. I didn't even think *about you. As far as I
was concerned, it was kill or be killed.'*

*Blackstone shakes his head – gently, because
it's still hurting.*

*'You could always have cut and run,' he says.
'In your place, there's many a man who would
have done.'*

*Tom Yardley grins. 'Didn't think of that. If I
had, maybe that's just what I* would *have done,'
he says.*

*Blackstone places his hand on the other man's
shoulder. 'Have the courage to admit to your
own bravery,' he says. 'I'm in your debt, Private
Yardley, and I promise you I won't forget it.'*

And the fact that he was there, on a cinder track
in Cheshire, was ample proof that he *hadn't*
forgotten.

Three

Blackstone reached the end of the cinder road, and saw the village of Marston spread out in front of him. Not that *spread* was quite the right word to apply to a hamlet that consisted of one main street, with a couple of truncated side streets running off it, he thought.

It was an ugly village, made up largely of squat terraced houses that looked quite bowed down under the weight of their heavy grey slate roofs.

It was an uncared-for village, with no gardens or fountains, no village green or duck pond – no evidence at all of civic pride.

But then, what had he expected to find? The village would have been built on the instructions of the same men who had sunk the gaping mines and constructed the disfiguring salt works, so had it ever been likely that the dwellings they created for their workers would be 'little palaces'?

A group of people – both men *and* women – were gathered at the closer end of the main street, clustered around some sort of cart. At first, Blackstone had no idea what they were doing, but as he drew nearer he saw the long, plain, wooden box resting on the back of the cart.

So it was a funeral.

He would have spotted that fact earlier if he'd been back in London. But then, if he'd been back in London, the funeral wouldn't have been like this at all. In the capital, even the poorest of the poor costermongers would not have wished to be seen dead at a funeral like this one!

The costermonger would have wanted – would have *expected* – a polished hardwood coffin with heavy brass handles. And that coffin would have been conveyed to the churchyard in a hearse pulled by four jet-black geldings.

The costermonger would have wanted it, and the costermonger would have got it – because his whole family, who had not had the money for medicines to keep him alive, would have plunged themselves deep into debt to some back-street moneylender in order to stage the appropriate funeral!

In contrast, here – in this world, which Blackstone was starting to find as alien to his experience as the dusty hills of Afghanistan – the coffin rested on the back of what was (for all that the floral tributes tried to disguise the fact) a simple farm cart. And the horses that would pull that cart to the churchyard were no shining and high-spirited geldings, but dull brown carthorses – surefooted but uninspiring – which would be back ploughing the fields before the soil had even settled on the grave.

The mourners, too, failed to live up to the

40

London example. Every man attending an East End funeral would first have paid a visit to his 'uncle' – the local pawnbroker – where he would have paid over a few pence to get his black mourning suit out of hock. And though, as soon as the funeral was over, the suit would go back on the pawnbroker's shelf, it would – for an hour or so – be getting an airing, as its owner wore it as a mark of respect.

No such effort had been made by the villagers of Marston. The men looked suitably respectful and solemn, but they were wearing their working clothes, and the only sign they were attending a funeral at all was the black bands wrapped around their forearms.

Blackstone, now twenty yards from the procession, came to a halt. He was not a part of this community, he told himself and, because of that, he had no right to intrude on its private grief.

The procession began to move slowly up the street, between houses in which all the blinds were tightly drawn. When it passed each house, it grew longer, as people joined it from their own doorways.

Blackstone lit up a cigarette. There was no point in going to Tom Yardley's home now, he thought, because there was no doubt that Tom himself would be part of the funeral cortège. There wasn't much chance of getting a drink, either – and he could really have used one after his longish walk in the hot sun – since the pub would probably be closed until the funeral was over.

So, all-in-all, he supposed he could use the time to get to know the village, the fate of which Yardley seemed so concerned about.

The naked man was lying on a stone slab in one of the laboratories of the University College Hospital. When alive, he had been seriously overweight, and perhaps that had worried him occasionally. Now, nothing concerned him, not even the deep incision that had been made in his chest, nor the pair of hands rooting around in the blubber.

There were two living people in the room, standing at opposite sides of the slab like bookends – though, if that had been what they actually were, they would have been considered a very ill-matched pair.

The woman was still on the comforting side of thirty. She was of medium height, and though her frame was wiry, she had a pleasantly rounded bosom. Her light brown hair would have cascaded over her shoulders, had she chosen to let it down, but at that moment it was constrained in a tight bun at the back of her head. There was evidence of laughter lines around her eyes and her mouth, but her firm jaw indicated that when she wanted to look serious, she could seem very serious indeed.

The man was older, taller and much stockier. His hair was cut short and, though still thick, was rapidly turning grey. He looked like the kind of man who could be deferential – though never subservient – when the situation called for it, but who in times of crisis would rise to the occasion and exert his natural authority. It would have been an exaggeration to say that he looked at the woman adoringly, but there was certainly nothing of indifference in his gaze.

The woman withdrew her hands from the corpse's insides, and said, 'It's poisoning all right, Jed, but it was self-administered.'

'Self-administered?' Jed Trent replied. 'So it's suicide?'

'In a way,' Ellie Carr agreed. 'If I had to make a guess about his diet, I'd say the man lived mainly off eel pies and glasses of milk stout, and in the end his heart decided it had had enough.' She paused for a moment. 'Did I mention the fact that we'll be going up north, Jed?' she continued.

'No, I don't think you did, Dr Carr. And who's this "we", anyway?'

'You and me, of course.'

Ellie Carr had spoken the words lightly, as if there were no question about it and – in a way – there wasn't. For whilst Trent had originally been hired by UCH to be a general factotum, he was rapidly turning – much to the annoyance of the other doctors – into Dr Carr's personal retainer.

'And why are we going up north?' Trent asked.

'I should have thought that was obvious,' Ellie Carr replied briskly. 'The forces of law and order, finding themselves once more unable to deal with the complexities of modern crime,

43

have again to resort to the subtleties of the scientific mind to rescue them from the mess.'

'In other words, we'll be working for the police again, will we?' Trent said dryly.

'Isn't that what I just said?' Ellie Carr asked.

'Yes. I suppose so. More or less,' Trent agreed.

He remembered the other jobs they'd done for the police, and more especially, the corners that Ellie Carr had made him cut to help her get her results – corners that could probably have landed them both in gaol if they had come under too much close public scrutiny.

'Who'll we be working with?' Trent asked. 'Will it be Inspector Blackstone again?'

Ellie Carr frowned. 'No, not Sam, this time,' she said. 'It's a Superintendent Bullock who says he wants our help.'

'A superintendent! Well, we are going up in the world, aren't we? And how does Sam Blackstone feel about it?'

'Why should he care, one way or the other?' Ellie asked sharply.

Trent shrugged.

'I asked you why he should care, one way or the other,' Ellie repeated.

'Well, it did look for a while back there as if you and him ... you and him would...'

'He and I would – *what*?'

Trent shrugged again. 'You know.'

'Would fall into bed together? Would make the beast with two backs all night long?'

Jed Trent tut-tutted disapprovingly. 'There's times you don't talk like a lady at all,' he said.

44

'That's because I'm *not* a lady,' Ellie Carr told him. 'Ladies are born, not created. Ladies sit around drinking tea – and sniping at absent friends. I'm a doctor and a scientist – a *woman* from the East End, who's left her background behind her and got on in life by using her brain.'

'And I'd better not forget that,' Trent said.

'And you'd better not forget it,' Ellie agreed.

Jed Trent grinned. 'Well, I suppose I'd better go and pack my bag, hadn't I?'

'Yes, that would be a good idea,' Ellie said.

She waited until Trent had closed the laboratory door behind him before lifting a clean swab to the corner of her eye, and wiping away a tear.

She did *miss* Sam Blackstone, she thought, and often – in the long dark hours of the night – she found herself wondering what had gone wrong between them.

The church was separated from the rest of the village by the Trent and Mersey Canal, and since the only way to cross the water was to go over the humpbacked bridge next to the Jubilee Salt Works, that was the route the funeral cortège took. As it reached the crown of the bridge, the huge steam whistle at the salt works released an ear-piercing scream. 'Even if the bosses don't come to the funeral themselves, at least they've got the decency to show their respect,' said one of the miners at the back of the cortège, as the sound of the whistle died away.

'Is that what you think it is?' asked the man walking next to him. 'A sign of respect?'

'Well, what would you call it?' the first miner asked.

'I'd call it a reminder to the lads workin' at the Jubilee that they've been given one hour to attend the funeral, an' if they're a minute late gettin' back to work, it'll be docked from their pay.'

The first miner did not want to argue about callousness of the bosses – not on an occasion like this – and turned instead to the only other subject of conversation that was readily available.

'Two funerals in three days,' he said. 'It's bloody tragic. I can't remember anythin' like that ever happenin' before. But at least Cedric Wilson died in his bed, which is more than you can say for the other poor bugger. Still, I suppose accidents do happen.'

'So they do,' his friend agreed. 'But there's accidents and accidents, aren't there? And some accidents are more preventable than others.'

'What do you mean by that?'

'Blasters are blasters, and drift masters are drift masters. A blaster knows what he *should* do, but he also knows that he has to do what the drift master *tells* him to do. So if anythin' goes wrong, whose fault do *you* think it is?'

There were places which, from a distance, seemed far less intricate than they actually were, Blackstone thought. An Afghan town could look like no more than a collection of mud walls when viewed from afar, for example, but once inside you became aware of its intriguing system of alleyways and of surprising areas of calm where small tea shops overlooked placid squares.

Marston was not like that. What you saw from a distance was exactly what you found when standing right in the middle of it. A canal marked its northern boundary, and the flashes (which had been working salt mines until they flooded) marked the southern one. A railway spur, running from the salt works to the town, provided its western border, and current salt-mine workings its eastern one. It was a working industrial unit, where the product came before the people – and it didn't pretend to be anything else.

And it was so ordinary – so mundane! So what did the place have to offer to a jewel-smuggler? Certainly not the bright lights and the high living! Then what other advantages *did* it have?

None at all, as far as Blackstone could see.

Master criminals knew that the best place to hide themselves was in a crowd, which was why they usually set up their operations in the middle of big cities. To choose a small village – where they would be under constant public scrutiny – was nothing short of madness.

Yet Tom Yardley had given the strongest possible hint in his letter that a jewellery-smuggling ring *was* at work in Marston, and Blackstone, who had once trusted the man with his life, was prepared to trust him on this, too.

* * *

The vicar was standing by the newly dug grave, but was looking in the direction of the church. The crack in the east wall was growing longer every time he looked at it, he thought. Longer – and wider.

But then that hardly came as a surprise, even to a man who professed as little interest in the physical world as he did. The church, like the rest of the buildings in the village, had been constructed over a honeycomb of mine shafts and brine workings. The whole village was slowly sinking, as the treacherous ground beneath it gave way. And there was no reason to assume that God's house would fare any better than the houses of the miners who had partly been the instruments of their own destruction.

One of the mine workers coughed, and the vicar was reminded that not only was life short for these men, but time was money to them too.

Ashes to ashes, dust to dust...

But not on *this* occasion, the vicar thought, turning his attention back to the plain wooden coffin. Here it was much more a case of a fine healthy frame being reduced to its component parts – with an arm recovered from one spot, a leg recovered from another, and the almost-intact – though bloody and battered – torso found in yet a third location.

It had been a very messy business, all right – but then that was only what you would expect when blasting went wrong.

The Number One Evaporation Pan in the Jubilee

Salt Works had an elevated position above the street, which made it a perfect vantage point for observing what was going on below, and it was from there that the two watchers had been following the movements of the man from London.

Both men were dressed in frock coats, though the taller man's was newer and more stylish than the one worn by the smaller man. But their manner of dress was not the major feature that distinguished between them. The taller man had an arrogance about him which suggested that he expected to be obeyed at all times. The shorter of the two, in contrast, had the hang-dog look of a man who would willingly embrace the protection of someone stronger than himself, even if, with that protection, came the prospect of the occasional beating.

The policeman from London had been walking up and down the lane for close to half an hour – as if by covering the same route over and over again he would find the answer to some question that had been troubling him – but now he came to a definite stop in front of the Red Lion Inn, not fifty yards from where the watchers had stationed themselves.

The taller watcher backed away from the observation post, turned and headed for the salt store. The shorter watcher obediently followed him.

Once inside the salt store, the taller watcher selected a block of salt, sat down on it and took a hip flask out of his pocket. He uncorked the flask and took a generous slug of whisky. He did not offer the flask to his companion, nor did the shorter man make any attempt to sit down in his presence.

'So our worst fears have been proved to be no more than correct,' the taller watcher said, though there was no evidence of any particular *concern* in his words 'Tom Yardley did indeed write to his old friend Inspector Blackstone. And now Blackstone is here in the village.'

'Perhaps he won't stay,' the shorter watcher said nervously.

'Won't stay? *Why* wouldn't he stay?'

'When he learns what's happened, he may decide there's no point in being here, and catch the next train back to London.'

The taller watcher laughed. 'Have you read anything at all about this Inspector Blackstone?'

'Well, yes, I—'

'Then you'll know all about him rescuing that little nigger prince?'

'Yes.'

'And how he caught the fire bug who threatened to burn the whole of London down?'

'Yes.'

'So having read all that, does he strike you as the kind of man who's *likely* to just walk away? Because that's certainly not how he strikes me!'

'But if you believe he'll stay, how can you remain so calm?' the smaller watcher wondered.

'I can remain calm because I am a planner – because when things happen, it is because I *want* them to happen.'

'You can't have wanted *this*!'

'True. But "this" – as you call it – may prove to be no more than a minor distraction. I've laid my plans very carefully, and thus far I've managed to fool the police, the customs-and-excise officials – and this whole village. So why should you assume that I can't fool him?'

'Because he's different! You said so yourself!'

'Yes, I did, didn't I?' the taller watcher agreed. 'And possibly you're right. Possibly he will have the perception and intelligence to see through all the camouflage I've thrown up around my little enterprise. In which case, we'll just have to deal with him, won't we?'

'Deal with him?'

'Stop pretending you don't know what I mean. When I say "deal with him", what am I talking about?'

'I don't know.'

'What am I talking about?'

The smaller man looked down his feet. 'You're talking about arranging a fatal accident,' he mumbled.

'Just so,' the other man concurred.

The blinds that had covered the pub windows had been pulled clear, and now Blackstone heard the bolts on the main door being drawn.

The door was opened by the landlord, a man in his late forties, with sandy hair. As he was pulling the pint of bitter that Blackstone had asked for, the Inspector noticed that he was still wearing a black armband.

51

'From your accent, I'd say that you're not from round here,' the landlord said, as he slid the foaming pint across the counter.

He sounded as if he were doing no more than making conversation, Blackstone thought. But was he?

Tom Yardley didn't trust the local police force, and maybe he didn't trust this landlord, either. So, until he'd spoken to Tom himself, it would perhaps be wisest to give away as little as possible.

'No, I'm not local,' he admitted.

'I'd guess you're a Londoner,' the landlord said.

'And you'd be right.'

'We don't get many Londoners in the village.'

'I imagine you don't.'

'If you think I'm being too nosy, you could just tell me to shut up,' the landlord suggested amiably.

Blackstone sighed. Despite his best efforts, the conversation had reached a point at which he would draw more suspicion on himself by saying nothing than he would by telling a half-truth or two, he decided.

'I've got a little bit of business that I need to attend to in the port of Liverpool,' he said.

'Then why aren't you *in* Liverpool?' the landlord asked. He chuckled. 'You don't think this village is Liverpool, do you? The little canal that runs through here *joins* the mighty River Mersey, but nobody's actually ever mistaken it *for* the Mersey before.'

52

Blackstone chuckled himself, as if he were sharing in the landlord's joke. 'No, I haven't made that mistake,' he agreed.

'Well, then?'

'I have a friend in this area, and since I had to be here anyway, I thought I'd take the opportunity to visit him.'

'A friend?'

'An old comrade from my days in the army.'

'Now who might that old comrade be?' the landlord wondered. 'There's quite a number of men from Marston who have served in the army, at one time or another, you know.'

Blackstone sighed again. In seeking to be discreet, he had only succeeded in turning himself into a man of mystery.

Was there any point in keeping his friend's name a secret any longer? Surely, in a village this size, everybody would know who he'd come to see the moment he talked to Tom. Besides, the important fact to hide was not that Tom was his old comrade, but that he himself was a police inspector, and it was because of that fact that Tom had practically *begged* him to come.

'You probably know the man I've come to see,' he said jauntily. 'It wouldn't surprise me if he wasn't one of your regulars, since he's a salt-miner, and I'm told that job's enough to give any man a raging thirst.'

The landlord was looking increasingly uneasy, as if, in his head, he was piecing together the bits of information about Blackstone's old

53

comrade's probable age and his occupation.

'This friend of yours...' he said, tentatively.

'Yes?'

'It's not Tom Yardley by any chance, is it?'

'As a matter of fact, it is.'

The landlord's face turned suddenly mournful. 'Then I'm sorry to tell you you've come too late,' he said.

'Too late?'

'That's what I said. We've just buried the poor bugger.'

Four

Blackstone, standing outside the pub, watched as the villagers came down the bridge, on their way back from the funeral. As the procession drew level with him, one man – a miner by the look of him – peeled free of it and made a beeline for him.

'Are you that inspector from London?' the man asked. 'Because if you are, Tom Yardley's told me all about how the two of you fought together in Afghanistan, and how you were the best sergeant he'd ever served under.'

'Did he mention that he saved my life once?' Blackstone asked.

The miner shook his head. 'Not that I can

recall.'

No, he wouldn't have, Blackstone thought. Not Tom.

'What if I am "that inspector from London"?' he said aloud. 'Why should that be any concern of yours?'

'Tom told me he'd sent you a letter,' the miner said. He checked quickly over his shoulder, to see if anyone was listening. 'And he ... and he told me that if anything happened to him before you got here, I was to let you know about it. I was goin' to write to you tonight, but now you're here...'

'Can I buy you a drink?' Blackstone asked.

The miner looked down the street at the slowly retreating column of mourners.

'I'm supposed to go straight back to work once the funeral's over,' he said, apologetically. Then he slashed his hand through the air in an angry gesture, and added, 'To hell with work. I *need* a bloody drink.'

The miner's name was Walter Clegg. He was around the same age as Tom Yardley, but there all resemblance ended. Tom had been a big man, broad-shouldered and inclined to beefiness, while Walter Clegg was small and wiry. And the differences were not only physical. The Tom that Blackstone had known could have become a leader in time, but this man had been born to be a faithful follower.

'Tell me what happened down the mine,' Blackstone said, as he placed the two pints and two whisky chasers on a table in the corner of

55

the pub where the other man was waiting for him.

Clegg picked up his whisky, and swallowed it in a single gulp.

'Ever been down a salt mine yourself?' he asked.

'No,' Blackstone admitted.

'Then before you can make any sense of it, I'll have to tell you what it's like down there.'

'Fair enough.'

'Salt mining's not like coal mining. Coal runs in seams, through other rocks. The seam can be narrow, or it can be wide. It can go on for miles, or it can come to a sudden stop not far from where it started. Salt comes in drifts that are twenty-six feet thick – sometimes even more – an' seem to go on for ever.'

Blackstone nodded. 'Understood.'

'Another way it's different is that we don't need to put up pit props, like they do in coal mines. When we're hackin' our way through the drift, we don't cut it all away. We leave pillars of salt behind us, to support the roof.'

'Is it really so important that I should know that?' Blackstone asked impatiently.

Walter Clegg nodded. 'Yes, it is – if you're to make sense of what I'm about to tell you.'

The 'hall' at the base of the main shaft is where the stables that house the pit ponies are located – ponies that will never again see the light of day, because they came down here as foals, and now are too big to be taken to the surface ever again.

It is Tom Yardley's habit to bring a little present for the ponies – usually in the form of lumps of sugar – and the first thing he does when he gets out of the cage is pay the ponies a visit.

As he strokes the animals and talks softly to them, the rest of his crew stand around smoking cigarettes. Though they are paid by the load for their work, they do not begrudge Tom his time with the ponies, because they have come to appreciate how lucky they are to have him as their blaster.

Tom knows just how much explosive charge to use – and just where to place it so that the rock crystal comes off the wall in manageable lumps, rather than in huge chunks that it almost cripples them to load into the wagons. It is not a talent that all blasters share, and there is not a rock-getter in the whole area who would not gladly change places with one of Tom's crew.

There are several tunnels leading off the hall, each one going to a different gallery. Tom's crew go down the one that leads to the gallery they have been working for some time.

The drift master, Mr Culshaw, is already at the rock face, standing next to the pile of crystal-salt boulders that the crew left behind them when they clocked off the previous week.

'You should have already shifted this,' he says, and the look on his face shows that he is in a foul mood this morning.

Tom shrugs. 'We didn't have time.'

'You should have made time.'

'My lads put in ten hours' solid graft on Saturday. By the time they were finished, they felt as if their backs were broken an' their throats were on fire. I wasn't going to ask them to do any more.'

'What about the big order that Mr Bickersdale's got to meet?'

'That's not our concern. If he can't meet it, he should never have taken it on in the first place.'

'You understand nothing about doing business,' Culshaw says contemptuously.

'Maybe not,' Tom Yardley agrees. 'But I understand how hard rock-gettin' is – which is somethin' you seem to have forgotten yourself, since your promotion to drift master.'

'What am I to tell Mr Bickersdale when he wants to know why we're falling behind?' Culshaw asks, almost wheedling now.

'Tell him that if he wants to increase production, he should put more men into that other mine of his,' Tom suggests.

'You know that would do no good. The Melbourne Mine's just a bloody white elephant – and the last thing I'm going to do is remind Mr Bickersdale that he was conned into buying it.'

'Then you've got a problem,' Tom says.

Culshaw's mood swings again, and now he is very definitely angry.

'No, you're the one with the problem,' he says. 'Because if you don't follow the new instructions I'm about to give you, I'll sack the lot of you and bring in a new crew.'

'You'd never do that,' Tom tells him. 'You'd

never get a crew that works harder than mine does.'

'I might.'

'You'd be takin' a very big gamble.'

'And why wouldn't I gamble? What have I got to lose by gambling? If I don't get the results Mr Bickersdale wants, I'll be out of a job myself.'

Tom thinks about it for a moment. He decides that Culshaw is right, and probably will carry out his threat if he's pushed.

'What do you want us to do?' he asks.

'Next time you blast, I want you to use a bigger charge that'll bring a hell of a lot more off the wall in one go. And then I want you to work a damn sight harder at loadin' the bloody stuff.'

'We're too close to the nearest pillars to use a much bigger charge,' Tom says.

'I'll be the judge of that,' Culshaw replies. 'I was a blaster while you were still sucking on your mother's tit – and I say it's all right.'

'Tom wasn't happy about the way things were turnin' out at all,' Walter Clegg told Blackstone. 'But he could see that Culshaw meant what he said, and he must have thought he could get away with using more explosives after all, because he finally agreed.'

While his crew load the rock crystal left over from the previous Saturday on to trucks, Tom Yardley drills a series of holes in the rock face, and then packs them with explosive charges.

59

Twenty minutes go by, then Tom says, 'I'm setting the fuse now, so take cover.'
The cover that he means is the salt pillars.
'Not there,' he shouts, when he sees the crew going behind the pillars nearest to the salt face. 'This is a bloody big charge I'm using. I want you all at the very end of the gallery.'

'We didn't think that was necessary,' Walter Clegg told Blackstone.

'Not even though he was using more explosive than usual?'

'No, they're massive things, them salt pillars – twenty-five yards square. They have to be that big, because they're supportin' several hundred feet of rock above them.'

'But you went anyway?'

'Tom was the boss. Tom knew what he was doin'.'

The crew retreat to the back of the gallery, as instructed.
Another two minutes pass, then Tom calls out, 'I'm going to light the fuse now.' And even before his words have stopped echoing around the vast cathedral of salt, there is a huge, deafening explosion.

'A good blaster knows how to set the fuse so it will give him more than enough time to take cover with everybody else,' Walter Clegg said.

'So Tom made a mistake, did he?' Blackstone asked.

Walter shook his head. 'No, I don't think he did.'

For a while, the crew are so stunned by the ferocity and unexpectedness of the explosion that they do nothing. And even when they do force themselves to move, the air is so thick with salt that it is almost like being caught in a snow storm.

Walter Clegg is the first member of the crew to reach the rock face, so he is the first to see the pile of boulders that the explosion has ripped away from the wall – and the first to notice that projecting from this pile is a human arm.

He knows he has no chance of pulling Tom clear – knows that the best thing he can do will be start clearing away the boulders – but his instincts have taken over, so he tugs at the arm anyway.

And it comes away in his hand.

'He was a mess,' Walter said, his voice choking as he spoke. 'There were bits of him all over the place. He just looked like so much meat. I was sick. We were all sick. But we collected him up as best we could.'

'And you don't think it was his own mistake that killed him?'

Walter shook his head again, more violently this time. 'It couldn't have been more than a second between him setting the fuse an' the explosion. He'd never have miscalculated it that badly.'

'So what *did* happen?'

'I can't be sure,' Walter Clegg admitted. 'I'm not an expert like Tom was. But it seems to me that them explosives had to have been tampered with – either by Culshaw or by some other murderous swine.'

Five

There were three people in the pony trap that was making its way down the narrow country lane. One was a uniformed police constable, who was sitting on the box and gently urging the pony on whenever it felt inclined to slacken its pace a little.

The other two people – a man and a woman – were sitting behind the box and looking around them. Jed Trent appeared to be enjoying the change of scenery and the fresh air. Dr Ellie Carr, on the other hand, looked at each and every new hedgerow suspiciously – as if expecting an ambush.

It was not her fault that she was so ill at ease, Ellie told herself. She was a city girl. She had been brought up in the slums of the East End, and though she now lodged in a much more salubrious area, it was *still* London – still very much a part of the metropolis.

The countryside, in her opinion, was something best viewed from a train window, on the way to a medical conference in Manchester or Glasgow. To actually find herself in the middle of it – surrounded by green fields, with not a lamp-post or tramline in sight – was bound to be rather disconcerting.

The constable reined in the horse and applied the brake. That done, he climbed down from the box and gallantly offered Ellie his arm to assist her in her own descent.

Ellie looked somewhat mystified, but took the arm anyway, and stepped down on to the lane.

'Why have we stopped here?' she asked.

'Because that's where the poor girl was murdered,' the constable replied, pointing into the drainage ditch.

Ellie Carr looked shocked. 'You are joking, aren't you?' she asked.

'Why would I want to joke, Doctor?' the constable wondered.

'It really *is* the scene of the crime?'

'Yes.'

'Then why isn't there anybody standing guard over it?'

The constable shrugged. 'Why would anybody want to stand guard? The body's been removed. There's nothing to see here any more.'

Ellie placed her hands squarely on her hips, so that – though she did not have the bulk for it – she somewhat resembled the bellicose fishwives of her childhood memories.

'Didn't it occur to any of the so-called detectives working on this case that, until I'd looked at the site, it shouldn't be disturbed?' she demanded.

'Doesn't seem to have,' the constable replied evenly.

Ellie Carr could have said more – undoubtedly *would* have said more – had not Jed Trent chosen that moment to position himself squarely between her and the local policeman.

Staring into his broad back – which he was clearly intending should block her out – Ellie heard Trent say, 'Thank you for bringing us here, officer. We'll find our own way back to the police station.'

'You'll walk?'

'We'll walk.'

'But it's over three miles.'

'Dr Carr won't mind that,' Trent told the constable. 'Like a lot of people who've never done a day's really hard work in their lives, she considers exercise to be good for the body.'

The local copper chuckled. 'It takes all sorts to make a world,' he said. 'Well, if you really don't need me, I'll be off.'

Ellie heard him walk back to the cart and climb up into the driver's seat, but she didn't actually *see* him do it, because every time she shifted her position, Jed Trent did the same.

It was only when the constable began to drive away that Jed turned to face her.

'How dare you mock me like that?' Ellie demanded furiously.

64

'I thought it was the best of the possible options that you'd left me,' Trent replied.

'The possible options *I'd* left you?'

'That constable could have gone away either laughing at you or furious with you. I thought that, for the good of the investigation, it would be better if he was laughing.'

'Explain yourself!' Ellie ordered.

'Gladly. You got right up that constable's nose with your high-handed manner, Dr Carr – and that certainly isn't the best way to get co-operation from the local force.'

'Really, Jed, I don't think you understand how—'

'No, I don't think *you* understand,' Trent said firmly. 'You can get away with playing the brilliant-but-volatile scientist with Inspector Blackstone, because I reckon he still fancies you. But if we're going to continue working with other policemen – who probably *don't* fancy you – then you'll just have to learn to be a little more tactful.'

'How *can* I be tactful when they allow this to happen to the scene of the crime?' Ellie protested, gazing down at the flattened grass and a dozen or so impressions of heavy police boots.

'It's a mess all right,' Trent agreed. 'But it probably wasn't that particular constable's fault.'

'But—'

'And even if it was his fault, it's done now, and it can't be undone – whereas the local coppers *could* undo the fact we've got rooms booked for the night, if they felt so inclined.'

'You have a point,' Ellie Carr conceded reluctantly. 'But look at what they've done, Jed! It's almost as if they'd held a bleedin' carnival here!'

'So I suppose that if they've destroyed all the evidence, there's nothing to be learned, and we might just as well head back to the town,' Jed Trent said, lifting his hand to his face to hide his slight smile.

'I never said they'd destroyed *all* the evidence,' Ellie Carr told him. 'It is just possible that a few shreds might remain – and that a brilliant young scientist just might be able to recover them.'

'If only we had one with us,' Jed Trent said softly.

'What was that?' Ellie demanded.

'Nothing,' Trent told her.

Ellie walked over to the ditch. 'Did you mean what you said earlier?' she asked.

'About Inspector Blackstone fancying you?' Trent asked.

Ellie frowned. 'No. About the local coppers probably *not* fancying me at all.'

'Of course I didn't mean it,' Trent said, the smile behind his hand broadening. 'With your graceful manner and your winning ways, what man *wouldn't* fall in love with you immediately?'

Ellie Carr nodded, as if acknowledging what was no more than the simple truth.

'That's all right then,' she said, stepping down

into the ditch – and seemingly oblivious of the fact that she was immediately plunging herself up to her ankles in dirty water.

It was twenty minutes before Ellie climbed out of the ditch again. As she stood dripping in front of him, Trent gave her a quick up-and-down inspection. It was not a pretty sight. The bottom half of her dress was soaking, and she had somehow contrived to get mud in her hair.

'Just look at the state you're in,' Trent said disapprovingly. 'You've probably caught your death of cold. And even if you haven't, it'll take a washerwoman hours to get all that filth off your dress.'

'Oh for heaven's sake, Jed, stop fussing,' Ellie said dismissively. 'What does a bit of dirt matter if the cause of forensic science has been advanced?'

'And has it?'

'I think so. What was the first thing that everyone told us about Emma Walsingholme when we arrived?'

'That she'd been killed and mutilated in a ditch?'

'Exactly! And the constable, whom you seemed so eager to defend, repeated that same error not half an hour ago.'

'So she *wasn't* killed and mutilated here?'

'Certainly wasn't *mutilated.*'

'How can you be so sure?'

'If she had been, I'd have found at least traces of it – splinters of bone, bits of tissue, the odd tooth...' Ellie paused. 'You really don't want to

67

know the details, Jed.'

'No, I probably don't,' Trent agreed. 'So she wasn't mutilated here. But was this where she was killed?'

'Highly unlikely,' Ellie Carr said crisply. 'Apart from the difficulty it would have caused the killer to move a girl who was spurting blood like a fountain, she'd have bled to death in a very short time. So there'd have been no need to strangle her, would there?'

'But if she didn't lose her hands and feet in the ditch, why were her gloves and shoes found next to her body?'

'You tell me,' Ellie suggested.

Trent thought about it for a minute. 'Because her killer wanted people to believe that this *was* where she met her end?' he said finally.

'That's just the conclusion I've reached,' Ellie agreed.

'But why would he give a damn what we think?'

'I don't have the slightest idea,' Ellie admitted. 'Maybe an examination of the actual body itself will give us some clue.'

Blackstone and Walter Clegg had already knocked back three pints of best bitter – followed by whisky chasers – when Clegg suddenly said, 'Why don't we go back to my house?'

Blackstone had no idea why Clegg should have made the offer, but he accepted it immediately, because, in his experience, men were much more comfortable on their home ground.

And whilst he did not think that Clegg had been lying to him so far, he was hopeful that the miner would become even more forthcoming from the safety of his own hearth.

They left the pub and walked down the lane towards the flashes. When they had gone about a hundred yards, Clegg turned into an alleyway, and Blackstone followed him.

They reached the back yard that contained the wash-house, outside lavatory and the house's only tap. Walter Clegg lifted the latch on the back door and pushed it open.

Blackstone was half-expecting to be greeted by a bunch of screaming kids, but instead there was only silence from inside the house.

'Are you there, Mam?' Clegg called out, and when there was no answer he said, 'She's probably gone off to visit one of her old cronies.'

'You still live with your parents?' Blackstone asked incredulously, before he could stop himself.

'Only with Mam,' Clegg said, not noticing his tone. 'Dad's been dead a good few years now.'

The room they entered was probably typical of the village. A cooking range dominated one wall, and though it was by no means a cold evening, there was a fire burning in the grate to keep the oven warm. Most of the rest of the space in the room was taken up by a heavy oak-veneer sideboard – which was covered with photographs – and a large kitchen table.

'Well, this is it,' Walter Clegg said proudly. 'This is the place that I call home.'

'Very nice,' Blackstone said, knowing that was what was expected of him. 'Very nice indeed.'

'Where are you plannin' to stay for the night?' Clegg asked, in a manner which suggested he had been waiting quite some time for the moment to spring this particular question.

'I haven't really thought about it,' Blackstone admitted. 'Is there a cheap boarding house in the village?'

Clegg laughed. 'A boarding house? In this village? There most certainly is not. If you want to find a room, you'll have to go back to town.'

'Well, since there doesn't seem to be any choice in the matter—' Blackstone began.

'Unless, of course, you wouldn't mind staying here,' Walter Clegg interrupted him.

'Here?'

'You could sleep in the front parlour, if you wanted to. I know Mam wouldn't mind.'

'I'm not sure...'

'There isn't a bed in there, I'm afraid, but I think you'll find the sofa quite comfortable.'

So that was what the invitation to his house was all about. It had been the first step in Clegg's campaign to get him to agree to spend the night there.

The reason for his eagerness was obvious, Blackstone thought. A police inspector who had come all the way from London was important – at least in the eyes of someone who had probably never been more than a few miles from this village – and having that inspector spend the night under his roof would make him feel important, too. And, when all was said and done, what was the *harm* in that?

'The sofa would do me just fine,' Blackstone said. He reached into his jacket pocket and pulled out the bottle of whisky he had bought from the off-sales in the pub. 'Why don't you find us a couple of glasses?'

Clegg produced two glasses from the mock-oak sideboard, and the two men sat down at the kitchen table.

'In the letter he sent to me, Tom sounded very worried,' Blackstone said. 'Did he seem worried to you?'

Clegg nodded. 'He did. An' it wasn't like him at all. Tom was the kind of feller who normally took difficulties in his stride.'

'He didn't tell you what it was that was on his mind?'

'No. I asked him, but he said it would be better for me if I didn't get involved.' Clegg's eyes watered slightly. 'I should have insisted,' he continued, with a note of anguish in his voice. 'I should have said that, as his best mate, I had a right – an' a duty – to share his burden with him.'

And maybe if he had shared it with you, you'd be dead as well, Blackstone thought.

'Did Tom ever mention smuggling to you?' he asked.

'Many a time. He said there was so much of it goin' on in Afghanistan that you couldn't move without trippin' over it.'

'But he never mentioned smuggling in *Marston*?'

Walter Clegg giggled. 'In Marston!' he repeated. 'Whatever would you smuggle out of Marston? Salt?'

It had been the reaction Blackstone had been expecting. The more he saw of the place himself, the more unsuitable it seemed as a centre of criminal activity. But Tom Yardley had been convinced that was just what it was.

And if he was wrong, then why was he now dead?

The two watchers stood at the head of the alley down which Blackstone and Walter Clegg had disappeared.

'They've been in there for over half an hour now,' said the shorter, more nervous one. 'What can they be talking about?'

'I've no idea,' his taller companion replied. 'And it doesn't really matter, anyway.'

'Are you sure about that?'

'Of course I'm sure. Clegg doesn't know anything.'

'Isn't it possible that Tom Yardley might have told him ...?'

'You've seen Walter Clegg for yourself. He's the kind of man you get to run errands for you – the kind you give the dirty jobs you don't feel like doing yourself. He's certainly not a man you'd ever think of entrusting with your deepest darkest secrets.'

'So if Clegg presents no danger, why are we

72

here?'

'Because Inspector Blackstone *does* present a danger – and I want to find out what his next move's going to be.'

'We should have him killed,' the smaller watcher said, 'right away. You said yourself that we could make it look like an accident, and nobody would ever know any different.'

The other watcher laughed contemptuously. 'A few hours ago, even talking about the possibility of killing him had you trembling – and now you can't wait to see him dead.'

'A few hours ago, I wasn't as frightened as I am now.'

'It's never occurred to you that we could use him, has it?' the taller watcher asked, with a superior air.

'Use him? For what?'

'To find what we're looking for, of course. Tom Yardley's beyond helping us with that, but maybe – if we handle him properly – Blackstone can take Yardley's place.'

'You really think he'll be able to find what we can't?'

'It's certainly worth a try, isn't it?'

'And if he does find it, can we kill him then?'

'Yes,' the tall watcher agreed. 'Then we *can* kill him.'

Six

Night was falling over the great city of London. The gas-lighters had completed their rounds, and all the gas lamps were burning brightly. The costermongers had locked away their barrows for the day and were heading for the nearest boozer at which they were not already seriously in debt. The music halls had just opened their doors and the respectable theatres were getting ready to open theirs. And in one of the better parts of town, a hansom cab was conveying a plump policeman – in disguise – to the destination he had never sought, but which the powers-that-be had decided it was necessary he should visit.

The frock coat didn't feel right, Archie Patterson told himself as the hansom got ever closer to the end of its journey.

It wasn't that the coat didn't fit properly. Far from it!

This particular operation, having been instigated by the Home Secretary himself, had almost unlimited funds at its disposal, and the expensive tailor to whom Patterson had paid a visit had done an excellent job of accommodating – and minimising – his unseemly bulges.

In fact, the frock coat was the finest piece of clothing that Patterson had ever worn. And that was just exactly the problem! Because when he said that it didn't feel right, what he really meant was it seemed all *wrong* that a detective sergeant like himself – a man who had to think twice before ordering a whisky on the day before pay day – should be accoutred in such an opulent piece of clothing. And if it seemed wrong to him, how would it look to others?

He had no doubt at all that the people he was going to visit would immediately grasp the fact that he was dressed well above his station – and therefore was nothing but a complete fraud.

He looked out of the window of the hansom cab. It would soon be arriving at his destination – Waterloo Road – where he would alight, knock on the door of number thirty-three, and immediately expose himself to ridicule.

He wished it had been Sam Blackstone, rather than Inspector Maddox, who was sending him out on this job. Blackstone would have set the right tone from the very start.

'You look every inch the young gent about town,' the inspector would probably have said.

'There's no call for sarcasm, sir,' his sergeant might well have replied.

And Blackstone would have said, 'No, I mean it. It's as much as I can do to stop myself making a small bow as you walk past.'

Patterson wouldn't have believed him, of course, and Blackstone wouldn't have *expected* to be believed, but – in some strange way – the

75

sergeant would have gained confidence from the exchange.

Maddox, in contrast, had inspected him in his new frock coat and then sniffed disparagingly.

He'd said, 'Well, since we seem to be quite unable to attract the better class of young man into the ranks of the Metropolitan Police Force, I suppose you'll have to do. You have your orders, Sergeant. You must carry them out to the best of your ability.'

And just how far would that ability take him? Patterson wondered. As far as the hallway of the brothel – if he were lucky. He was a policeman, not an actor – handy in a fight, but absolutely hopeless at pretending to be what he wasn't.

Mrs Clegg – Walter's mother – was a lively old woman, with a tongue that fired off words more rapidly than a Maxim machine gun could fire off bullets. After half an hour of her relentless questioning – 'What's it like living in London?' 'Do you see the Queen often?' 'I've heard they've got railways that run underground down there, but that can't be true, can it?' – Blackstone politely excused himself on the grounds that he needed a breath of fresh air before he went to bed, and set off up the lane towards the humpbacked bridge.

The lane was bathed in the pale light of an almost-full moon, but there were no street lights – as there would have been in London – to add to the glow, because street lights required gas to burn, gas came through underground pipes, and

– in a village where any stretch of ground might give way at any time – gas-filled pipes were too great a danger to even contemplate.

He reached the crown of the humpbacked bridge. Ahead of him, bathed in the ghostly moonlight, he could see the churchyard where Tom had been laid to rest only hours earlier, and – though he had not seen it coming – he felt a sudden wave of personal failure wash over him.

Could he have reached Marston any sooner than he had done? he asked himself. And if he had arrived earlier, would he have been able to prevent Tom Yardley's death?

He retraced a few of his steps, then took the dog-legged path that led down to the towpath that ran alongside the Trent and Mersey Canal.

A number of narrowboats had moored close to the bridge for the night. They were, in their own idiosyncratic way, as impressive and intriguing as ocean-going liners and paddle steamers, Blackstone thought, almost whimsically. They were called *narrow*boats for a good reason – none of them being more than seven feet wide – but what they lacked in width they made up for in length, and the ones he was looking at were at least seventy feet from bow to stern.

Through the still night air there came the sound of a horse whinnying softly to itself.

Blackstone turned in the direction the sound had come from, and saw that there were several horses tethered in a nearby meadow. When morning came, each one would be harnessed up to its owner's narrowboat and soon they would

77

be gone – plodding slowly and steadily towards their next destination, towing the boat behind them.

He turned again and took a closer look at the nearest boat. The cabin – which would be the home of the boatman and his entire family – looked to be about ten feet long, and was elaborately decorated with paintings of roses and castles, much as gypsies' caravans were. Indeed, these people *were* like gypsies in many respects, Blackstone told himself. They were constantly moving up and down the country, carrying their cargoes along a network of canals that was almost as extensive as the railway network. They shifted coal from Newcastle to the factories in Birmingham, salt from Cheshire to the Liverpool docks – anything and everything that was in one place and needed to be in another.

Blackstone lit up a cigarette, inhaled deeply, and wondered what Patterson was doing at that moment. And then, suddenly, though he neither heard nor saw anything to arouse his suspicions, he got the distinct impression that he was being watched.

The house on Waterloo Road was part of a terrace which also contained the embassies of some of Britain's less prosperous allies and the homes of merchants and traders who had not yet climbed to the very top of their particular commercial tree. From the outside, it gave an appearance of being highly respectable without being overly ostentatious, which was – of course

– exactly what the people who were running it would have wanted.

Patterson climbed the steps to the front door. He lifted his cane, which had a silver knob on the end of it, and knocked.

Even this simple action made him feel slightly ridiculous, because, though he knew that fashionable young men of his age did carry canes, he'd never been able to understand why they did it – especially canes with a silver knob on the end, for God's sake!

The man who answered his knock was tall and broad. He was dressed in a butler's uniform, but he looked no more at home in this outfit than Patterson did in his, and his broken nose was a much fairer indication than his uniform of how he *actually* earned his living.

The 'butler' ran his eyes quickly up and down Patterson's frame, and though his arms remained by his sides, he balled his hands into fists.

'Yes?' he said contemptuously. 'What do you want?'

'I – I was told there would be young ladies here,' Patterson said.

The stutter had been unintentional, but it had the effect of relaxing the bruiser anyway, and his hands unclenched.

'There may – or may not – be young ladies here,' he said. 'Why should that matter to you, one way or the other?'

'I'd – I'd rather like to meet one of them,' Patterson said, and this time the stutter was more art than nature.

'And maybe they'd like to meet you,' the bouncer conceded, unbending just a little. 'But before that can happen, I need to see the colour of your money,' he concluded, his voice hardening again.

'Of – Of course,' Patterson said, reaching into his pocket and producing a thick wad of banknotes that he had signed out of Scotland Yard less than an hour earlier.

The bruiser looked duly impressed. 'Wait here,' he said, closing the door and retreating down the hallway.

The next person to open the door was a young, rather unattractive woman in a maid's uniform.

'If yer'll foller me, sir, Madam is waitin' for yer in her parlour,' she announced.

Patterson had to suppress the sigh of relief that was attempting to fight its way out of his corpulent frame. 'It's very kind of her to spare the time,' he said.

Seven

Madam – or perhaps it would have been more accurate to call her *the* madam – was a woman in her early fifties. She was wearing a deep-blue velvet dress with a plunging neckline – though her cleavage had been discreetly covered with fine lace – and had about the same amount of make-up on her face as would have been used by the entire cast of a major production in the Theatre Royal, Drury Lane.

Her parlour was decorated with very heavy red-and-gold wallpaper, and a number of subtly pornographic paintings of half-naked nymphs hung from the picture rail. The air was thick with the smell of perfume. There was a small side table in the corner of the room, but most of the available space was taken up by a series of chaises longues, on one of which 'Madam' was reclining.

'Take a seat,' she said, and Patterson perched himself awkwardly on the edge of a chaise longue some distance from her.

'It's always a pleasure to be visited by a fine-looking, well-set-up young man like yourself,' the woman continued, though the expression in her eyes clearly said that she saw him as no

81

more than a fat boy with money in his pocket.

Patterson cleared his throat, partly because he was still pretending to be nervous – and partly because it was no real pretence at all.

'Thank you, ma'am,' he said thickly.

'What's your name?'

'Archibald.'

'Just Archibald? Don't you have a second name?'

'Not one that I'd be willing to use here.'

'Cautious, aren't you?' the madam asked tartly.

'Very,' Patterson agreed.

The madam nodded. 'When you get to know us better, you'll come to see just how discreet we can be, but for the moment I suppose there's no harm in you being a little careful.' She paused for a second. 'Might I ask you, Archibald, who recommended us to you?'

'No,' Patterson said.

'No?'

'The person in question would only give me this address if I promised not to use his name.'

'But he has been here himself, has he?'

'So he claims.'

Madam reached for a feather fan, and wafted it a few times in front of her face.

'Yer not a copper, are yer?' she asked, with a sudden hard edge – and rough accent – entering her voice.

'Of course not!' Patterson protested.

'Then what *are* you?'

'I'm a gentleman.'

82

The madam looked at him speculatively. 'What do you do for a living?' she demanded.

Patterson had his top hat on his lap, and now he ran his hands nervously around the rim. 'Nothing,' he said.

'Then where does the full wallet – which my manservant assures me you have in your pocket – come from?'

Patterson looked down at the floor, as if in embarrassment, and embarked on the story he had prepared in advance.

'My father gives me all the money I need,' he mumbled.

'And why would he do that?'

'He likes me.'

'He likes you!' the madam repeated sceptically. 'And where does *his* money come from?'

'He owns plantations in the West Indies.'

'Makes his money off the niggers, does he?'

'In a manner of speaking.'

'And what about your grandfather? What did he do?'

'We don't talk about him.'

'Why would that be? Because he was poor?'

'As I said, we don't talk about him.'

'So your granddad didn't have a pot to piss in, but you can swan around town like you were the Prince of Wales himself?'

'I – I suppose so,' Patterson agreed. 'Though I'm nowhere near as rich as he is.'

'Got a lady-friend?' the madam demanded, out of the blue.

Patterson looked flustered. 'No, I – I find it

difficult to talk to any of the young ladies I meet socially.'

'Besides which, none of the ladies you meet socially would ever think of giving you what you really want, now would they?'

'No,' Patterson agreed, guiltily.

'So what *is* it you want?' the madam asked. 'We've got all sorts in here. Fat ones, and ones that are so thin you can hardly see them when they turn sideways. Tall ones and small ones. Black ones and yellow ones. We cater for every taste, and if we haven't got it now, we can get it for you.'

'I – I like the young ones,' Patterson mumbled.

The madam cackled loudly. 'Do you know, if I'd had to make a wager on it, that's where I'd have put my money,' she said. 'Well, we can certainly provide for your needs if that's what you're after. We've a lovely young girl upstairs who can't be more than fourteen, and as soon as she's finished entertaining her present gentleman caller—'

'I like them untouched,' Patterson interrupted.

'Untouched? You mean you like them to be *virgins*?'

'Well, yes, I suppose I do,' Patterson admitted.

'And why is that?' the madam wondered, with a smile playing at the corner of her heavily painted lips.

'There's no chance of disease that way,' Patterson said.

The madam's smile widened. 'That's not it at all, is it?' she asked. 'Or, at least, not all of it.'

'I assure you—'

'What you really like is the way they're all aquiver because they've never done it before, and they don't know quite what to expect. What you really like is the way they cry out in pain when you enter them for the first time. I'm right about that, aren't I?'

'Perhaps a little right,' Patterson said.

'Well, that's nothing to be ashamed of,' the madam said easily. 'There's many a man walking the streets of London with the same desire as yourself. It's as natural to want a virgin as it is to want a fresh egg. But since they can only lose their cherry once, it does come expensive.'

'I appreciate that,' Patterson told her. 'I believe it can cost anything up to twenty-five pounds.'

The madam threw back her head, and laughed loudly. 'Twenty-five pounds!' she repeated.

'That's what I've been told.'

'Well, yes, I suppose it could cost only twenty-five pounds if you were willing to accept a snotty-nosed ragamuffin who'd just been picked up from the docks. But the pleasure is so much more intense when it's a better class of girl you're deflowering – a shopkeeper's daughter or tradesman's daughter, for example. That's the kind of girl we like to offer our gentleman callers here – and that kind of girl will cost you at least *fifty* pounds.'

Patterson licked his lips. 'Can I see her?' he asked.

The madam laughed again. 'It's not like

85

ordering up towels or linen, you know. We haven't got a big cupboard upstairs marked "Virgins".'

Patterson started to stand up. 'Then if you haven't got what I—' he began.

'Sit down, Archibald,' the madam ordered. 'I can get you exactly what you crave – but it might take some time.'

'How long?'

The madam shrugged. 'Could have her tomorrow, might take a week or so. You can never tell in these matters. But whenever she gets here, she'll have been well worth waiting for. All right?'

Patterson nodded, and sat down again. 'But how will I know when you've got your hands on one?' he asked.

'I'll tell one of the maids to take a message to your club. Which one is it? The St James's? White's? You do *have* a club, don't you?'

Patterson nodded. He did indeed have a club – the Peckham Domino and Whist Club, where he had first met Rose, his fiancée – but that didn't quite fit in with the role he was currently playing.

'Well, which one is it?' the madam asked.

'I'd rather not be contacted at my club,' Patterson said. 'I'll give you a telephone number, instead.'

'That would be perfectly acceptable,' the madam agreed.

Patterson made a great show of taking a case containing his visiting cards out of his pocket.

He opened it, then – as if having second thoughts – snapped it shut again.

'I'll write the number down for you,' he said, taking a slip of paper and pencil out of his other jacket pocket. 'That will be much easier.'

'What you really mean is that not only don't you want me to know your full name, you don't even want me to know where I can contact you. Isn't that right?'

'No, I—'

'Of course it is, and I've already said that I don't blame you. I didn't trust *you* when you first walked in here, did I? But now I've got the measure of you, and I do. And in time, when you've become a regular customer, you'll learn to trust me, too, and we'll develop what's called a "mutually beneficial relationship".'

'I'm sure we will,' Patterson agreed, handing her the slip of paper.

'Is this your home?' the madam asked, glancing down at the numbers he'd written down.

No, Patterson thought. Not my home at all. In fact, it's a special number that the London Telephone Company has just assigned to Scotland Yard, and you're the only one who can ring it.

But aloud, he said, 'It's a friend's home.'

'And will you tell this friend of yours to be expecting a call from me?'

'No, I'll tell him to expect a call from my sister's dressmaker, about the dress I'm having made for her as a surprise.'

The madam looked at him with fresh suspicion. 'You're not quite as bubble-headed as you

87

seemed when you first walked in here,' she said.

Damn, Patterson thought; he'd made the mistake of sounding too much like himself – and too little like the spoiled rich boy with a weakness.

'I'm – I'm not bubble-headed at all,' he said, improvising wildly. 'I just act like an idiot when I'm nervous – and who *wouldn't* be nervous in a house of ill-repute?' He put his hand over his mouth. 'I'm sorry, I didn't mean to suggest that you're...'

The madam laughed again. 'Let's call a spade a spade,' she said. 'This *is* a house of ill-repute. A whorehouse, if you like. You wouldn't be here if it wasn't, now would you? And now we've got any little misunderstandings we might have had out of the way, I'm sure the two us will get on famously.'

'I'm sure we will,' Patterson agreed, standing again. 'Well, since we seem to have finished our business for tonight—'

'We haven't quite finished,' the madam interrupted. 'I will have to go to a great deal of expense to obtain the girl you want, and if you don't turn up, as you've promised...'

'If virgins are as rare and prized as you claim they are, you can always sell her to one of your other customers,' Patterson said.

He was sounding too clever again, he thought in a panic – too much like a policeman. But fortunately, Madam seemed more interested in defending her own position than examining his.

'It's true there'll be a ready market for the

girl,' she agreed, 'but I've taken rather a shine to you, and I'd like you to have her.'

'Thank you.'

'Still, as I said, business is business, and I'd feel much happier if you'd leave a deposit, just to show good faith on your part.' The madam paused for a second, as if assessing how much she thought she could get away with. 'Shall we say, twenty-five pounds?' she ventured.

'Why not?' Patterson agreed, reaching into his pocket for the money that the Home Office had so willingly provided.

It was a mixture of sympathy and annoyance that finally made Cathy approach the girl huddled in the corner – sympathy because she could still remember how she'd felt herself when first brought to this place, and annoyance because the girl's sobs were really starting to grate.

'What's yer name?' she asked.

The other girl looked up. 'Lizzie.'

'An' I'm Cathy. How did yer get here, Lizzie?'

The new girl had stopped crying, but was still sniffling. 'I was an inmate at the workhouse,' she said. 'A lady came to visit an' said she was lookin' for a girl she could train up to be her personal maid.'

'Tall woman, was she, this lady?' Cathy asked. 'Black hair? Little mole on her chin?'

Lizzie nodded. 'The master said I was very lucky she'd picked me, an' I really thought I was myself. But she never took me to her home, like she'd promised. As soon as we left the work-

house, she handed me over to this man, an' now
... an' now I'm here.'

'That's the same as happened to all of us,'
Cathy said.

'All of you?'

'There was some other girls here when I
arrived, but they've gone now. The place is not
so bad, once you get used to it.'

'But it's so dark an' cold!'

'They'll give yer warm clothes later. An'
blankets – lovely thick blankets, like yer'd
never get in the workhouse.'

'But what will they do with me?'

'For a start, they'll feed yer up. Yer'll never
feel hungry while yer in here. They'll let yer
take a bath every day in lovely warm soapy
water – an' when yer get out of the bath, they'll
give yer creamy lotions to rub into yerself. It's a
real treat, I can tell yer.'

'An' do they watch you while you're takin'
this bath of yours?' Lizzie asked, in horror.

'Not if yer don't want them to – an' some of
the girls didn't. I don't mind meself. I've got a
nice little body, an' if it gives them pleasure to
look at it, then I don't see why they shouldn't.'

'An' do they ever try to ... try to...'

'Have their wicked way with yer?'

'Yes.'

'Never. The boss don't allow that kind of
thing. So yer see, yer've nothin' to worry about
at all, an' my advice to you is to stop frettin' an'
enjoy yerself while yer here.'

'But what about when I go?' Lizzie asked.

'Where will they take me? Where did they take the other girls?'

'I don't rightly know,' Cathy admitted. 'I haven't asked, an' the people what run this place haven't told me.'

'But what do you *think*?'

'My guess would be a brothel somewhere.'

'An' doesn't that frighten you?'

'Not really. I've got used to sleepin' in a feather bed, and eatin' real meat every day. I like not havin' to scrub floors until me hands are red-raw, like I used to have to do in the workhouse.'

'I know, but—'

'An' if all it takes to have the good things – an' avoid the bad ones – is to spread me legs now an' again, then I'm perfectly happy to go along with it.'

It was a relief for Patterson to be out in the night air again – to be smelling healthy horse dung and smoke, instead of being overpowered by the stink of perfume, greed and desperation. The sergeant walked quickly away from the house on Waterloo Road, and didn't stop until he had turned the corner.

A mixture of emotions was rushing through his body – his earlier nervousness, which he had still not quite managed to quell; a relief that he had, against all odds, pulled the deception off; a pride that, even without Blackstone to guide him, he still seemed to be a pretty good copper. But gradually all these emotions retreated, and all that was left was anger.

91

He thought of Rose, his fiancée. She might sometimes torture him with her unreasonable requests that he should diet, but, all in all, she was a good little soul. When he did eventually marry her, she would still be a virgin, and any discomfort she felt on their first night together would at least be made easier for her to bear by the knowledge that he loved her and would not willingly hurt her.

It would be different for the poor girls that people like the madam procured for their customers. They would be deflowered by men they had never met before – men who would treat them roughly and take pleasure from the pain they were causing them.

Patterson had not wanted this case initially, but now he discovered that he was glad it had been assigned to him. He knew he could not clean up the whole world – or even the whole street – on his own. He knew that prostitution had existed since the dawn of time, and would continue to exist until the last second before the world came to an end. But even given those limitations, he could at least see to it that this particular bitch of a madam paid in full for her crimes.

Wednesday: Gone, but not forgotten

One

The Northwich Police headquarters was a large black-and-white building – the black part being a timber framework, the white part the plastered-over bricks that had been used to fill in the gaps. It was very much like the buildings being erected around the time that King Henry VIII was using the executioner's axe as a speedy and convenient method of making himself a bachelor again. And Blackstone, who had already noticed quite a number of similar structures on his way to the station, found himself wondering why a modern industrial town like this one would ever choose to ape a style that was already being considered old-fashioned three hundred years earlier.

But he was not there to speculate about architecture, he reminded himself, as he entered the police station and asked the duty sergeant if it would be possible to see the inspector in charge.

Inspector Robert Drayman was in his early thirties. He had light brown hair, pale-green eyes and a generous mouth. Drayman's handshake was firm and welcoming, and – despite his avowed intention to treat all the local coppers he met with suspicion – Blackstone found

95

himself immediately warming to the man.

'Is this an official visit?' Drayman asked, when he'd invited his guest to sit down.

Blackstone laughed lightly. 'Official? Certainly not. It's simply that I was in the area and I thought I'd call on you purely as a professional courtesy.'

'I'm glad you did,' Drayman told him. 'I know that you bobbies who work in the big cities regard those of us based in small towns as little better than country bumpkins...'

'No, no,' Blackstone protested.

'...and though I hate to admit it, you're probably quite right to. We don't have your experience of dealing with serious crimes, because there isn't any serious crime to deal with.'

It was too good an opening to miss and Blackstone seized it with both hands. 'I wouldn't have thought there was a town in the whole country where there isn't *some* serious crime,' he said.

'I suppose any crime's serious – if it happens to you,' Inspector Drayman said earnestly, 'but perhaps what I really meant was that we've no experience of *complicated* crimes.'

'Complicated crimes?' Blackstone repeated.

'If there's a murder here, it's almost always either the result of a domestic disturbance or a fight in a pub. We usually have more witnesses coming forward than we could shake a stick at, and even when there are no witnesses, the murderer himself – full of remorse – is more than likely to give himself up.'

'Sounds an ideal situation to be in,' Blackstone said.

'Do you really believe that?' Drayman asked, sounding a little disappointed.

'Absolutely,' Blackstone confirmed. 'The simpler a murder is to solve, the happier I am.'

'Perhaps you're right,' Drayman agreed. 'At the end of the day, I suppose it's our job to bring the guilty to justice as quickly as possible. But once in a while I do catch myself wishing that I had a real challenge – a crime I needed to do some serious thinking about, rather than one with a solution that just falls into my lap.'

He paused for a moment, as if considering whether or not he dared voice the next thought that was in his mind.

'Look,' he continued, 'I know you must be a very busy man, but I wonder if you could spare the time to have a meal with me tonight. I'd be most interested to hear about the cases you've had to deal with.'

'I'd be more than willing to dine with you,' Blackstone said.

Drayman smiled gratefully. 'Excellent. I'm sure I'll find it invaluable to hear your ideas. And, naturally, you'll be my guest.'

They fixed a time when they would meet, then both men stood up and shook hands again.

'Before I go, there is one thing that's been puzzling me about this town,' Blackstone said. 'I can't help wondering when—'

Drayman held up his hand to stop Blackstone saying any more, and smiled again.

'Don't tell me!' he said. 'Let me see if I can

use what few detection skills I actually have to guess what you were about to ask.'

'All right.'

'You've just arrived in town, and most things you've seen here will be just like the things you'll see every day in London – except that they'll probably be smaller and more old-fashioned. But there's something that has aroused your curiosity – something you *don't* have in London. Am I right so far?'

'You're spot on,' Blackstone said.

'It has to be our black-and-white buildings. You've been wondering why this police station – and so many other buildings in the town – look as if they belong to some time in the dim and distant past.'

'That's right,' Blackstone agreed.

'The answer's really very simple: they're built like that because they have no foundations.'

'Why don't they—'

'And the reason they have no foundations is because that makes it much easier to move them.'

'But why should you want to move them?'

'In this area, we never know where the ground's going to subside next, so we have to be prepared for it to happen anywhere and everywhere. If it started to give way under this station, we'd simply jack the building up, put it on rollers and move it elsewhere. It's not exactly an easy job to undertake, but I can assure you that it's a damn sight easier – and a damn sight less expensive – than pulling the station down

98

and building a new one.'

'It must be,' Blackstone agreed.

He had almost convinced himself that Drayman was as honest and straightforward as he appeared to be, but there was one test he needed to put the man through before he could really be sure.

He walked towards the door. If Drayman *was* hiding something, now would be the time he would begin to relax his guard.

Blackstone reached towards the doorknob, then suddenly turned around. 'By the way,' he said, 'I don't think I ever told you what had brought me to Northwich, did I?'

'No,' Drayman agreed. 'I don't think you did.'

'I came to attend the funeral of a good friend of mine.'

Inspector Drayman looked sympathetic, but not overly interested. 'Oh yes?' he said.

Blackstone looked the other man squarely in the eyes. 'He was an old army friend,' he said, with slow deliberation. 'A man I owe a considerable debt of gratitude to. His name was Tom Yardley. Have you heard of him?'

'No, I don't think I have,' Drayman confessed. 'Wait a moment! He wasn't that salt-miner who blew himself up, was he?'

'That's right.'

Drayman shook his head slowly from side to side. 'It's always a terrible thing when an able-bodied man is cut down in his prime.'

His eyes had not so much as flickered as he spoke, Blackstone thought.

If there was something rotten going on in Marston – something that involved members of the local police force – then Inspector Drayman was definitely not a part of it.

Ellie Carr and Jed Trent had spent the night at a boarding house in Tunstall, one of the six pottery towns which ran in a north-to-south line along the Trent and Mersey Canal and produced the china crockery that had made Staffordshire world-famous.

'*Trent* and Mersey,' Ellie had said mockingly, the first time they'd crossed over the canal on their way to the town. 'What an honour to have a long thin stretch of water named after you, Jed.'

'There's a river named after me, as well,' Jed Trent had said, pretending to take her seriously, 'though there are those who claim that the river got its name before either me *or* the canal.'

Ellie had laughed, and said, 'People can be so jealous, can't they?'

Tunstall was not more than three or four miles from the drainage ditch in which Emma Walsingholme's body had been found, but seemed almost to be on a different planet. There were no hedgerows or lush meadows there. It was a town dominated by chimney stacks and bottle-shaped kilns, and even when these were shut down, the smoke they produced hovered around like an unwelcome relative.

'Just like being back home,' Ellie told Jed, as she sniffed the air just after breakfast.

Yet when Superintendent Bullock arrived in a pony and trap to take her to Walsingholme Manor, she was surprised to discover that she was quite looking forward to the prospect of seeing green fields again – so perhaps she could grow to like the countryside after all.

'In the olden days, potters always used charcoal in their kilns, you know,' Superintendent Bullock said, as they left the smoky town behind them. 'But the problem with that was that England's quickly running out of the wood to make the charcoal from. Which is how this place started to come into its own. It had the right sort of clay, you see, but it also had coal mines to provide an alternative fuel to fire the kilns.'

'Very interesting,' Ellie Carr said politely.

'The only thing that was holding the potters back was a decent transport system,' continued Bullock, who appeared to have a real enthusiasm for the subject. 'Then, around a hundred and thirty years ago, they built the canals that connected us to all the major cities – Liverpool, Manchester, London – and all obstacles were removed. So now you can travel to almost any part of the world and be confident you'll find Staffordshire pottery.'

'You said "us",' Ellie pointed out.

'I beg your pardon?'

'You said, to connect *us* to all the major cities.'

Bullock grinned, sheepishly. 'Caught me out, haven't you?' he said. 'Yes, you're quite right – I was born and brought up round here.'

'So you know the area well,' Ellie said.

'Like the back of my own hand.'

'That must be a great help in the investigation.'

The smile disappeared from Bullock's face and was replaced by a look of deepest gloom.

'*Nothing* helps in this investigation,' he said, 'nothing at all. I've investigated eight murders of eight innocent young girls so far, and I know no more about the killer now than I did when I started.'

One of the men had taken Cathy away, and once she had gone, Lizzie felt the fear starting to return.

She found herself wishing she was back in the workhouse, because though she had hated the institution, she'd at least known the rules – at least known what to expect.

Here there was only an uncertainty that stabbed into her gut like a knife – which made her jump when there was even the slightest noise. And when she heard the sound of footsteps approaching her cell – heavy, decisive footsteps, like the ones she was hearing now – she almost wished she was dead.

The cell door opened and she saw one of the men standing there. He was very big and very ugly, and she could smell the stink of alcohol on his breath even from a distance.

'Take your clothes off,' he ordered her.

'What?'

'Take your bleedin' clothes off, you little bitch!'

'Is it – Is it time for my bath?'

'Maybe later. Right now, I'm goin' to do what I've been dreamin' about all night: I'm going to *have* you.'

'Please, no!' Lizzie begged.

The man laughed.

It was the most evil laugh that Lizzie had ever heard, and she understood immediately that the man was pure evil himself, and that the more frightened she was, the more he would enjoy what he was about to do.

'If you don't do what I tell you – and right away – I'll not only have you, but I'll whip you into the bargain,' the man said. 'And I promise you, little girl, you wouldn't enjoy a whipping from me. So do as I say: let the dog see the rabbit, before I lose my temper.'

He *wanted* her to resist, she thought. He *wanted* to give her a whipping. But she would at least deny him that satisfaction. With tears streaming down her face, Lizzie lifted the workhouse smock and pulled it over her head.

'Nice,' the man said, licking his lips with his thick slimy tongue. 'Very nice indeed. Now let's see the rest of it.'

'What the hell's going on here?' demanded an angry voice.

Both Lizzie and her tormentor turned towards the doorway.

The new arrival was a well-dressed man, carrying a walking cane in his hand. He was nowhere near as big as the brute who wished to violate her, yet he was clearly the one who was in control.

'I asked you what was going on in here,' the man repeated, in an icy tone.

The tough looked down at the floor. 'I was ... er ... just inspectin' the new girl, boss,' he mumbled.

'You were just doing *what*?'

'Inspectin' the new girl.'

The boss stepped into the cell.

'Liar!' he said. He sniffed the air. 'You're drunk! It's eleven o'clock in the morning, and you're already drunk!'

'What if I am?' the tough demanded. 'A man's entitled to a bit of pleasure, ain't he?'

'And if I'd arrived a few minutes later, your "bit of pleasure" would have included deflowering this girl.'

'I ain't had a woman for weeks, boss,' the drunk said, wheedlingly. 'Not for weeks.'

'Then go out and find yourself a cheap whore!'

'I don't like payin' for it. Anyway, they ain't the same as a sweet little thing like her.'

The boss lifted his hand and pointed his index finger directly at the drunk's face. 'You will leave her alone,' he warned. 'You will not damage her. Do you understand? You will not damage *any* of the goods.'

'It ain't as if anybody's likely to notice – not where she's goin',' the drunk argued.

The boss moved so quickly that it was almost a blur to Lizzie. One moment he was standing near the door, the next he'd crossed the room and was slapping the drunk in the face.

Once! Twice! Three times!

The drunken man finally seemed to understand the predicament he had got himself into, and sank to his knees.

'I'm sorry, boss,' he said, almost sobbing. 'I didn't mean it. I swear I didn't mean it.'

The other man took three steps back, and raised his cane in the air as if he were about to strike the drunk.

'No, boss, please!' the drunk moaned.

The boss lowered the cane. 'You disgust me! You truly disgust me. Get out of my sight – and don't let me see you again for the rest of the day.'

The drunk scrambled to his feet and rushed out of the open door.

When he'd gone, the boss turned to Lizzie and said, in a kindly voice, 'I'm very sorry about that, my dear. I promise you that nothing like it will ever happen again.'

'Why are you keepin' me locked up here?' Lizzie asked.

'Because I have plans for you, and you must stay here until those plans come to fruition.'

'You what?'

'There's something I need you to do for me – but I don't need you to do it for me yet.'

'Couldn't you – Couldn't you just let me go?' Lizzie pleaded.

'I'm afraid not,' the man told her. 'I've already got too much invested in this operation to do that.'

'What operation?' Lizzie asked. 'I don't have no idea what you're talking about.'

'Be patient, and all will be revealed to you,' the man said soothingly. 'And in the meantime, my dear, try to learn to savour the things that you're being offered here. The food, for example. If I remember correctly, there's best beefsteak on the menu tonight.'

He smiled at her, then stepped out of the cell. Once he was outside, he slammed the door behind him and locked it.

Inspector Maddox was so smilingly friendly when he greeted Archie Patterson that, for a moment, the sergeant toyed with the idea that the real Maddox must have been disposed of overnight and this unconvincing replica left in his place.

'I had my doubts about you initially, Sergeant, as I'd have had my doubts about any officer who'd been working for Inspector Blackstone for any length of time,' Maddox told him. 'But, from what I've read in your report, you seem to have pulled the whole thing off rather splendidly.'

'Thank you, sir,' Patterson replied.

'Yes, rather splendidly,' Maddox repeated. 'As soon as the madam has managed to get her hands on a suitable girl, she'll ring you. And as soon as you've made the second payment, we can arrest her. I can see no difficulty at all in bringing this case to an entirely satisfactory conclusion.'

'And do you think she'll be convicted?'

'I don't see how she could fail to be, as long as you make sure that the money you hand over has been marked and recorded first.'

'But will she go to gaol?'

'Ah, that depends,' Maddox said evasively.

'On what?'

'On any number of things.'

'For example?'

'For a start, on whether or not the newspapers still have an interest in the case by the time it comes to trial. If they have, then an example will certainly have to be made of her.'

'And if they haven't?' Patterson asked.

'Then there's the question of her barrister,' Maddox continued, ignoring the sergeant's question. 'If he's good – if he knows how to spin his story well – the madam could end up looking only slightly less of a victim than the girl herself.'

'She can probably afford the best lawyer around,' Patterson said miserably. 'Are there any other factors which might affect the outcome?'

Maddox chuckled. The miserable bastard actually *chuckled*! 'And then, of course, there's the judge,' he said.

'You mean that some judges are more severe in their sentencing than others?' Patterson asked-ed.

'I mean that if the judge she comes up before is one of her clients – or one of his close colleagues on the bench is one of her clients – he'll probably be inclined to take a more lenient view than he might otherwise have done.'

'And how likely is that?' Patterson wondered.

Maddox chuckled again. 'If you'd known some of the judges I've known, you'd think it *very* likely.'

'So all the effort we'd put into this operation could turn out to be a complete waste of time?' Patterson asked despondently.

'Not at all,' Maddox said, still buoyed up by his own good humour, and not even noticing that Patterson was not sharing the mood. 'We will have done everything that the Home Secretary asked us to do, won't we?'

'Yes, I suppose so.'

'And that will be duly noted, so that when it comes round to the time to be considered for promotion, we'll both already be ahead of the field. I'd rather like to be a superintendent, you know.'

'Would you, sir?' Patterson asked flatly.

'I would indeed. And given the cock-up that Superintendent Bullock seems to be making, there may very well soon be a vacancy.'

'So, the madam could walk away scot-free, could she?'

'Not scot-free, no. There'll have to be a fine – probably rather a hefty one – which, in my opinion, is punishment enough, considering that all she was doing was striving to meet her clients' needs.'

Two

Walsingholme Manor could not strictly have been called a stately home. It did not dominate the surrounding landscape like the ancestral piles of some of England's oldest families did. It did not have an east wing and a west wing attached to the main building, each of them as long as – and far more impressive than – the average London working-class street. But, even allowing for that, it was still a very substantial edifice of perhaps forty or forty-five rooms, which had been built in a pleasant and reasonably unostentatious neo-classical style.

'Sir John Walsingholme's great-grandfather was a master potter,' Bullock told Ellie, as the pony trotted up the long driveway to the front entrance of the house. 'I've seen some of his work on display in the museum. Very impressive. He was a real craftsman!'

'I'd be willing to wager he didn't earn enough to buy this place, though,' Ellie Carr said.

Bullock laughed. 'You're right. It was Sir John's grandfather who had the head for business. He ended up *owning* the pottery factory in which his own dad had worked.'

'And, from then on, the family's never looked back?'

'More or less. Sir John's father sold the factory – lock, stock and barrel – for an absolute fortune, and then bought as much land as he could lay his hands on. I knew him – though not, of course, to speak to. He was the master of the local hunt and the sheriff of the county. You'd never have guessed, to look at him, that his granddad had made his money by getting his hands dirty.'

'What's Sir John himself like?' Ellie asked.

'Two days ago, I'd have said that he was a fine figure of a man – a real man's man. He nearly won the Wimbledon Tennis Championship a few years ago, you know. *Would* have won it, if he hadn't come up against William Renshaw, who was at the top of his game at that time. But like I said, that was two days ago.'

'And what's he like now?'

'Now,' Bullock said sombrely, 'the man's a wreck.'

The pub was called the Hanging Tree. And, for all Blackstone knew, there might well once have been a tree on the site from which rebellious peasants and other malcontents had been hanged by the neck until dead.

But if that *were* so, there was certainly no trace of the grisly history to be seen now. Instead there was just a perfectly ordinary working boozer, which stood in the shadow of the town's covered market hall.

When he opened the door of the public bar, he saw that the place was already packed out

110

with customers.

He navigated his way around the various groups of drinkers, and when he reached the bar he ordered himself a pint of bitter.

It was while he was reaching into his pocket for his cigarettes that the accident happened. His elbow knocked into one of the pint pots sitting on the bar and sent it flying. The pot hit the floor on the bar side of the counter, spilling what little beer was left in it, and bouncing once before coming to rest.

'That's was my bloody drink you just spilt,' said an angry voice to Blackstone's right.

The inspector turned. The speaker was a huge, barrel-chested man with a three-day growth of beard on his face that did not quite hide the scar running down his cheek.

'Sorry about that, mate,' Blackstone said easily. 'Let me buy you another one.'

'Are you a foreigner?' the other man demanded.

Blackstone shook his head. 'No, I'm not,' he said. 'But even if I was, I'd still be more than willing to buy you that drink.'

'You sound a lot like a bloody dirty foreign swine to me,' the other man growled.

'Now, now, Mick, we don't want any trouble in here,' said the landlord soothingly, from the other side of the bar. 'Accidents will happen, and you'd all but finished that pint anyway, hadn't you?'

The man he'd called 'Mick' whirled round towards him.

111

'You keep out of this,' he warned. 'I want to know if this bastard who's spilled my beer is a foreigner.'

Blackstone sighed. He'd dealt with enough aggressive drunks in his time on the Force to know that this man was looking for trouble, and whatever he himself said would make no difference. Still, he supposed he might as well try to smooth things over.

'I'm from London,' he told Mick.

'From London!' the drunk repeated. 'From bloody *London*! Then you've no business bein' here, have you?'

He was speaking so loudly – and so unpleasantly – that people were already starting to edge away.

And it was just as well that they were, Blackstone told himself. Because this Mick character was big and heavy, and even in a half-drunk state, he would still take a lot of handling.

'I said, you've no business bein' up here in Cheshire, have you?' Mick repeated.

'Why don't you let me buy you that drink, to show how sorry I am about spilling yours?' Blackstone suggested. 'And let me get you a whisky chaser, while I'm about it.'

'I want you to show me just how sorry you *really* are,' Mick said. 'I want you to get down on your knees – an' lick my boots.'

Blackstone shook his head, almost regretfully. 'I'm afraid I can't do that,' he said.

'Can't you, by God!' Mick roared. 'Well, we'll soon see about that, won't we, now?'

He feinted with his left arm, and led with his right fist. The deception might have worked on a man with little experience of street fighting, but it didn't work on Blackstone. He blocked his opponent's attack with his right arm and punched with his left. His fist connected with a jaw-bone that felt as hard as iron. Mick's head rocked, and then he toppled over backwards, hitting the floor with a heavy thud.

For a second he looked completely dazed, then a smile came to his face.

'You're tougher than you look, you long streak of piss an' wind,' he said to Blackstone.

'A lot of people have told me that,' Blackstone replied. 'Can I buy you that drink now?'

There was some spittle and blood around Mick's mouth, and he wiped it away with the sleeve of his jacket.

'Why not?' he asked. He held his arm in the air. 'You help me back up on to my feet, you can buy me that drink – or maybe I'll buy you one instead – an' we'll pretend that none of this has ever happened.'

'I shouldn't think you need any help from me to get up,' Blackstone said flatly.

'You're probably right,' Mick agreed.

He put his hands on the floor and raised his torso off the ground. He winced, said 'Ouch', then smiled again. And still Blackstone did not move.

The big man made quite a show of the difficulties of standing up, but once he was on his feet, he came back to life immediately.

With his right hand, he grabbed a pint glass, smashed it against the counter, then jabbed the jagged edge of the glass in Blackstone's direction.

'Now we'll have some fun,' he snarled. 'Now we'll see how you Londoners bleed.'

'You really don't want to do this,' Blackstone warned him.

'Don't I?' Mick asked. 'An' will you still be tellin' me that when you're screamin' like a stuck pig?'

He lunged forward, the jagged edge aimed at his enemy's throat. Blackstone sidestepped, and as Mick blundered past him he struck out with his boot and caught the big man a heavy blow squarely on the kneecap.

Mick came to a halt, let the broken glass in his hand fall to the floor, and sent an urgent message from his brain to his body that it should forget the pain in his knee and concentrate on maintaining his balance.

It was at that moment – just as the message was getting through – that Blackstone kicked the kneecap a second time, so hard that the sound of the crack echoed off the walls.

'You bastard!' Mick screamed, as his leg gave way underneath him and he fell to the floor for the second time.

Two uniformed police constables appeared in the doorway and elbowed their way through the crowd.

'It was the man on the floor – Mick Huggins – who started it all,' the landlord told them. 'This gentleman was doin' no more than defending himself.'

The constables bent down, took one of Mick's arms each and pulled him up off the floor.

'We're arresting you for causing a public affray,' one of them told the big man, who was, of necessity, putting all his weight on one leg and looked as if he might collapse again.

'We may be needin' you as a witness, sir,' the constable said to Blackstone.

The inspector nodded. 'My name's Blackstone. Your Inspector Drayman knows where I can be contacted.'

The constables frogmarched Mick out of the door.

When they'd gone, Blackstone turned back to the bar. 'Nice quiet little town you've got here, isn't it?' he said conversationally to the landlord.

Superintendent Bullock had been no more than accurate when he'd described Sir John Walsingholme as a wreck, Ellie Carr thought, looking down at the man slumped in the armchair.

Walsingholme's eyes were bloodshot, his skin was grey and there was a tremble in his hands over which he clearly had no control. If she hadn't previously been told he was in his mid-forties, Ellie could easily have taken him for at least seventy.

'We're very sorry to bother you at a distressing time like this, sir,' Superintendent Bullock told the shadow in the armchair.

Walsingholme raised his head slightly, though it seemed to cost him a great deal of effort.

'You have your job to do, Superintendent. I quite understand that,' he said in a voice that fell somewhere between a whisper and a croak.

'We're concentrating most of our efforts on looking for any suspicious strangers who might have been spotted in the area just before your daughter disappeared,' Bullock said. 'We've had no reports of any so far, but we mustn't give up hope yet.'

'Hope!' Walsingholme repeated hollowly. 'There is *no* hope now that my darling Emma's dead.'

'If we catch her killer...'

'Even if you did catch him – even were you to subject him to such pain as no man has experienced before – it still wouldn't bring her back.'

'That's true,' Ellie Carr said, sympathetically. 'But at least it would ensure that other girls didn't suffer the same fate.'

Though she had been standing right in front of him, Walsingholme only now seemed to notice she was even there.

'Who are you?' he asked.

'This is Dr Carr,' Bullock said.

Walsingholme laughed bitterly. 'You're too late,' he said. 'My daughter is beyond your help now.'

'Dr Carr is a a forensic pathologist,' Bullock said. 'She'd like to examine your daughter's body.'

'Why?' Walsingholme asked.

116

'It might help us to learn more about the nature of her death,' Ellie explained.

'But we know what killed her. She was strangled, and then she was ... and then she was...'

'Her body may hold more clues to her murder than are obvious to the naked eye,' Ellie said evenly.

'I don't understand,' Walsingholme confessed wearily.

'A more detailed examination of her remains might well reveal...'

A look of pure horror came to Sir John's face, as he finally understood what Ellie was saying.

'You want to cut her up!' he exploded.

'That might well be a part of the process,' Ellie admitted. 'But I can assure you that if any incisions are necessary, her remains will be granted all the respect and dignity that—'

'The poor child has lost her hands and her feet!' bellowed Walsingholme, finding new strength from the rage that was engulfing him. 'Her face – and most of her body – has been slashed to ribbons! And you want to mutilate her further? What kind of monster are you?'

'Whatever I may do to her, can't hurt her now,' Ellie said gently. 'And it might just help to bring her killer to justice.'

'I've already told you, that won't bring her back!'

'And by arresting the man before he can do any more harm, we'll be sparing other parents the suffering that you've had to endure.'

'Let them suffer!' Walsingholme said. 'Let the

117

whole world suffer, if sparing it suffering means defiling my dear sweet daughter even further.'

'We should be leaving,' Bullock told Ellie, with a sudden urgency in his voice.

But Ellie stood her ground. 'We've come to ask your permission as a matter of courtesy, Sir John...' she began.

'Courtesy!'

'... but the truth of the matter is that I'm afraid you have no choice but to accept that the autopsy will go ahead. In the case of violent death, the law is quite clear about our right to do whatever—'

'To hell with the law!' Walsingholme said. 'It has been arranged that my poor daughter will be buried tomorrow, and that arrangement stands. And between now and then, no one – not even the Lord Chancellor himself – will go near her. I will give up my life before I will allow any of you to touch her.'

'Sir John...' Ellie said.

But she was already moving away from him – not because she wanted to, but because Superintendent Bullock was half-pushing, half-carrying her towards the door.

Three

'If you ever behave in that way again, I'll not only kick you off this case, I'll see to it personally that you never get anywhere near another Metropolitan Police investigation,' Superintendent Bullock said, as he bundled Ellie Carr out of the main door of Walsingholme Manor.

'If *I* behave in that way again,' Ellie asked angrily, breaking free of his grip. 'What about the way that *you* behaved?'

'I had to do *something*,' Bullock told her. 'It doesn't do to make an enemy of a man like Sir John Walsingholme.'

'Are you afraid it might damage your promotion prospects?' Ellie asked, sneeringly.

'No, I'm afraid he might use his influence to have *me* taken off this case!' Bullock countered.

'Would that be such a loss?' Ellie demanded, still furious. 'You haven't exactly made a great deal of progress so far, have you?'

'No,' Bullock admitted, his fury matching her own. 'But at least I know the ins-and-outs of the case now, and if there's a lead to be found, I might recognize it for what it is. Could you say the same about anybody else coming in from the outside and starting from scratch?'

The logic of his argument made Ellie Carr feel as if she had suddenly been doused with a pail of icy water.

'You're right,' she said, calmer now. 'You're the best man to lead the investigation.'

'So now you understand why I had to remove you before you could do any more damage?'

'Yes, and I'm sorry that my actions in there have made your life more difficult for you.'

'You only did what you thought was right,' Bullock said, somewhat mollified. 'You only wanted to catch the killer.'

They walked over to the pony and trap, almost friends again.

'But I really *do* need to see that body,' Ellie said, as she climbed into the passenger seat.

'I thought I'd already made it plain to you that that simply isn't possible,' Bullock replied.

'Can't you get some sort of warrant from the local Justice of the Peace?' Ellie wondered. 'Whatever his personal feelings – and whatever he told us a few minutes ago – Sir John would have to respect that.'

A smile, which could have been bitter and could have been darkly amused – and was probably both – came to Bullock's lips.

'And you think that the local JP would give us such a warrant, do you?' he asked.

'I don't see why he wouldn't, once we've explained the necessity of it to him,' Ellie said earnestly.

'Oh, don't you? I wonder if you'll still think

that way when I tell you the JP's name.'

'It's Sir John Walsingholme, isn't it?' Ellie asked.

'That's right,' Bullock agreed. 'It's Sir John Walsingholme.'

'Name?' the booking sergeant at Northwich Police Station demanded.

The big man with a scar on his cheek glowered down at him. 'It shouldn't be me that's here,' he said. 'It's that other bastard you should have arrested. He nearly broke my soddin' knee.'

'Only after you tried to rearrange his face with a broken glass,' the sergeant said, unsympathetically. 'Now, for the second time of asking, tell me what your name is.'

'Mick Huggins,' the prisoner said, sullenly.

'Michael Huggins,' the sergeant said, writing the name down in his ledger. 'Address?'

'Haven't got one.'

'So you're homeless?'

'I didn't say that,' Huggins replied, grinning as if this were a game he had played a hundred times, but never tired of.

'You just told me that you don't have any address,' the sergeant said impatiently.

'So I did. But I've still got a home. I'm a narrowboat man. I live on my barge.'

Blackstone stood at the crown of the humpbacked bridge, in the village that had been raised on salt – in all senses of the word – and

121

sometimes sank because of it, too. Ahead of him lay one of the mines, and beyond that the church and the school. Behind him were the houses and more mines.

There was no escaping salt, he thought. Even this bridge was not free of it, for the Jubilee Salt Works had been built right alongside it, and, at its upper level, actually opened on to the bridge.

He turned to walk back down the bridge, and saw that a man – stripped down to his vest and enveloped in steam – was standing at the open salt-works doors and watching him.

'Are you that Mr Blackstone?' the man asked.

'I don't think I know you,' Blackstone replied cautiously.

'No more you do,' the man agreed. 'I'm Ted Littler. I'm a mate of Walter Clegg's. An' *you*, unless I'm very much mistaken, were an army mate of Tom Yardley's.'

'That's right,' Blackstone said.

'He was a good man.'

'One of the best.'

There was a pause, as there sometimes is when men who don't know each other have run out of things to say.

Then Ted Littler spoke again. 'Do you want to come inside, and have a look around?'

Blackstone shrugged. Littler may have offered the invitation as nothing more than a way of breaking the awkward silence, but now it had been made, it would seem impolite to refuse it.

'Yes, I'd like to,' he said.

Littler led him through the double doors into a

room that was so steamy it would have put a Turkish baths to shame. The room was dominated by a huge metal pan – Blackstone guessed it was at least sixty feet long – which was made of large iron plates bolted together. And in the pan was a bubbling milky liquid which was responsible for all the steam.

'That's brine,' Ted Littler explained. 'Do you know what brine is, Mr Blackstone?'

'A mixture of salt and water?'

'That's right. We pump the water into the ground, and it dissolves the salt and makes brine. Then we pump the brine out again, and heat it up to boiling point in this pan. And when the water evaporates, what we're left with is salt. It's almost like magic, isn't it?'

If it was, it was a very sticky sort of magic, Blackstone thought, for though he'd been standing there for less than a minute, he was already starting to sweat heavily and had the tang of salt on his tongue.

There were several other men, besides Littler, working on the pan, and Blackstone found himself watching them with a growing fascination.

The main tool of their trade appeared to be an almost-flat sieve on the end of a long pole. The men skimmed these sieves through the milky solution, then lifted them clear of the surface and held them there while the liquid drained away. That done, they swung the sieves clear of the pan and tipped their contents into wooden moulds, which were around two feet long and nine inches square.

'That salt would strip the flesh off your bones right now,' Littler said, obviously pleased that Blackstone was taking an interest. 'But by the time it's cooled down in the moulds, it'll have turned as hard as a brick. So the next time you see a block of salt resting on the shelf of your local shop, just remember all the effort that's gone into makin' it.'

'I will,' Blackstone promised.

'Funny thing, isn't it?' Ted Littler continued. 'I've never been out of Cheshire myself, but the salt that I make in here travels all the way round the world. Take the blocks you've just seen us making. They might go no further than Manchester, but it's just as likely they could be in South Africa a month from now.'

Blackstone said nothing, but he was doing some rapid thinking. Ever since he'd arrived in this village, he'd been asking himself why a jewel-smuggling ring would ever base itself here. And now he thought he had the answer.

The King Charles's Arms was the most convenient pub for the boarding house at which Ellie Carr and Jed Trent were staying, but even from the outside it was obvious to Trent that it was a rough-and-ready place.

'Why don't we see if there's somewhere a little more salubrious further down the road,' he suggested.

'There's no need to,' Ellie replied firmly. 'This place will serve our needs perfectly well.'

Trent had begun to learn to distinguish between the times when there was some point in arguing with Ellie and the times when there wasn't, and judging this to be one of the latter times he merely shrugged and said, 'On your own head be it then, Dr Carr.' He opened the door to the saloon bar and gestured her inside.

Ellie looked around her.

'Changed your mind?' Trent asked over his shoulder.

'Not at all,' Ellie said. 'You find us a nice table, Jed, and I'll get the drinks in.'

'There are no "nice" tables,' Trent told her. 'And if anybody's getting the drinks in, I think it had better be me.'

But he was speaking to empty air, because Ellie was already striding towards the bar counter.

'We don't serve women,' the landlord said, speaking to her, but looking over her head.

'That's all right, I don't want to buy one,' Ellie said cheerily. 'But what I *would* like is a pint of your best bitter and a large port and lemon.'

'Listen, love—' the landlord began.

'I'm not your love now, nor do I ever consider it a very likely – or enjoyable – prospect,' Ellie interrupted him.

'You what?'

'Look at me!' Ellie said.

For a second the landlord resisted, then he slowly lowered his eyes until they were resting on her.

'What you have to ask yourself is whether or not it's worth the trouble to refuse to serve me,'

125

Ellie said. 'Or, to put it another way, how much trouble do you think I could cause if I *don't* get served?'

She wasn't that big, the landlord thought, but she was scrappy. And she looked as if she'd rather lose a leg than give way now.

'A pint of bitter an' a port an' lemon, you said, didn't you?' he asked.

'That's right,' Ellie agreed.

As she took the drinks over to the table that Jed had found for them, she discovered that she was angry. But not angry with the landlord. She'd never really been angry with him.

'That's the trouble with you,' Jed said, when she sat down.

'What is?'

'If you can't fight the battles you want to fight, you'll fight any battles that happen to come to hand.'

He was right, of course. She recognized now that she'd picked this pub deliberately, because she'd been looking for trouble as a way of relieving the frustration that had been eating away at her. But she couldn't help it! She'd always been a fighter, and that was why – despite her background – she'd ended up as a medical researcher rather than a flower girl.

'It's the bleedin' injustice of it wot gets me,' she said, not even noticing that she was slipping back into the Cockney of her childhood.

'What injustice are you talking about?' Jed Trent said.

'The injustice of there being one law in this

country for the rich – and quite another law for the poor. If Emma Walsingholme had been a domestic servant or a milkmaid, her dad wouldn't even have been *told* that I was going to perform an autopsy. The body would just have been delivered to the nearest morgue, and that would have been that.'

'That's possibly true, but—' Jed Trent began.

'But because her bleedin' dad's got a title – and an estate that it would take you half a day to walk round – I've been told I can't even get near her. It makes me sick to my stomach, Jed.'

'Put yourself in her father's place.'

'I'm not here to put myself in his place. That's his clergyman's job. *I'm* here to examine the body of his daughter. I'm here to come up with information that might possibly prevent more murders.'

'Oh, is that why you're getting so het up?'

'Of course it is!'

'And it has nothing at all to do with the fact that you *always* get frustrated when somebody blocks you from furthering your own research?'

'There may be a bit of that to it as well,' Ellie admitted, a little guiltily. 'But that's not to say I don't want to help catch this madman. I really *do* want to do that!'

'I know you do.'

Ellie thought for a moment. 'If we could just learn where they're keeping the body until the funeral, we could probably find a way to break into the place, and—'

'No!' Trent said forcefully.

'You've no need to worry. However much I might want to cut her open, I wouldn't. I'd just *look* at the body.'

'The answer's still no.'

Ellie gave Trent a black look. 'You do work for me, you know. It's not the other way around.'

'I work for the University College Hospital,' Trent pointed out. 'But even if you *were* the one who paid my wages, I still wouldn't let you do a crazy thing like that.'

Ellie Carr sighed. 'You're probably right,' she agreed. 'Breaking into the house would be going too far – even for me. So we'll just have to hope we get more co-operation the next time, won't we?'

'The next time what?'

'The next time some poor bloody girl is murdered. Because it will happen again, Jed, I can assure you of that.'

Four

When night falls over London, the mighty River Thames scoops up reflections as misers are popularly believed to scoop up their gold coins. Lights of all kinds bob on the water – the yellow light of the moon; the orange light of the gas-lit street lamps; the blue and green light that comes from the warning beacons of ships at anchor in the centre of the river.

It sometimes seemed to Archie Patterson – in one of his more fanciful moods – as if these small lights (buffeted by waves, sidelined by ripples), were engaged in a valiant struggle to stay afloat, but that, despite their noble efforts, they would eventually give way to exhaustion – and sink.

But they never *did* go under, as the more practical side of his mind always recognized. They stayed exactly where they were, surfing the water, until the sun came up again – and they simply faded away.

Patterson was not thinking about the lights on the water that night, as he walked along the Embankment. He was not even thinking about his fiancée, Rose, though the forceful way she was clinging to his arm must have made her hard to forget. Instead, much as he fought against it, his thoughts kept returning to the brothel in Waterloo Road.

He would make an arrest – he was sure of that. But to what end? So that the madam could pay a *fine*?

'What are you thinking, Archie?' Rose asked, poking him in the ribs with the index finger of her free hand.

'I was thinking that, in this life, people don't always get what they deserve,' he said.

'And what exactly is that supposed to mean?' Rose wondered. 'That you don't deserve me? Or

I don't deserve you?'

'Oh, that I don't deserve you,' Patterson said, taking hold of the hand with which she poked him, raising it to his mouth and kissing it lightly. 'Everybody knows that. It's as plain as the nose on your face.'

'My nose isn't plain!' Rose said, with mock-indignation.

'No,' Patterson agreed. 'It's a wonderful nose.'

'Tell me more,' Rose demanded.

'It's a beautiful nose. A nose that easily caps all other noses that have gone before it. When I'm arrested for not being worthy of you – as I'm bound to be eventually – that nose will be one of the prime pieces of evidence to be held against me.'

Rose giggled. 'Well, I'm certainly glad we've got *that* particular question straightened out,' she said.

They walked a little further along the Embankment.

The madam *should* get what she deserved for ruining a young life even before it had time to properly get started, Patterson told himself. She should be made to suffer as the girls who had passed through her hands had been made to suffer. But she was like one of those lights that never sank, whereas the girls were stones that went straight to the bottom.

'I know they say that two wrongs don't make a right,' he said to Rose, 'but do you think that's always true? Aren't there sometimes occasions when you need to turn the enemy's own weapons on him, if you're ever to defeat him?'

Rose giggled again. 'Whatever are you talking about now, Archie?' she asked him.

Patterson shrugged his beefy shoulders. 'Nothing really,' he admitted. 'Or if it is something, it's probably rubbish.'

'That's more than likely,' Rose agreed. 'You're a sensible chap most of the time, but when you *do* talk rubbish, you're really very good at it.'

Blackstone was enjoying his meal with Inspector Drayman, and the more he talked to the man, the more he found himself liking him. Drayman was not a brilliant copper, he'd soon decided, but he was certainly a conscientious one, and could probably deal more than adequately with any cases that were likely to come his way. But his strongest point, from Blackstone's perspective, was that he was a nice bloke – a thoroughly *decent* bloke – and there were far fewer of them in the police force than the public ever realized.

It was as the meal was drawing to a close that Blackstone decided to be a little more open with the local copper.

'Just before Tom Yardley died, he wrote me a letter,' he said, 'and in that letter, he hinted there was a jewellery-smuggling ring operating in his village.'

Drayman looked thoughtful for a second. 'Well, that certainly clears up one mystery.'

131

'And what mystery might that be?'

'The mystery of how an experienced blaster somehow managed to blow himself up.'

'You think he might have been murdered, too?' Blackstone asked.

'Too?' Drayman repeated. 'Why, who else do you think thinks that?'

'I do.'

'I'm afraid you've misinterpreted what I said completely. What I was meaning to suggest was that if Yardley thought there was some kind of smuggling ring in Marston, then he was clearly losing his mind in some way. And if he was losing his mind, that would explain why he made his fatal error with the explosives.'

'So you dismiss the possibility of a smuggling ring out of hand?'

'Absolutely.'

'Let me explain to you a little about robbery and fencing,' Blackstone suggested. 'It isn't always *easy* to steal really valuable jewels, but it's *never* easy to sell them on. Say you've got a diamond necklace, worth hundreds – or even thousands – of pounds. If it's that expensive, it will also be that *well known*, and there'll be no market for it in England. So the thief's faced with two options. Would you like to take a guess at what those options are?'

'I suppose he could break up the necklace and sell the individual diamonds.'

'He could, but if he does that, already he's reducing its value – because the parts will never be worth as much as the whole.'

'And his other option, I imagine, is to try and sell it abroad.'

'Exactly! But he's got to *get it* abroad first, and the only way to do that is by ship. Now, at each and every stage of the journey, there's the possibility of things going seriously wrong...'

'I'm sure there is.'

'...but the danger's greatest at the British customs and the foreign customs. Because these customs officers are highly trained. They know all the likely places they'll try to hide them – in suitcases with false bottoms, in hidden compartments in baby carriages which actually have a baby in them at the time, crammed up the smuggler's own back passage...'

'They don't really do that, do they?' Drayman said, horrified. 'They don't really stick them up their own back passages?'

'Indeed they do,' Blackstone said. 'You'd be surprised how much you can hide up an arsehole if you really want to.' He paused to light a cigarette. 'But we're getting off the point. Let's suppose that a group of very smart criminals put their heads together and come up with an *unlikely* method of smuggling – a method that the customs officers would never even think of.'

'I'm all ears,' Drayman said.

'In a way, this new method is no more than a variation on the false-bottomed suitcase trick, but before they can implement it, they have to get the goods themselves to Marston.'

'Why?'

'I'll come to that in a minute. Now, getting the

133

jewels here *could* be a problem, because the chances are that they'll have been stolen from houses and shops that are hundreds of miles from the village.'

'I still don't see—'

'But it's no real problem at all, when you think about it – because the goods can be brought here, quite safely, by narrowboat.'

'Good God, that's a ludicrous idea!'

'You're wrong about that. It isn't ludicrous at all. In fact, it's a very sensible and a very practical plan, given that Marston is connected to large parts of the country through the canal network.'

'But it would be so slow!' Drayman protested.

'That's all to the thieves' advantage, because no one – and that includes the police who are trying to track the jewels down – would ever *expect* them to move the goods slowly.'

'So they bring the jewels to Marston and hide them in this new variation of a false-bottomed suitcase?' Drayman asked sceptically.

'That's right. They take the jewels to the salt works—'

'And hide them in at the bottom of a big pile of loose salt?' Drayman said, chuckling. 'And then, I suppose, they all go to church and pray that when they need the jewels again, they'll be able to find them.'

'They don't hide them *under* a *pile* of salt,' Blackstone said. 'They hide them *in* a *block* of salt.'

'What?'

'They put the jewels on top of a heap of hot salt in a mould, pour more hot salt on top of it, and then let the salt set into a hard block. Once that's done, they load the block – along with thousands of other blocks which are almost identical – on to a narrowboat, which takes it to Liverpool, where it's loaded on to a ship that is sailing to wherever it is they've got a buyer for the goods.'

'It's a very clever idea,' Drayman admitted, 'but it's so incredible that I would have thought it belonged more to the realms of fiction than to real life.'

'Ten minutes ago you thought it was incredible that smugglers would make use of their backsides to hide the goods, but you've come round to the idea now, haven't you?'

'Well, yes.'

'So maybe in another ten minutes, the salt-block idea won't look so fanciful, either.'

'You've only got this Tom Yardley's word that there's a smuggling operation in the village.'

'Tom Yardley's word is all I need.'

'Perhaps it is. But you knew him and you trusted him, whereas I never even met the man, so his word carries no weight with me at all.'

'What are you saying? That before you'll even consider taking me seriously, you're going to need to see a lot more in the way of solid evidence?'

'Yes,' Drayman agreed. 'I think that's exactly what I'm saying.'

* * *

Though Jed Trent had tried to start up a conversation several times during the course of the meal, Ellie Carr had either not heard him at all, or – if she had – had grunted as few words as possible in reply.

Now, as the waiter cleared away the last of the dishes, Trent said in a very loud voice, 'Would you like to tell me what the problem is, Dr Carr?'

Ellie jumped. 'Do you have to shout, Jed?' she asked.

'Yes, I do – if I'm ever to get through to you,' Trent told her. 'I don't know where your mind's been all night, but it certainly hasn't been here with me.'

'I've been thinking,' Ellie said defensively.

'I've worked that out for myself. *But what about!*'

'About Emma Walsingholme's corpse.'

'Don't start that again,' Trent warned her. 'There'll be no breaking and entering while I'm around.'

'Of course there won't,' Ellie agreed primly. 'I would never suggest anything like such a course of action.'

'But you did suggest *exactly* that course of action,' Trent reminded her, '– just this afternoon.'

'This afternoon, I was much younger – and much more foolish – than I am now,' Ellie said.

'I beg your pardon?'

'For heaven's sake, Jed, let's stop talking about what *might have* happened – but never did

– and try to concentrate our minds instead on something that has actually occurred.'

'All right,' Trent agreed.

'I've been looking at the police reports on the condition of Emma's body when they found it, and it's pretty gruesome reading.'

'I imagine it is. There's no pleasant way to describe a girl who's had her hands and feet cut off, and her face slashed.'

'Yes, that is pretty horrific,' Ellie Carr agreed, almost indifferently, 'but I'm much more interested in the rest of her injuries. There were cuts and slashes all over the body – and I'm wondering why.'

'Do you really *need* a reason? The man who did it was a lunatic. Shouldn't that be enough for you?'

'It would certainly be enough – if he hadn't been such a very *methodical* lunatic.'

'What's methodical about slashing a woman to pieces?'

'Nothing at all. But if he'd done it while she was wearing her clothes, the dress would have been reduced to ribbons. And from what I've read, it wasn't.'

'So he took the dress off her. Maybe he got a bigger thrill out of killing her when she was naked.'

'Maybe he did. But why did he then put the dress *back on* her?'

'It beats me.'

'It beats me as well. What was the point of all those cuts?'

'To demonstrate that he had contempt for women in general, and pretty young rich girls in particular?'

'I would have thought he'd have made that point quite clearly enough with all the other mutilation,' Ellie said. 'The way I see it, there has to be some other reasoning behind the body-slashing – some message that couldn't be sent by simply cutting off her hands and feet.'

'That doesn't make any kind of sense,' Jed said.

'Not to you, no,' Ellie agreed. 'But perhaps it made sense to him.'

She suddenly slammed her hand down on the table, so hard that two of the waiters stopped in their tracks and turned around to see what had happened. 'Or perhaps he wasn't trying to *tell us* anything at all,' Ellie continued. 'Perhaps, on the contrary, he was trying to hide something *from* us!'

'Like what, for example?' Trent wondered.

'I don't know,' Ellie admitted gloomily. 'I really don't even have the faintest glimmering of an idea.'

Thursday: The White Devil

One

Blackstone was back in Afghanistan – back in the deep, deep cave where Private Tom Yardley had saved his life.

He had the stink of cordite and blood in his nostrils. He could see both the dead Pathan warriors and his own dead comrades in the flickering light of the oil lamp. His head ached from the blow that had been so recently delivered to the back of his skull. Yet there was at least a part of his brain that knew full well that none of it was real.

He did not mind that he was only dreaming. Dreams had often been useful to him in the past. They had warned him of dangers he had not been aware of when he was conscious. They had given him clues that his awakened self had followed. It would be going too far to suggest that they had served as actual signposts in his investigations, but they had at least given hints as to where those signposts might be found.

So dreams were welcome. Dreams were old friends and allies.

His head is throbbing and his vision is blurred. When he hears the footsteps in the connecting passageway, he gropes for his rifle. But he knows he is in no shape to fight, and that if more Pathans are coming, then he is already as good as dead. Then he hears Tom Yardley speak, and it is like hearing the voice of an angel.

'There were six of them, but there's only five here!' Blackstone says urgently. He is still groggy, and needs to lean on Tom as they make their way back down the passageway and out through the first cave. The sunlight outside is blinding, and for a moment, he thinks he will lose consciousness again.

The Pathan is lying on the ground, where Tom shot him.

And why shouldn't he be? Blackstone's befuddled brain asks. What did you expect him to do? Get up and walk away?

The Afghan is undoubtedly dead, but there is something not quite right about the wound in his chest, something that — however much he tries — Blackstone can't put his finger on.

But why is he even trying to discover what's wrong, he wonders. The Pathan warrior — a sworn enemy — no longer poses a threat, and that is really all he needs to know about him.

It was the furious knocking on the front door which brought him back to the present – which made him aware that the barren rocks of Afghanistan were no more than a memory, and that reality was a sofa in Walter Clegg's front parlour.

The knocking ceased, and a man's voice called

out, 'Inspector Blackstone? Are you in there?'
Official title, official business, Blackstone thought.

He reached for his gold watch, flicked opened the lid with his thumb, and saw that it was a quarter past five in the morning.

'Inspector Blackstone?' said the voice on the other side of the door, with increasing urgency.

Blackstone swung his body off the sofa and, clad only in his long johns, padded across the parlour and opened the door.

A uniformed constable was standing on the front step. 'Inspector Drayman would like to see you, sir,' he said, without preamble.

'Why? What's happened?'

'A girl's gone missing.'

Dear God, not another one, Blackstone thought.

'Is she from the local gentry?' he asked.

'No, sir,' the constable replied. 'She's a baker's daughter.'

Inspector Drayman was sitting at his desk. He was red-eyed through lack of sleep, and his skin had turned deathly pale with worry. When Blackstone entered his office, Drayman gave him the kind of look that a drowning man might give to the possessor of a lifebelt.

'Do you remember, when we were talking yesterday, that I said I wished I had more interesting crimes to deal with?' he asked bitterly. 'Well, I promise you, I never meant anything like this.'

143

'Give me the details,' Blackstone said crisply.
'The missing girl's name is Margie Thomas and she's thirteen years old. Her father has a small bakery down by the river.'
'So where did she—'
'I'm coming to that. Her grandmother lives in Great Budworth, which is a small village a couple of miles the other side of Marston. The grandmother's not been feeling too well recently, so it was arranged that Margie should spend the night with her. The girl was supposed to be setting off at around three o'clock in the afternoon, when she'd finished her chores in the bakery, but at the last minute her father decided he'd let her go earlier, so she could spend more time with her granny. She left home at about eleven thirty yesterday morning, but she never reached the grandmother's house.'
'When was the alarm raised?'
'Not until after you and I had finished our meal together.'
'Why did it take so long?'
'The grandmother didn't know anything was wrong. She assumed that the reason Margie hadn't turned up was either because she wasn't feeling well herself, or because the bakery had been busier than usual and she'd had to stay and help her dad. And for all the father knew, the girl was safely with her grandmother.'
'So what finally alerted them?'
'A postman called Tibbs. He's a friendly feller, the sort who'll talk to anybody. When he made the afternoon delivery, the grandmother happen-

ed to mention to him that Margie hadn't turned up, and when he met her dad in the pub, later in the evening, he asked him if anything was wrong with her. That's when Mr Thomas came to the police station.'

'Do you have any idea what kind of girl Margie is?' Blackstone asked. 'Is she wilful? Flighty?'

Drayman shook his head. 'From what we're told she seems to be a very quiet – almost timid – girl. Very responsible and very obedient. It's almost inconceivable to any of the people who know her well that she would ever have disappeared voluntarily.'

'What action have you taken?'

'I've had men out searching for her all night, but I knew from the start that, in the dark, it was almost bound to be a fruitless task. I felt a complete fool for even issuing the order.'

Blackstone nodded sympathetically. 'But you issued it anyway. And you were right to – because, in a situation like this one, you can't afford to ignore even the longest odds.'

'And what do I do now it's come light?' Drayman asked, 'Get the men to go over the same ground again?'

'Yes, but this time they should be on the lookout for anybody who might have seen the girl at some stage on her journey, because if we can pin down the point at which she was last sighted, we might be in a better position to work out exactly where she was when she vanished.'

Inspector Drayman produced a packet of

145

cigarettes from his pocket. His hands were trembling so violently that half a dozen of the cigarettes spilled on to his desk.

'She's already dead, isn't she?' he asked.

'We don't know that yet,' Blackstone replied evenly.

'Be honest with me, Sam. Please!'

'Miracles have been known to happen,' Blackstone said gravely, 'but if they happened too often, they wouldn't be miracles at all. Which means you're right, and the chances are that she's already dead.'

When Archie Patterson discovered, to his amazement, that he couldn't face the thought of eating the generous fried breakfast his landlady had just placed in front of him, he knew immediately that something was seriously wrong.

It was true that there had been a few – a very few – occasions in the past when he'd deliberately skipped a meal. But that had been different. That had only been to compensate for the fact that he'd strayed from the path of righteous dieting on which Rose had set him. Then, he had never *wanted* to abstain – had never felt any *inclination* not to eat. Now, even looking at the eggs swimming in lard was enough to make him feel slightly queasy.

'Whatever's the matter with you, Mr Patterson?' asked the landlady, who had returned with a second helping of fried bread, only to find that he hadn't even touched the first. 'You're not ill or anything, are you?'

'No, I'm not ill,' Patterson said.

'It's not like you to leave your food untouched like that,' the landlady persisted. 'Are you sure you haven't got a temperature?'

'I'm fine,' Patterson said gruffly. He slid his plate across the table. 'Could you take this away please?'

His landlady picked up the plate and walked over to the window. For a moment, Patterson thought that she was intending to examine the rejected food in a better light, but instead she lifted her eyes upwards to the sky.

She turned back towards him. 'Well, I was wrong,' she said.

'Wrong about what?'

'It's not raining fire and brimstone after all.'

'I beg your pardon?'

'I thought that if you turned down the perfectly good food I'd put in front of you, Mr Patterson, it must mean the end of the world was coming. But it seems quite a normal day outside.'

'Thank you, Mrs Barnes, I won't be needing anything else,' Patterson said frostily.

'Thank you, he says,' the landlady grumbled to herself, as she made her way back to the kitchen. 'If he won't touch his food, he's got nothing to thank me *for*, has he?'

Left to himself, Patterson lit up a cigarette – and even *that* didn't taste quite as it should have done.

Mrs Barnes had been quite right in her assertion that the world was not actually coming to an end, he thought, but it was also true that his experiences of the previous two days had certainly soured his own vision of it.

The madam of the brothel on Waterloo Street would not get off lightly, he promised himself. He simply would not allow that to happen!

Every single police officer in the Northwich area had been drafted into the search for Margie Thomas, and the station itself would have been completely deserted had not Blackstone insisted that he and Inspector Drayman stay behind to hold the fort.

And so it was that when Horace Crimp entered the police station, he encountered not the duty sergeant he would normally have expected, but two detective inspectors.

'What can I do for you, Mr Crimp?' Drayman asked, in a tone of voice that immediately alerted Blackstone to the fact that the small bald man with a mouth full of bad teeth was not one of the inspector's favourite people.

Instead of answering, Crimp produced a dirty toothpick from his waistcoat pocket and began probing his rotting teeth with it.

'I've no time for your usual theatricals, Mr Crimp,' Drayman said, impatiently. 'A girl's gone missing.'

'So I hear, and very sad it is, too, I'm sure,' Crimp said, removing the toothpick from his mouth, examining the results of his oral exploration that rested on the end of it, and returning it to his pocket. 'Unfortunately, Inspector Drayman, the wheels of justice cannot cease to turn on one matter simply because another one has arisen.'

'Mr Crimp's a solicitor,' Drayman told Blackstone.

'I'd gathered that much already,' Blackstone replied, sourly.

'Are you going to tell us why you're here, Mr Crimp?' Drayman asked.

'You have a client of mine locked up in one of your holding cells and—' Crimp began.

'I'm afraid you've been misinformed,' Drayman interrupted him.

'I think not.'

'The only man in the holding cells is a narrow-boat man by the name of Mick Huggins.'

Crimp nodded. 'Just so. Mick Huggins. He is precisely the client to whom I was referring.'

'You can't be serious!' Drayman exploded.

'I can assure you I am *quite* serious. He is my client, and I would like him to be released on bail immediately.'

'A child is missing!'

'I've already made it clear to you, Mr Drayman, that I am perfectly well aware of that.'

'And yet being "perfectly well aware", you still expect me to take one of my men off the search, just so he can escort your thug of a client to the magistrate's court?'

'I object to my client being called a thug...'

'I don't *care* what you object to!'

'...but that is neither here nor there, as far as

149

the matter in hand goes,' Crimp concluded.

He reached into his jacket pocket, produced a piece of paper and handed it to Drayman without a word.

The inspector scanned the sheet. 'This is an order from the magistrate to release Huggins on bail,' he said flatly, when he'd finished.

'Indeed,' Crimp agreed. 'That is exactly what it is.'

'But when did you ... How did you...'

'I paid a personal call on the magistrate. I explained to him you might find it difficult to provide an escort for my client while you have this other pressing matter to deal with. I suggested that, in order to make life a little easier for everyone concerned, it might be possible to circumvent the normal procedures if I were willing to post a bond of surety. He considered my proposition and came to the conclusion that that would be perfectly satisfactory.'

'And how large was this bond you posted?' Drayman asked.

'That is really none of your business, Inspector,' Crimp said. He paused for a second. 'But since you seem so interested – and since I am always willing to co-operate with the police whenever it is practicable – I can see no harm in telling you it was fifty guineas.'

'Fifty guineas!'

'Indeed.'

'A guttersnipe like Huggins couldn't raise fifty guineas.'

'You may be right.'

150

'I doubt he could raise five shillings.'

'Possibly not.'

'So where did the money come from?'

Horace Crimp smiled, revealing both his rows of disgusting teeth in all their full gory glory. 'Now that, Inspector, really *isn't* your business,' he said.

Drayman and Blackstone stood at the window of Drayman's office, watching Horace Crimp lead his client down the police-station steps and out into freedom.

'Now there's a man who knows how to turn his weaknesses into strengths,' Blackstone said, with something akin to admiration in his tone. 'I particularly like what he did with the toothpick.'

'Yes, that is one of his better tricks,' Drayman agreed. 'He uses it in court all the time. He gets both the prosecuting counsel and the witness so transfixed on the revolting things he's doing in his mouth that when he finally asks his knock-out question, it catches them completely off guard.'

'I'd be right in thinking he regards honesty as an unnecessary luxury, would I?' Blackstone asked.

'You would,' Drayman agreed. 'He's as bent as a corkscrew. If you want the law trampled on, twisted, perverted or otherwise made a fool of, then you go straight to Horace Crimp. Not that I can prove any of that, you understand, because no man's better at covering his own back than our Horace.'

'I'm guessing he doesn't come cheap,' Blackstone said.

'And you're not wrong. Any man who goes to Crimp for help needs to be earning at least a thousand pounds a year, or he'll never even get through the office door.'

'Mick Huggins doesn't earn a thousand pounds a year.'

'No, he doesn't.'

'And Mick Huggins didn't ask for Crimp's help, either. How could he have done, when he's spoken to no one outside this station since the moment you locked him up?'

'I'd dearly love to know who his mystery benefactor is,' Inspector Drayman said.

'It's an intriguing question,' Blackstone agreed. 'But it's not half as intriguing as the other question I'd like an answer to, which is *why* this mysterious benefactor thought it was worth springing a toe-rag like Huggins.'

Two

Horace Crimp's office, much like the man himself, was run-down and slightly disgusting, but Crimp had never seen the need to spend money on it. Why should he, when most of his important clients had never been there – and never would go there – since, though they clamoured for his services, they shrunk away from having any close association with him?

Sitting in that sordid office now, Crimp looked across the scarred table at the narrowboat man who was standing at the opposite side of it.

'Do you know what most of your business associates wanted to do when they learned you'd been arrested, Huggins?' Crimp demanded. 'They wanted to have you eliminated!'

'Pardon, Mr Crimp?'

'They wanted to have you *killed*, you cretin! Murdered! Done away with! But I talked them out of it.'

'Thank you, Mr Crimp.'

'There's no need to thank me. I didn't do it because I care a tuppenny damn about your worthless hide. I did it because your death would only have complicated matters – and they are complicated enough already.' He slammed his fist down on the table. 'Do you realize how delicately balanced this whole deal is? Can you grasp the fact that it only needs one little thing to go wrong for the whole structure to come toppling down on all of us?'

'Yes, Mr Crimp,' Huggins said.

But he didn't realize at all, Crimp thought. Huggins had absolutely no concept of the intricate nature of the machinery that had been constructed to see this operation through.

And how could he have been *expected* to have a concept of it? The man was little better than an animal, motivated solely by a primitive instinct to survive. Yet, paradoxically, it was the mindless beast in him that made him so valuable. For having absolutely no sense of right or wrong, he would cheerfully carry out tasks that would have turned most normal men's stomachs.

'You were specifically told not to draw any attention to yourself,' Crimp said. 'And what did you do? You not only got into a fight, you got into it with a bloody *police inspector*.'

'I didn't know that he was a bobby,' Huggins replied. 'He didn't look like one.'

'And what do bobbies look like? Do they all have pointed heads to fit under their pointed helmets?'

'No, Mr Crimp, but—'

'Besides, even if he'd had a notice strapped to his chest that *said* he was a policeman, you were too drunk to even notice.'

'That's not fair. I admit I'd had a drink or two—'

'You were rat-arsed. Blackstone would never have beaten you so easily if you hadn't been. But what's already gone is no longer the point. We must concern ourselves with what happens next.'

'Can you keep me out of gaol, Mr Crimp?'

'I don't know, Huggins. I really don't,' Crimp admitted. 'But let's assume that I can't. If the worst does come to the worst, I've been authorized to tell you that for as long as you're serving your sentence, you'll continue to be paid, and that when you come out, there'll be a nice bonus waiting for you. That is, of course, if you can keep your big mouth shut.'

'You can rely on me, Mr Crimp.'

'I hope so, Huggins. I really do. Because you know what will happen if you don't.'

'Yes, Mr Crimp.'

'You just have to say one word out of place, and I'll be unable to restrain your associates any longer. It won't matter where you are – in gaol or on the run – they'll find you, and when they do, they'll finish you off. So you're going to have to tread very carefully between now and your trial. Do you understand?'

'Yes, Mr Crimp.'

'You're certain?'

'I swear on my mother's life.'

'I didn't know you'd ever had one,' Crimp said cuttingly. He waved his hand in a gesture of dismissal. 'You can go.'

Huggins got up, head bowed, and shuffled over to the door, but the moment he was outside the building he straightened up and began to walk with a much firmer step.

You had to act like these clever lawyers expected you to act, he told himself, but it didn't mean anything. He hadn't been half as worried as he'd pretended to be – hadn't believed for a second that his assosh— assoch— whatever Crimp had called them would have him murdered. How could they, when they needed him to do the dirty work for them? Besides, he would be a very hard man to kill, and they must already know that.

But though he wasn't scared, he'd continue to play their game, if that's what they wanted. He'd p his head down, as he'd promised in imp's office. But not before he'd settled one utstanding score – not before he'd dealt with that skinny detective from London.

Ellie Carr had darkly predicted there would soon be another murder, and she had been proved right.

The girl had been discovered in some bushes, on a piece of waste land between two of the pottery factories, not four miles from where Emma Walsingholme had been found. She was wearing an expensive silk dress, and – like the previous victims – she had been horrendously mutilated. When Ellie Carr and Superintendent Bullock arrived, she was still lying where she had been found, though a police ambulance had arrived and would soon remove her.

'Do you mind if I take a look at her?' Ellie asked.

'That's why you're here,' Bullock replied. 'But until we've got permission to go further, make sure it's *no more* than a look.'

Ellie knelt down beside the body. The hands and feet had been removed, as with the other victims, but there was not an excessive amount of blood to be seen, so – again, like previous victims – the amputations had probably been carried out elsewhere.

She lifted the dead girl's skirt. Her legs and thighs had deep slashes in them, probably made by an axe or machete. From her reading of the medical reports on the other dead girls, Ellie had been expecting that, but she was still shocked to see just *how* regular they were, and *how* methodically they seemed to have been inflicted.

She expanded the area of her examination to cover the ground around the body. She had hoped to find some footprints, but instead of earth there was hard clay, and even if a man had stamped down as hard as he could, he would have made very little impression on it.

Had the killer known the ground would be so hard? she wondered. Had that been another part of his calculation?

She searched around for other clues – a thread of clothing, a personal item that might have fallen out of the murderer's pocket – but she had very little expectation of finding anything.

The man who had done this was careful – *bloody* careful.

But then why had he chosen to dump the body in such a public place? Why not leave it somewhere in the countryside, where there was much less likelihood of him being caught in the act?

'We need to remove the corpse now, ma'am,' said a voice beside her and, turning, she saw a uniformed constable.

'Of course,' Ellie agreed.

She climbed back to her feet and walked over to where Superintendent Bullock was waiting for her.

'I've been on the Force for nearly thirty years and I've never come across cases like these,' Bullock said mournfully.

'Have you identified the girl?' Ellie asked.

'Oh yes,' Bullock replied. 'She was carrying a bag – some kind of reticule – and it was left right next to her body. Inside it there was a letter addressed to her.' He frowned. 'The killer always seems to want to make it as easy as possible for us to identify his victims. Have you any idea why?'

'None,' Ellie said.

'Anyway, her name's Lucy Stanford, and she is – or rather, she was – fifteen years old.'

'Which makes her a couple of years older than the rest of the victims, doesn't it?'

'Yes.'

'But does she come from the same background as all the others?'

'More or less. Her father owns a pottery factory a few miles from here. It's one of the smaller ones in the area, but he's still a great deal wealthier than you or I are ever likely to be.'

'Perhaps the killings aren't about the victims at all,' Ellie suggested. 'Perhaps your murderer has something against the rich in general.'

'Go on,' Bullock encouraged.

'If you hated a rich man, and wanted to make him suffer, what would be the best way to do it? I think it would be to rob him of something he truly loved and could never replace. In other words, to kill his daughter – and not *just* kill her, but do it in the most ghastly way possible.'

Bullock toyed with the idea for at least a couple of minutes.

'You could be right about that,' he said finally. 'But, in all honesty, I'd have to say that you could also be completely wrong. The problem is, Dr Carr, I've no idea at all what makes this man tick – and that really frightens me.'

'Will you be going to see the parents yourself?' Ellie asked.

'I will. It's not a duty I enjoy, but it's not a duty that I feel I can pass on to some other poor bugger, either.'

'Would you mind if I came along with you?'

Bullock hesitated again. 'I don't want another scene like the one we had yesterday.'

'You won't get one. I promise you I'll behave this time. But could I ask you one small favour in return?'

'I wasn't aware that promising me not to misbehave could be counted as a favour,' Bullock said.

Ellie grinned. 'You know what I mean.'

'What's the favour?' Bullock asked, resignedly.

'Don't bring up the subject of an autopsy with them.'

'And what if they bring it up themselves?'

'Then try to give the impression that they have no choice about whether there is one or not, which legally *is* the case...'

'True.'

'...and would also be *practically* the case, if we didn't live in a society where, if you happen to be born with a silver spoon in your mouth, you can get away with anything.'

Bullock smiled. 'You're beginning to sound like a bit of a radical to me, Dr Carr,' he said.

'I'm a *scientist*, Superintendent Bullock,' Ellie countered, with just an edge of rebuke in her tone, '– a scientist who is dedicated solely to searching out the truth.' She suddenly realized that she must be sounding pompous, and grinned again. 'Which I suppose is another way of saying that whatever gets in the way of my doing my job properly is to be considered a Bad Thing,' she continued.

'Did Inspector Blackstone find it *difficult* working with you?' Bullock wondered.

'He might have done at first,' Ellie said airily. 'But he soon got used to it.'

Three

The previous evening Inspector Drayman had said he needed evidence before he'd entertain the idea of a smuggling racket in Marston, Blackstone thought, as he sat alone in Drayman's office.

Well, now he *had* evidence – or something that came damn close to it – in the form of Mick Huggins. Because Huggins, a man of no importance in his own right, must be important to somebody *else*'s plans. Why else would that 'somebody' not only have posted a fifty-guinea

160

bail bond, but also retained a crooked – but expensive – attorney to represent him?

And in what way could Huggins *be* important to anyone's plans? There was only one answer to that: he had a narrowboat, and was needed to transport the stolen jewels!

Now was not the time to point all this out to Inspector Drayman, Blackstone accepted. But later there would be an opportunity, and Drayman would be forced to admit that the man who had saved Blackstone's life was no fantasist, but a hero who had forfeited his own life in an attempt to see justice done.

Inspector Drayman appeared in the doorway of the office, looking very agitated.

'We finally have a report of a definite sighting of Margie Thomas yesterday,' he said.

'Who's your witness?'

'The landlord of the Townshend Arms.'

'Where's that?'

'Just before you reach the flashes, on the road to Marston. He says he was standing in his yard when she walked past the pub.'

'And he's sure it was her?'

'Absolutely sure. He knows the girl well enough for her to have stopped and told him she was going to stay at her grandmother's.'

'Does he know roughly what time it was when he saw her?'

'It was just before noon. He remembers that because, as she was walking away, he heard the grandfather clock chime in the bar. And that fits in with the other things we know about her

161

movements. She left the bakery at about a quarter to twelve, and it would have been a fifteen-minute walk from there to the Townshend Arms.'

Blackstone checked the clock on the wall. It was twenty-five minutes to twelve.

'Why don't we try covering the same route at roughly the same speed as the girl did?' he suggested.

'Will that do any good?' Drayman asked hopefully.

'Well, it can't do any harm,' Blackstone replied, trying to sound encouraging.

They reached the Townshend Arms at noon, just as Margie Thomas had done twenty-four hours earlier, and then they walked towards Marston at the pace that they calculated a thirteen-year-old girl – in no particular hurry to reach her destination – would have gone at.

Blackstone was struck afresh by the sheer *concentration* of industry in the area that fringed the flashes on either side of the road, but while the smoke from the chimneys of the mines and salt works was clear evidence there were a great many people in the immediate vicinity, he noted that there was not a single soul on the cinder road.

'It's always like this at this time of day,' Drayman said, reading his thoughts. 'Give it half an hour and all the salt works will be knocking off for their dinner break. Another half an hour and the market will close. By quarter past one this road will be as busy as any of your posh London thoroughfares, but, at the moment, nobody's got any reason to be here.'

At the edge of Marston the mineral railway line cut across the road on its way to the mines beyond the village. As Blackstone and Drayman reached that point in their journey, they saw that a railway signalman was in the process of pushing the gates on to the street, in order to open up a passage for the train and block that same passage to road-users.

'Do you do this at the same time every day?' Blackstone asked.

'No,' the signalman replied. 'We take Sunday off. But every other day of the week, the train comes through here at twenty past twelve, on its way to the mines.'

'And once it's gone through, what happens? Do you open the gates immediately?'

'No, that'd be a complete waste of my time an' energy.'

There was a roaring sound in the near distance, and a steam train, pulling half a dozen empty salt wagons behind it, came rushing into view. As it thundered over the road, the crossing gates rattled furiously, and when it was gone, the air was filled with the smell of burnt cinders.

'Why would it be a waste of time to close them?' Blackstone asked, when his hearing had returned to something like normal.

'Because I'd only have to shut them again twenty minutes later, when the train comes back.'

'So you leave them closed for the full twenty

163

minutes?'

'That's right.'

'And you're here the whole time?'

'Not much point in going away, is there? There's not a lot you can do in that time.'

Blackstone felt a dark foreboding in the pit of his stomach.

'When you were here yesterday, you didn't happen to see a girl, did you?' he asked.

'She'd have looked twelve or thirteen. She'd have been wearing a green dress and carrying a basket.'

The railway official shook his head. 'There was no one like that,' he said confidently. 'I'd have noticed if there had been.'

So Margie Thomas had never reached Marston, Blackstone thought.

He turned to Inspector Drayman. 'Have you had the flashes dragged yet?'

The local policeman looked worried. 'Do you think I need to?'

'Yes,' Blackstone said. 'I rather fear you do.'

The Stanford family lived in a large and pleasant detached house on the edge of the town. It was a maid – rather than a butler – who answered the door, but even so, Superintendent Bullock had been quite right when he'd suggested that they were not short of a bob or two.

Bullock and Ellie were shown into a large reception room, where Lucy's mother and father were waiting to receive them. The wife was sitting in a high-backed chair and was gripping

164

the armrests so tightly that her knuckles had turned white. Her husband was standing by her side, with his hand resting comfortingly on her shoulder.

'I'm sorry to bother you at a time like this, but there are some details I need to take down,' Superintendent Bullock said softly. 'If I could leave it until later, believe me I would.'

The father nodded gravely. 'Of course.'

'When did you first discover your daughter was missing?' Bullock asked.

'This morning, when one of the maids took a bowl of hot water up to her room. The girl saw right away that Lucy's bed hadn't been slept in, and immediately reported the matter to me.'

'Did your daughter often leave the house without informing you?' Bullock wondered.

Mr Stanford stiffened. 'Certainly not. This is a very respectable household, and Lucy was a very well-brought-up young lady.'

His wife emitted the smallest of sobs. 'Tell them the truth, Reginald,' she said.

'This is all very distressing for you, my dear,' her husband said solicitously. 'Don't you think it might be much better if you were to retire to your day-bed for a while?'

'Our daughter is dead!' Mrs Stanford screamed. 'What's the point in lying about her now?'

'Really, my dear, I do think you should—'

'Tell them the truth, Reginald! For God's sake, just tell them the truth!'

Mr Stanford cleared his throat. 'As I said, my daughter was well bred and well mannered,' he began, 'but she was a little headstrong, as girls of her age can sometimes be.'

'She was seeing a young man,' Mrs Stanford said.

'A hooligan!' her husband unexpectedly exploded. 'A lout! I should have had him horse-whipped.'

Mrs Stanford reached up and grasped her husband's hand. Her anger appeared to have drained from her, but she seemed even more distraught than she had when they'd first entered the room.

'Please let me speak, Reginald,' she begged. 'Please let me tell them what it is that they need to know.'

Her husband looked up at the ceiling. 'Very well,' he said, in a distant voice. 'If you feel you must, then you have my permission.'

'Lucy met the young man – his name's Jamie Green – at the home of the Carlisle family,' Mrs Stanford said shakily. 'The Carlisles have stables, and Elizabeth Carlisle is – was – a great friend of Lucy's, so Lucy often used to go there to ride.'

'And did this Jamie Green also go there to ride?'

'No, he was a ... a groom in their stables.'

'I see,' Bullock said.

'I can understand why she was attracted to him,' Mrs Stanford continued. 'He's a very handsome boy. And, by all accounts, he's a very *nice* boy, too – sensitive and understanding. Only ... only...'

'Only, he's simply not from the right background to know your daughter socially,' Bullock supplied.

'Exactly,' Mrs Stanford agreed gratefully. 'They had no future together, and she'd have known that if she'd taken the time to think about it. But the young simply don't do that, do they? They *never* think about the future. All they care about is the present.'

'When you found out what was going on between them, you forbade her to see him again?'

'We did more than that. My husband told Augustus Carlisle – Elizabeth's father – about it.'

'Carlisle should have dismissed the young ruffian on the spot,' Mr Stanford said, his eyes still directed at the ceiling. 'That's what I would have done – thrown him straight out on to the street without a reference, and warned him that if he attempted to go near Lucy again, he'd end up in gaol.'

'But Augustus didn't do that,' Mrs Stanford continued. 'He's a very kind man and—'

'He could *afford* to be kind!' her husband interrupted. 'It wasn't *his* daughter the hooligan was making eyes at.'

'And he used his contacts to find the boy a new position in a racing stable near London.'

'So instead of being punished, he got a promotion of sorts,' her husband said. 'So much for "the wages of sin", eh?'

'So Jamie left the area, and we thought that

was the end of it,' Mrs Stanford told the superintendent.

'But it wasn't?' Bullock asked.

'No, I'm afraid it wasn't. I was in the centre of town a few days ago, and through my carriage window I caught a glimpse of him.'

'You never told me!' her husband said, outraged.

'I know that, my dear, and I'm very sorry for it,' Mrs Stanford said. 'I knew at the time you should have been informed, but I wanted to save you the distress.'

'So you think that when your daughter left the house last night, she did it of her own free will, and for the purpose of seeing this young man?' Bullock asked.

'I'm sure of it.'

'And do you think it's possible that it was this same young man who killed her?'

Mrs Stanford raised her hand to her mouth in horror. 'Oh, good Lord, no,' she said; 'Jamie wouldn't have harmed even a single hair on Lucy's head. He loved her.'

Four

Blackstone and Drayman watched as the uniformed constables clumsily manoeuvred unfamiliar rowing boats back and forth across the flashes that lay on each side of the raised cinder road.

They had been there for over an hour, and in that time the sky overhead had turned from bright blue to slate-grey. Blackstone hoped that wasn't an ill omen – but rather feared that it was.

'Even if the poor little bugger *is* somewhere down there – and I pray to God she isn't – we might never find her,' Drayman said gloomily.

'What makes you say that?' Blackstone wondered.

'I say it because I know the history of these flashes. When I was a kid, they weren't even here. Where the flashes are now, there used to be a fair number of mines.'

'*Working* mines?'

'Some of them were still working, yes, but most had been abandoned long ago. Anyway, early one morning – and totally unexpectedly – the ground started to give way.'

'Was it quick?' Blackstone asked.

'Not at first. At the beginning it was such a

169

gradual process that there was time enough for word to get around, and when the real slippage eventually got under way, quite a crowd had gathered – and I was part of it.'

Blackstone grinned, despite their sombre mission. 'So you were a witness to history?' he said.

'You could call it that if you wanted to,' Drayman agreed. 'Or you could call it being a witness to man's folly – to his inability to understand that if you keep on raping and pillaging nature, then eventually nature is going to start fighting back.' He coughed, somewhat embarrassedly. 'Sorry about that, Sam. I didn't really mean to get on my high horse.'

'That's quite all right; we all have horses we feel like jumping on occasionally,' Blackstone assured him. 'What happened next?'

'The more the land slipped away, the faster the process became. I remember one old pumping station that went in no time at all. A solid brick building it was, but one minute it was there, and the next it was gone. And the people who were watching cheered – as if they were watching a circus, instead of being given a foretaste of what could well be the future of their own homes and businesses.'

'People are like that,' Blackstone said, philosophically.

'Then it all went,' Drayman continued: 'the other buildings, the winding gear, any trucks they hadn't been able to remove in time – all of it – straight down into a bloody big hole.'

'When did it start to fill up with water?'

'Almost immediately. There was a brook running across part of the land, you see, and that brook was connected to the river. Well, once the water found it had a hole to fill, it bloody well filled it. Do you know, the river actually ran *backwards* for a few hours while the crater was filling up.'

'Now that *certainly* must have been something to see,' Blackstone said.

'It was. But it's a bit like watching a man cut his own right arm off – you can only see him do it once.' Drayman coughed again. 'Anyway, now you know the history, you can probably understand why dragging these flashes is more difficult than dragging any normal stretch of water.'

Blackstone nodded. 'A normal lake is shallow at the shoreline and deep in the middle, but I imagine the same rules don't apply here.'

'That's right,' Drayman agreed. 'At some points around the edge, the flashes plunge straight down, thirty or forty feet. Or even further, for all I know. And at some points in the middle you run a risk of scraping the bottom of your boat on some of the old mine buildings, which didn't quite collapse. Then, of course, there are the tunnels from the old mine workings. We can only see the water on the surface of the flashes, but there must also be underground lakes, several hundred yards below where we're standing.'

A constable in the furthest rowing boat called

171

out across the water to them. They were too far away to hear what he was saying, but from his frantic gestures it was obvious that he'd found something.

They laid the girl out on a tarpaulin on the ground. It was always difficult to form a clear picture of quite what a victim must have looked like before she went through her ordeal, Blackstone thought sadly, but he would guess that Margie Thomas had been a rather pretty child.

The dress she was wearing was made of cotton and had daisies on it, set against a green background. It was probably her best one – or, at least, her second-best – because she'd been on her way to see her grandmother. It had been ripped in several places during the struggle, and a further strip had been torn off the bottom and twisted to form a crude rope. Then the killer had used this rope to attach a large stone to her so that, once he'd thrown her in the water, he'd be sure she would sink.

'He must have picked her up over his head and flung her as far out as he could,' Inspector Drayman said. 'It's pure luck she landed on top of one of the old buildings.'

Lucky for them, but not for her, Blackstone thought. *Her* luck had run out long before she hit the water.

There were bruise marks on the girl's upper thighs, her upper arms and around her neck. There was no doubt that she had been raped and then strangled – or possibly the two had

172

occurred simultaneously.

'Bastard!' Inspector Drayman said, as much to himself as to Blackstone and the constables who were gathered around him.

'Easy now,' Blackstone cautioned.

'Filthy, *evil* bastard!' Drayman said.

The constables took the girl's body to the morgue, and Blackstone took Drayman to the Townshend Arms.

'Do you have any idea who might have done this?' Blackstone asked, when they'd both rapidly downed double whiskies at the bar. 'Anyone in your records with a history of rape – or anyone who you've only collared for sexual interference before, but who might have progressed to rape?'

Drayman shook his head. 'Nobody at all. That kind of thing doesn't happen in this town.' He laughed, bitterly. 'Sorry – what I meant to say was, "That kind of thing *didn't used to* happen in this town."' He ordered two more whiskies. 'What do you think are the chances of me catching the swine, Sam?'

'It depends,' Blackstone said, cautiously. 'Nobody saw Margie after she'd gone past this pub, but it's just possible that somebody did see the rapist, either going the same way or coming from the other direction.'

'Possible, but not likely,' Drayman said. 'I'm right, aren't I?'

'We won't know until we've made more inquiries.'

'Come on, Sam! We covered the same route today that he must have covered yesterday. And at exactly the same time! *We* didn't see anybody, did we? And nobody saw us.'

Drayman put his head in his hands. 'I'm never going to get my hands on him, am I, Sam?'

'The odds are against it,' Blackstone admitted. 'It's the killers who *plan* things that we usually catch – the ones who go to such elaborate lengths to hide their crime that they eventually end up tripping over their own cleverness. They set up a fake alibi, for example, but it's never as watertight as they think, and once we've broken that down, we've got them. Or they try to lay the blame on someone else, but there's always some overlooked detail in the trail they set that leads us straight to them rather than the man they're trying to frame.'

'But there's nothing like that in this case,' Drayman said.

'Exactly. This is what you might call "a crime of opportunity". The killer had no more idea that Margie would be walking along that particular road at that particular time of day than Mick Huggins had that I'd walk into the Hanging Tree just when he was in the mood for a fight.'

'What makes you so sure of that?'

'I'm sure because even *Margie* didn't know she'd be going to her grandmother's at that time. If you remember, it was only at the last minute that her father decided to let her leave early.'

'Of course,' Drayman agreed. 'So the killer came across the girl purely by chance.'

174

'Yes. And that's the problem in a nutshell, you see,' Blackstone said. 'Because nothing was planned, there's nothing for us to get our teeth into.'

'What about the murders of all those girls who had their hands and feet cut off?' Drayman asked. 'Were they carefully planned?'

'Yes, I think they must have been.'

'The killer can't have known *all* the girls.'

'No, but he must have known *of* them. If they'd been random murders, or crimes of opportunity, the victims would have come from all kinds of backgrounds. But they didn't. They were all young ladies. And that means that they were carefully selected. That means that he knew exactly what he was going to do long before he actually did it.'

'In other words, those cases are the exact opposite of this case. Is that what you're saying?'

'More or less.'

'Which means, according to what you've told me, that the bobbies investigating them must have *one hell of a lot* to get their teeth into. So what progress are *they* making?'

'The last I heard, they'd made about as much progress as we have,' Blackstone said gloomily.

Five

There was nothing he could have done to save the girl, Blackstone told himself, as he walked up Marston Lane. Nothing at all! She had been dead even before he'd known that she was missing.

Yet, despite the logic of the argument, he was still weighed down by a sense of personal failure. As if it were *his* fault that he was not godlike and all-seeing – as if he could have actually have done something to prevent the tragedy, if only he'd tried a little *harder*.

The numbing effect of the whisky he had drunk with Inspector Drayman in the Townshend Arms was already beginning to wear off, and what he needed most in the world, he decided, was to go straight to the Red Lion and get a top-up of the golden anaesthetic.

His heart sank when he saw Walter Clegg standing at the top of the alley that led to his back yard, the more so because Clegg wore an expression on his face which clearly stated that Blackstone's return was just the event he had been waiting for.

'You've timed that well, Inspector,' Clegg called out, as Blackstone drew level with him.

'The kettle's just about to come to the boil. We can go inside an' have a brew.'

In all probability the kettle had been on the boil for hours, Blackstone thought. It may even have boiled itself dry a couple of times, while Clegg waited for his honoured guest from London to return.

The problem with Walter, he decided, was that while he was a nice enough bloke, he worked far too hard at trying to be your mate, and the result was that you quite soon found his presence almost suffocating.

'Yes, I could just fancy a cuppa,' Walter Clegg said.

'If you don't mind, I don't really feel like a cup of tea right at the moment,' Blackstone said.

'Fair enough,' Walter Clegg agreed easily. 'Now I come to think about it, I'm not sure I fancy one myself. But there's still some whisky left in that bottle you bought the other night. We could put that to rest instead.'

What a persistent bugger the salt-miner was, Blackstone thought.

'I've got some thinking to do, Walter,' he said aloud, 'and I'd really much rather do it alone.'

Walter Clegg looked crushingly disappointed. 'But I've got something to show you,' he said. 'It may be important.'

Blackstone sighed inwardly. Clegg had taken him under his roof and entertained him as best he could, so he supposed he owed it to the man to spend a little time with him. But – with the image of the dead Margie Thomas still fresh in his mind – it would *have to be* a little time. Then he'd have that drink he had been promising himself – and when he did, it would be without Walter hovering at his elbow like a faithful puppy.

Walter Clegg seemed much happier once they were safely inside the house.

'Well, what's it to be?' he asked. 'Tea? Or whisky?'

It would be easier to make his excuses and leave if they weren't drinking whisky, Blackstone thought.

'Tea,' he said.

'Right-oh,' Clegg agreed chirpily.

Blackstone sat down at the kitchen table that was the centre of Walter Clegg's home, while Walter busied himself moving the hob back over the open fire and fetching the teapot.

'I've had all sorts of people askin' me about you, Inspector, but I promise you I haven't told them anythin' at all,' Walter said, as the heavy iron kettle came to the boil.

'No?'

'No! I just said that you were up here on private business, and I couldn't discuss it with them.'

Thus leaving them with the impression that I'd taken you into my confidence, Blackstone thought.

Walter brought two of the best china teacups from the sideboard and placed them on the table. Then he lifted the kettle off the hob and poured the scalding water into the teapot.

178

'You said you've got something to show me that might be important,' Blackstone said.

'Oh, that's right,' Clegg agreed.

He said it as if it had slipped his mind entirely, but the inspector was not fooled. The 'something important' was his trump card – the hook on which he was keeping his guest dangling – and he was reluctant to give it up until he absolutely had to.

'Well?' Blackstone said firmly.

Walter Clegg sighed, walked over to the sideboard again, and came back with a sealed envelope.

'It's a letter of some sort,' he explained.

The envelope was cheap and flimsy. Blackstone's name was written on the front in block capitals. He slit it open and extracted the single sheet of paper that lay inside.

The note, like the envelope, was written in capitals, and though the writer did not appear to be an educated man, the message was clear enough:

WHY DON'T YEW ASK MISTER BICKERSDALE
WHY HE PAID MICK HUGGINS BALE.

'Where did you get this from?' Blackstone asked.

'It was lyin' on the mat. Somebody must have slipped it under the door while we were all out.'

'Who's Mr Bickersdale?'

'Why? Is the letter from him?' Walter asked, and he was almost bursting with curiosity.

Tom Yardley had been curious, too, Blackstone reminded himself – and that had probably

179

cost the poor devil his life.

'No, it's not from Mr Bickersdale,' he told Walter, 'but it mentions him. So who is he?'

'He's a mine-owner,' Walter Clegg said sullenly.

'Where's his mine?'

'His *mines*. He's got two of them. They're about a mile an' a quarter from the village.'

'So he's a local man, is he?'

'No.'

He'd hurt the other man's pride, Blackstone realized, which was something he'd never intended to do.

'Listen, Walter,' he said, 'the reason I'm not telling you more is because, like Tom, I think there's something nasty going on in this village – and I don't want to get you involved.'

'So you're protectin' me?'

'That's right.'

Walter puffed out his chest. 'I don't need your protection,' he said. 'I can look after myself.'

'I know you can,' Blackstone agreed, 'but you've got your mother to consider. How would she cope if anything happened to you? Besides, Tom kept you out of it, and I think he'd want me to do the same.'

'Well, if you're sure that's what Tom would have wanted...'

'I am.'

Walter Clegg nodded, and seemed to reconcile himself to the thought that he'd be kept in the dark.

'Mr Bickersdale's not from round here,' he

said. 'He turned up out of nowhere, about two years ago now. People do say that, before he came to the village, he'd already made himself a fortune somewhere abroad. Anyway, he obviously wasn't short of money, because the first thing he did was to buy himself a share in the Jubilee Salt Works. That was quite a smart move, because when there's a demand for salt, it's not a bad little business.'

'I thought you said he was a *mine*-owner, not a *salt works*-owner.'

'I'm comin' to that. The second thing he did was to buy the two mines off old Seth Updyke. The Victoria Mine, which is where Tom an' me work ... where Tom *used to* work, before he ... before he...'

'Where Tom worked before he was killed,' Blackstone said gently.

Walter Clegg nodded. 'That's right. The Victoria Mine isn't a bad little business either, but the Melbourne Mine, which is the other one he bought, is an entirely different matter. He should never have touched that – not even with the end of a six-foot barge pole.'

'It was a bad purchase, was it?'

'About as bad as it could be. Even if the Melbourne had been the going concern that he thought it was when he bought it, he'd still have paid more for it than what it was worth. But the simple fact is that the mine hasn't made a profit for years, an' is never likely to again.'

'Didn't anybody warn him of that before he bought the mine?'

181

'Somebody probably would have done – if he'd bothered to ask. But he didn't.'

'So what's wrong with the Melbourne Mine?' Blackstone asked.

'Everythin'. Some mines are easy to work, an' some mines aren't – the Melbourne Mine's one of the hardest there is. You see, when you're...' Walter Clegg paused for a second, as if searching for the right words. 'Maybe the easiest way to explain it to you would be to draw it,' he continued.

'All right,' Blackstone agreed.

Walter Clegg stood up, walked over to the sideboard and rummaged around in the drawers. When he returned to the table, he had a piece of paper and a pencil in his hand. He put the sheet of paper flat on the table and drew a series of parallel lines on it.

'These are your beds of rock,' he said. 'The top one is made up of sand and clays. I did hear that it was laid down in the Ice Age, but I've no idea when that was, except that it was before my time.'

Blackstone smiled. '*Well* before your time,' he said.

'Now below the clays, you got the marlstone,' Walter Clegg continued. 'An' below the marlstone you've got the seam of salt. Do you see how level an' regular all the layers are?'

'Yes,' Blackstone said, 'I do.'

'In a mine like this one I've just drawn, all you have to do is sink your shaft down to the drift, then hack away to your heart's content.'

Walter drew another set of lines on the paper, and this time the lines were stepped.

'But there's places where the layers of rock aren't regular, because of a slippage that probably occurred when Moses was a lad,' he continued. 'An' if you try to mine there, you've got problems.'

'What kind of problems?'

'As you can see from my second drawin', the drift doesn't run flat. Some times it goes up, an' sometimes it goes down. So gettin' the salt out takes a lot more time an' a lot more labour, and that means it's costin' you more to extract it than you can sell it for.'

'And the Melbourne Mine's like that?'

'Yes. An' it's not its only drawback. The Melbourne has always had a seepage problem. Mr Bickersdale has got a lot more pumps down there than you'll find in any other mine, an' he has to keep them runnin' twenty-four hours a day. An' that's extra expense, an' all.'

'But even so, he still keeps it running, does he?'

'In a manner of speakin'.'

'What do you mean – in a manner of speaking?'

'There were only a few lads workin' there when he took over, an' he moved them to the Victoria Mine. Then he brought in some fresh miners from outside to take over their jobs in the Melbourne.'

'Why would he have done that?' Blackstone wondered.

'Beats me. The local lads were quite happy with the new arrangement, because it's easier work in the Victoria, but even they couldn't see the sense in bringin' in strangers to mine the Melbourne.'

But maybe they were never intended to mine the Melbourne at all, Blackstone thought. Maybe that was just a cover to explain the presence of outsiders in the area – outsiders who knew nothing about rock-salt mining, but a great deal about smuggling stolen jewels!

'Have you ever talked to any of these men that Bickersdale brought in from the outside?' he asked.

'No, I haven't,' Clegg said. 'They keep themselves pretty much to themselves.'

'But they must come into the village in the evening, if only to have a drink in the pub.'

'Not as far as I know.'

'What about their provisions? They have to buy them somewhere.'

'Maybe. But they don't buy them here.'

Which made sense, Blackstone thought. If they weren't real miners, then the last thing that Bickersdale would want was to have them talking to men who were.

'I'd rather like to have a word with this Mr Bickersdale,' he said. 'Where will I find him? At the salt works?'

'I shouldn't think so. He's more of what you might call a silent partner in that business. Mr Watkins is the feller what actually runs it.'

Bickersdale wouldn't need to run it in order to

use it for his own purposes, Blackstone thought. All he had to have was unquestioned access – which was exactly what his silent partnership would give him.

'So he'll be at the Victoria Mine, will he?' he asked.

But he was not all surprised when Walter Clegg said, 'No, he seems to spend more of his time at the Melbourne Mine.'

Of course he did. It was only natural that he would want to stay close to the centre of his *real* business.

'How do I get to the Melbourne Mine?' Blackstone asked.

'Your easiest way would be to go to the bridge, take the path down to the canal, turn left, an' keep walkin' for about fifteen minutes,' Walter Clegg told him. 'If you do that, you can't miss it.'

Six

From his elevated vantage point on the canal bank, Blackstone raised his field glasses to his eyes and gave all those parts of the Melbourne Mine which were above ground a sweeping examination.

In many ways it looked very much like all the other mines in the area. It had its winding shed,

185

and a boiler house with a brick chimney, which was belching out thick black smoke. There was a solid brick structure, which had a sign on it announcing that it was the office, and two other brick buildings – one half the size of the office, the other much smaller – neither of which gave any indication of its function at all. And the mine had its salt store, a big wooden building with a domed roof. It was only when the sweeping examination was completed, and a slower, more careful one begun, that the ramshackle nature of much of the complex became clear. The salt store – which should have been the very heart of the business – was clearly rotting away from neglect, and Blackstone was in no doubt that in a heavy rainstorm it would leak like a sieve. The carts and wooden trucks scattered haphazardly around the yard looked to be in very poor repair. And though he had been standing there for over half an hour, Blackstone had not once seen the winding gear bring any rock salt to the surface.

The door of the middle-sized building opened and a man stepped out. He was wearing a jacket and trousers, rather than miners' overalls, and there was something about the way he walked over to the corner of the yard that told Blackstone that, while he might be a hard man in himself, he was not a man habitually involved in hard physical work.

Once he had reached the end of the yard, the man unbuttoned his trousers and urinated.

A second man stepped out of the shadows. He

was not dressed like a miner either, and he was holding a double-barrelled shotgun in his hands.

The two men talked for a while. Then the man who had been relieving himself buttoned his trousers again and returned to the building he'd recently emerged from, and the man with the shotgun stepped back into the shadows.

So the middle-sized brick building was a hostel for the men that Bickersdale had brought in from outside the village, Blackstone thought. They could eat there and sleep there, without ever once risking meeting a villager and revealing how truly ignorant they were about rock-salt mining.

And the man with the shotgun was a guard – though why a salt mine should actually *need* an armed guard was an interesting question.

But, of course, it wasn't a real salt mine, any more than the men whom Bickersdale employed were real salt-miners.

'If this place produces enough salt in a day to flavour a workhouse soup cauldron, I'll eat my hat,' Blackstone said to himself, as he took the track that led down to the mine.

As he crossed the yard, Blackstone was aware that the man on guard duty was probably watching him from his hiding place. But he gave no outward sign that he was even aware of the man's existence, and instead marched straight up to the office door and knocked on it as loudly as if he were executing a warrant.

The man who answered the imperious knock was in his middle-to-late forties, and balding.

187

He had pinched features, and half-moon spectacles were resting on his nose. But what Blackstone noticed most about him – as he stood blocking the doorway of the outer office – was the fear in his eyes when he saw who it was who'd come calling.

'What ... What do you want?' he asked.

'I'd like to see Mr Bickersdale.'

'Do you have an appointment?'

'You're his clerk, are you?' Blackstone demanded.

'I asked if you had a—'

'Just answer the question!'

'Yes, I'm ... I'm his clerk.'

'And what's your name?'

'Robertson. Hubert Robertson.'

'So tell me, Mr Robertson, if I *did* have an appointment with Mr Bickersdale, wouldn't you know about it?'

'I suppose so.'

'Then I can't have one, can I? But if you were to go into Mr Bickersdale's office, and ask if I could see him, and if, you having asked him, he then said yes, I would have an appointment. Isn't that right?'

'Yes, but—'

'Then you'd better go and ask him, hadn't you?'

Robertson bit his lip indecisively, and looked down at his feet.

'What's the matter?' Blackstone asked, hectoringly. 'Can't move because you've got a bone in your leg?'

Robertson looked up again. He seemed terrified of doing what Blackstone had asked him to do, but equally terrified of *not* doing it.

'Wait here,' he said finally. And with that, he disappeared into the office.

'Just a minute!' Blackstone said.

The clerk returned to the doorway. 'Yes?'

'If I was on my way to ask my boss if he'd agree to see a bloke who'd turned up unexpectedly, I'd at least want to know the bloke's name. But you never asked me, did you?'

'No, I...'

'Why is that? Because you forgot to ask my name? Or because you already know it?'

'It's ... It's because I forgot to ask,' the frightened clerk said.

'Then it's a good job one of us is on the ball, isn't it?' Blackstone asked. 'You can tell him that it's Sam Blackstone wants to see him – *Inspector* Sam Blackstone.'

Lawrence Bickersdale was in his mid-forties. He was a tall, distinguished-looking man, with a skin that looked as if it had seen more than its fair share of sunshine. He had a wide brow, strong jaw and quick eyes, which had been assessing Blackstone since the moment he had stepped into the office.

The office itself was almost spartan in its furnishings. A large mahogany desk – which was not so much antique as merely *old* – dominated the centre of the room. There were two chairs – one on each side of the desk – and a cheap sofa in one corner. If Blackstone had been expecting to see charts on the walls, showing production and sales figures, he would have been disappointed, because the only thing that Lawrence Bickersdale seemed to consider worthy of display was a large map of the world.

'Take a seat, Mr Blackstone,' Bickersdale said, indicating the chair in front of the desk. 'My clerk told me that you'd requested an appointment with me, but he appears to have been negligent in furnishing me with a reason for the meeting.'

'What you mean is, you asked him why I wanted to see you, and he said he couldn't tell you because I hadn't told him,' Blackstone countered.

Bickersdale smiled. 'I can see you are a man who favours the direct approach,' he said. 'Very well, then, I can be direct, too. You are a police inspector. Is that right?'

'Yes, sir.'

'But not a *local* police inspector?'

'No, I'm from London.'

'Which means, unless I'm very much mistaken, that you are a long way outside your own jurisdiction.'

'That's quite true – I am,' Blackstone agreed. 'The local police have a lot on their hands at the moment. A young girl has been murdered.'

'Yes, I heard that,' Bickersdale said, regretfully. 'But I still don't see what you're...'

'They've asked me to help out with the inquiry – and with a few other matters besides.'

'But not officially?'

'No, not officially.'

'So you are here, *unofficially*, about the death of that poor girl, are you, Inspector?'

'As a matter of fact, I'm not. The inquiry I'm pursuing at the moment is one in which I've had some personal involvement. Yesterday, a man called Mick Huggins attacked me in a pub in Northwich.' He paused.

For a while there was silence.

Then Bickersdale said, 'Yes?'

'The attack was totally unprovoked, and, as a result of having made it, Mick Huggins was arrested and placed in the cells to await his appearance before the magistrates. Do you have any comment to make at this stage, sir?'

Bickersdale seemed to be considering the matter.

'I don't think so,' he said finally, 'unless it's to express my deepest regret to you that your introduction to our fair town had to involve an encounter with a hooligan.'

'Do you know the hooligan in question, sir?'

'I don't believe so.'

'That's strange.'

'Is it?'

'Yes, I really think it is. Because, you see, his bail was posted this morning – and we've been informed that you were the one who posted it.'

Bickersdale smiled again. 'Have you, indeed? And might I ask what the source of that information was?'

'I'm afraid I'm not at liberty to say, sir.'

'I would guess it was an anonymous letter,'

191

Bickersdale said. 'But no matter. What does this man, Higgins...'

'Huggins.'

'What does this man *Huggins* do for a living? If, indeed, he does anything at all?'

'He operates a narrowboat.'

'Ah, then I may well have met him. I may even have done business with him. But I can't recall the name, which is hardly surprising since my clerk, Robertson, handles the trivial details. And I would certainly never have even considered posting a fifty-guinea bail bond for him.'

The expression on his face showed he realized he'd made a mistake, but it was only there for an instant before it was replaced by a blander look.

'Fifty guineas,' Blackstone repeated. 'Now where did you get that figure from, I wonder?'

'I believe you mentioned it yourself.'

'I didn't.'

'I'm sure you did.'

'I was most careful not to.'

'Then perhaps I just assumed that for such a serious offence as attacking a policeman – even one from London, with no official standing here in Cheshire – a bail of fifty guineas would be the least that would be required.'

'You talked earlier about "our fair town",' Blackstone said. 'But it's not really *your* town at all, is it? You've only lived here for two years.'

'True,' Bickersdale agreed. 'But one's attachment to a particular location cannot be measured merely by the calendar. There are some places that just feel like home – and this place felt like home to me the moment I arrived.'

'And so you bought a couple of mines and a share in a salt works?'

'That's right.'

'Which has me puzzled,' Blackstone admitted. 'Oh, I can see why you bought the mines. Any man would like to have businesses that he could truly call his own.'

'Quite so.'

'It's the share in the salt works I don't understand. That's just putting money into somebody *else's* business.'

'A business from which I derive profits.'

'True, but you don't have control over the business, do you? And you strike me as a man who likes to be in control at all times. So I was wondering whether there might be some other – what you might call *subsidiary* – reason for your investing in the works.'

'I'm afraid that I have no idea what you're talking about,' Bickersdale told him.

'No, I'm not making much sense to myself, either,' Blackstone said easily. 'Where did you live *before* you came here, Mr Bickersdale?'

'I fail to see how that could be relevant to either the attack on you by this man Huggins, or to the murder of that poor girl.'

'It isn't relevant,' Blackstone admitted. 'I was just curious.'

'Would you reveal to me the details of *your* background, if I asked you to, Inspector?'

'Willingly.'

'Then by all means feel free to do so.'

'My mother died when I was a nipper,' Blackstone said. 'I was brought up in an orphanage. As soon as I was old enough, I joined the army. I served in India, fought in Afghanistan and rose to the rank of sergeant. When I left the army, I joined the Metropolitan Police.'

Bickersdale nodded. 'Very concise,' he said. 'And I will try to be equally brief in return. Before I came to live here, I travelled extensively abroad for a number of years.'

'That *is* concise,' Blackstone said.

'Yes, it is, isn't it?' Bickersdale agreed. 'Did your travels take you to the United States of America?'

'Yes, I've certainly been there.'

'India?'

'There, too.'

Lawrence Bickersdale stood up and walked over to the map hanging on the wall. 'In order to save you the trouble of having to list every single country in the world, Inspector, I'm quite willing to specify I've been here...' (he pointed at Australia), 'here ....' (he circled the Middle East with his index finger), 'and here...' (he jerked his thumb in the general direction of South Africa).

'Do you know much about diamonds?' Blackstone asked, as the other man was walking back to his seat.

Bickersdale said down quite heavily. 'I beg your pardon?'

'I would have thought my question was simple enough to understand. I asked you if you knew

194

much about diamonds. You certainly look to me like a man who'd know his jewellery.'

'Perhaps if I'd married I would have known about it – the ladies like their men to take an interest in things they're interested in themselves – but since I've always been a bachelor, I've never really felt the need to acquaint myself with the subject.'

'Do you still keep in contact with any of the people you met on your travels?'

'No, I'm afraid I've lost touch with them all. How about you, Inspector? Do *you* still keep in contact?'

'I did hear from *one* of my old comrades,' Blackstone said. 'A bloke called Tom Yardley.'

Bickersdale blinked. 'Was that the same Tom Yardley who blew himself up at one of my mines, just a few days ago?'

'Well, it was certainly the same Tom Yardley who *got* blown up,' Blackstone replied.

Bickersdale took his watch out of his waistcoat pocket and made some display of consulting it.

'It has been most entertaining to talk to you, Inspector,' he said, 'but, as I'm sure you must appreciate yourself, a man who has a business to run can only afford to spend so much time on idle chit-chat, so I think it's the right moment to bring this conversation to a close.'

Blackstone stood up. 'Of course, sir. And thank you so much for sparing me the time.'

'It was my pleasure,' Bickersdale said, unconvincingly.

Seven

It was late afternoon when Archie Patterson paid his first visit to Marlin Street in what had been a long time. The street was at its quietest at that time of day, as Patterson had known it would be. In fact, he had deliberately chosen to make his visit *when* it was quiet – because when a man is doing something that might well cost him his job, he wants to be observed by as few people as possible.

As he passed the pawnbroker's establishment – a depressing place, in which the pledges were household effects scarcely worth redeeming even had the pledgers had the money to do it – he found he was asking himself if he was doing the right thing in following this plan of his.

As he reached a small corner shop – dirty windows, and only a few battered tins of stew in evidence on the shelves – he had almost persuaded himself that he should abandon the whole crazy idea. But then he reached his destination – a place that had once been a printer's shop, but had long ceased to function as such – and he found his resolve returning to him.

He knocked on the door, and his knock was answered by a bent old man wearing very thick spectacles. The man peered up at him, and when he saw who it was standing there, his jaw began to quiver.

'I ain't done nuffink wrong, Mr Patterson,' he said.

'Did I *say* you had done anything wrong, Gabriel?' Patterson inquired.

'I served my time without complaint, an' when I come out, I'd learned my lesson. You know that.'

'You're not in trouble,' Patterson said. 'I'm here because I've got some business for you.'

The old man looked really frightened now.

'Business?' he said. 'What kind of business?'

'Shall we go inside?' Patterson asked – and it was more of an order than a request.

Lizzie had lost track of the amount of time she had spent in the cell. She missed Cathy. The other girl had horrified her with her willingness to embrace prostitution, but she had been a cheerful soul – full of life – and this bleak prison seemed even harder to bear now she had gone.

Lizzie wondered where Cathy was *now*. Probably in some house of ill-repute, spreading her legs – as Cathy had so crudely put it herself – for any man with a little money to spend. She hoped that the other girl's new life was equal to her rosy expectations – that she really didn't mind what was being done to her, hour after hour, night after night – but she knew that as far as she herself was concerned, she would absolutely hate it when her own turn came.

She heard footsteps in the corridor, and im-

197

mediately feared it was the man who had tried to rape her, returning. But when the door swung open, she saw that it was only the boss, and that he had brought with him another man – a thin, middle-aged one – who really looked quite harmless.

'Hello, Lizzie,' the boss said cheerfully. 'Are you being looked after properly?'

'Yes, thank you, sir,' Lizzie replied, because that was what she had been taught to say in answer to such questions in the workhouse – however bad things *really* were.

'They've been feeding you well, and letting you have nice warm baths every day?'

'Yes, sir.'

'And no one's tried to take advantage of you?'

'Not since that first time.'

The boss nodded. 'Excellent. Now be a good girl and sit quietly on your stool while this gentleman does your hair.'

'What do you mean – "while he does my hair"?' Lizzie asked, gripped by a sudden panic. 'He's not goin' to cut it all off, is he? Like they do in the workhouse, when you have nits.'

The boss laughed. 'No, of course he's not going to cut it all off. Far from it, in fact.'

'Then what *is* he goin' to do?'

'He's just going to give it a little more shape.'

'An' why would he want to do that?'

'To make you look even prettier than you already are. You want to look prettier, don't you?'

'Yes, sir,' Lizzie said obediently.

198

Gabriel Moore's home would have made the average hovel almost anywhere else look like a miniature palace, but on Marlin Street it was probably no better and no worse than most of the houses.

'Would you like to sit down, Mr Patterson?' Moore asked.

Patterson looked at the chair he was being offered and decided not to take the risk of catching something.

'I won't be here long, so I'll stand,' he said. 'The purpose of my visit is very simple. As I intimated when we were outside, I want you to do a little job for me, Gabriel.'

'What kind of job? Like the ones I used to do?'

'That's right.'

Moore spread out his hands in gesture of hopelessness. 'I can't do it, Mr Patterson.'

'Didn't your old mother ever tell you it wasn't a good idea to turn down a request for help – especially when that request came from the Filth?' Patterson wondered.

'Honest, I can't. I ain't got the equipment no more.'

Patterson laughed, disbelievingly. 'An artist like you doesn't just throw his equipment away,' he said. 'Even if he knows he may never use it again, he just can't bear to get rid of it.'

'Even if I'd got the equipment – an' I ain't sayin' I have – I couldn't do the job,' Moore protested.

'Of course you could,' Patterson assured him. 'It's a bit like riding a bike – once you've learned how to do it, you never forget.'

'Look at me, Mr Patterson,' Moore implored him. He held up his hands for the sergeant to inspect. 'Can't you see how they're shakin'?'

Patterson nodded. 'Yes, they certainly do seem to have a bit of a tremble about them, don't they? With hands like those, any work I asked you to do for me now would be vastly inferior to what you've produced in the past.'

'That's what I'm sayin', Mr Patterson. It wouldn't pass muster. It wouldn't fool a blind man.'

'Ah, but you see, that's the point,' Patterson said. 'I don't *want* it to fool a blind man.'

Blackstone and Drayman had agreed earlier to meet in the Townshend Arms. Their plan had been that the local inspector would outline the progress that had been made in the investigation, and his more experienced colleague from London would analyse what he'd been told and suggest further lines of approach based on that.

It would have been a good plan, if there'd *been* any progress to analyse. But there hadn't.

'It's just as you predicted it would be, Sam,' Drayman lamented. 'Margie Thomas's murder was nothing more than a crime of opportunity, and we're never going to find the bastard who did it.'

Blackstone wasn't really listening. Instead he

200

was thinking of the meeting he had had with Bickersdale.

The man had seemed so calm and in control – friendly enough, in a cold, amused sort of way – but even if he hadn't let it slip that he knew exactly how much Mick Huggins's bail had cost, Blackstone would have had his card marked anyway, because he knew a villain when he saw one.

'*The problem is that any man in town between the ages of sixteen and sixty could have done it,*' he heard Inspector Drayman's voice echo dreamily in the back of his mind.

But why had a smart bloke like Bickersdale ever allowed himself to be saddled with a white elephant like the Melbourne Mine, Blackstone wondered – a mine in which the drift was irregular, and the seepage continual; a mine that was never going to show a profit, whatever he did?

'*I can't question the whole town,*' Inspector Drayman was saying, somewhere in the far distance. '*I simply haven't got the manpower available for that.*'

The trick to understanding any man was to see the world as he saw it through his own eyes, Blackstone told himself. So how *did* the world look through Bickersdale's?

The mine-owner had been abroad for a number of years, probably working in places where advancement was less dependent on a man's ability than on the colour of his skin. And that – as Blackstone knew from his own observation

201

of English merchants in India – led to arrogance. So Bickersdale returns to England with a pocketful of money and an almost overpowering belief in his own infallibility. He has already decided that he wants to buy himself a business that will give him both an income and a certain standing in the community, and he decides that owning salt mines will answer both his needs. He doesn't ask anyone else's advice. Why should he, when he already knows it all? And it is only when he has actually purchased the Melbourne Mine – and been running it for a while – that he comes to see that he might just as well have taken his fortune and thrown it straight down the mine shaft.

'Besides, who's to say that the killer's from this town at all? He could be a visitor.'

There were many men who would simply admit their mistake and write it off to experience, Blackstone reasoned. There were many others who would be crushed by what had happened and spend the rest of their lives haunted by bitter regret. But Bickersdale did not strike him as falling into either of these camps.

Bickersdale was quite a different breed altogether. For him, being cheated by one man would seem exactly the same as being cheated by life in general. And he would not tolerate that. He would want his wealth returned to him, and if the only way to achieve that objective was to embark on a life of crime, then it wouldn't bother him at all.

Inspector Drayman, having reached the end of

his litany of woes, had now fallen silent and was obviously waiting for some sympathetic response from his listener.

'What do you know about a man called Lawrence Bickersdale?' Blackstone asked.

'Bickersdale?' Drayman replied, clearly knocked completely off balance by the unexpected question. 'I ... I believe he owns a couple of the salt mines in Marston.'

'That much I already knew,' Blackstone said. 'What else can you tell me about him?'

'Not a great deal, I'm afraid. He seems to keep himself pretty much to himself.'

'You haven't heard any whispers about him?'

'Whispers?'

'Rumours that he's not quite as respectable as he appears – that he might perhaps be involved in something a little shady?'

'Look here, Sam, I don't really see how any of this fits in with the investigation into Margie Thomas's tragic death,' Drayman said.

'It doesn't,' Blackstone admitted.

'In that case, it must have something to do with this diamond-smuggling theory of yours, and I'm sorry, but I've got much more important matters to deal with at the moment than your pet obsession. *I* have a murderer to catch.'

'I appreciate that,' Blackstone told him. 'But if you could just take five minutes to fill me in on—'

'Five minutes or five hours, it makes no difference,' Drayman said, with growing irritation. 'My mind's focused – as it should be – on

Margie's murder. I simply can't deal with anything else.'

Archie Patterson could, Blackstone thought. Patterson could be right up to his elbows in a serious crime, yet still find a moment or two to admire the latest piece of technical gadgetry or make a new contact who might just be useful during a future investigation. If Patterson were sitting opposite him now, he would dismantle his boss's theory, examine every small part of it individually, and then see if it still fitted together. If Patterson was sitting there, there'd already be at least five or six other theories lying on the table by now.

But Patterson *wasn't* there – and Blackstone found himself missing the chubby sergeant more than he'd ever thought he would.

Eight

Ellie Carr did not see the point of re-fighting battles she had already won and, having proved to her own satisfaction that she *would* be served in the King Charles's Arms whenever she wanted to be, she was quite content, that evening, to let Jed Trent go up to the bar and order the drinks.

Trent returned to the table with a pint for himself and a port and lemon for Ellie. He sat down, took a healthy swig of his beer, then said, 'Have the powers-that-be decided whether to allow you to examine Lucy Stanford's body yet?'

'No, they haven't,' Ellie replied. 'The local police surgeon isn't very keen on the idea at all and is being very difficult about it. He claims that performing the autopsy is *his* job.'

'And, strictly speaking, he's right.'

'Perhaps so. But the man's a positive dodo, Jed. He might once have known his way around an autopsy table, but I doubt he's opened a medical textbook in the last thirty years – and there've been a lot of significant advances in that time. So even if there is something to be learned from the body, I very much doubt that he's the man to learn it.'

'Still, if he doesn't want you to...'

'Superintendent Bullock's arguing that I should be allowed to see it. And the superintendent can be very persuasive when he wants to be. In fact, I think he's rather a good copper.'

'And what's this "good copper" *doing* about catching the murderer?' Trent asked.

'As far as I know, he's following pretty much the same procedure as he has in all the other cases.'

'So he's putting all his faith in finding eyewitnesses?'

'Yes.'

'It didn't work before,' Trent pointed out.

'I know that,' Ellie agreed, 'but what else *can* he do?'

'Given the lack of any other evidence, probably not a great deal,' Jed Trent conceded.

'And it's *because* the police are getting nowhere that it's even more vital than ever that I'm given the opportunity to examine the body. Because I'm the only real hope.'

'You always did have a high opinion of yourself, Dr Carr,' Jed Trent said dryly. 'What about the boy – the one Lucy Stanford was supposed to be sweet on?'

'He's gone missing. The local police are looking for him, but even if they find him, I can't see he'll have much to contribute.'

'Unless he turns out to be the actual murderer himself.'

'I don't think he is, not for a second. He has no connection with the other dead girls and, from what Lucy's mother said, he did seem to be genuinely fond of Lucy herself.'

'You're probably right,' Trent agreed. 'Chances are, he'll turn out to be no more than another dead end.'

Ellie was thoughtfully silent for a moment, then she said, 'Did you mean what you said about me having a high opinion of myself?'

'I suppose I did.'

'But is it justified?'

'You sound a bit unsure of yourself all of a sudden,' Jed said, surprised. 'What's brought that on?'

'I'm *always* unsure of myself – though, to give myself due credit, I usually manage to hide it very well.'

'Well, I'm blowed,' Jed Trent said.

'I'm working in a new field of science, and I'm making up half the rules as I go along,' Ellie said earnestly. 'Many of the people I have to deal with treat me as if I were some kind of witch doctor or circus freak. So sometimes I do have a crisis of confidence. Sometimes I do find myself wondering if a good percentage of the work I do is any more than mumbo-jumbo.'

'I'd never have guessed.'

'But I do respect your opinion, Jed. So tell me honestly: am I as good as I think I am?'

Jed Trent smiled at her fondly. 'You're better!' he said. 'You're the best there is.'

Ellie breathed a sigh of relief. 'Thanks, Jed,' she said. 'I really needed to hear that.'

Blackstone disliked the telephone almost as much as his chubby sergeant loved it, but there were times when it was necessary to put his prejudices against the infernal machine to one side and make use of it – and this call to London was one of those times.

Patterson came on to the line almost immediately. 'It's good to hear your voice, sir,' he said.

And it was good to hear Archie's, Blackstone thought, even if the sergeant's *was* so crackly and metallic that it hardly sounded human.

'I need some information,' he told Patterson. 'I doubt you'll be able to provide it, but you're the best shot at finding it that I've got.'

Patterson chuckled. 'Best shot you've got?

Then you'd better "fire away", hadn't you, sir?'

Blackstone grinned. He really *did* miss Patterson.

'I'm interested in a man called Bickersdale, who seems to have spent a great deal of his adult life travelling abroad,' he said. 'I don't know where you'll need to go to find out about—'

'Bickersdale?' Patterson interrupted. 'Lawrence Bickersdale?'

'Yes, his first name *is* Lawrence,' Blackstone said cautiously.

'There's *a* Lawrence Bickersdale who's a bit of a legend among my pals at the Foreign Office,' Patterson said, 'but I don't think they've heard much about him for the last two or three years.'

'They won't have,' Blackstone told him. 'What do they know about him *before* then?'

'They've been tracking his movements all over the world for years. It became a sort of hobby for them – a bit like playing armchair detectives.'

'Yes, but what did they *tell* you?' Blackstone asked impatiently.

'Bickersdale was particularly famous – or maybe I should say infamous – for what he did in Africa, while he was working as a mercenary in the Congo Free State, for King Leopold of the Belgians.'

'Go on,' Blackstone encouraged.

'The natives used to call *all* the Europeans white devils – which is hardly surprising, considering the way they treated them – but according to my pals at the FO, Bickersdale was such a vicious, ruthless bastard that he was *the* White Devil.'

'Did he have anything to do with the diamond trade?'

'Not in the Congo, no. I don't know if there are any diamonds there. But he may have been involved in diamond trading later, when he moved on.'

'So what *was* he involved in while he was in the Congo?'

'You name it, he probably did it. Slavery was big business, and so was ivory smuggling. And then there was the rubber harvesting.'

'What about it?'

'Rubber grows on vines there, and they used to force the natives to slash through the vines and lather themselves in rubber latex. Then, when the latex had dried, it would be scraped off them, which was a very painful process, because all their bodily hair would come with it.'

'Yes, I can well imagine it would be painful,' Blackstone said, grimacing slightly.

'Still, at least the ones involved in rubber production got to stay alive as long as they were useful,' Patterson continued, 'which is more than you can say for a lot of other poor buggers. There've been literally millions of people killed out there, and my pals believe that Bickersdale's probably responsible for quite a number of those deaths.'

'If he is, however did he get away with it?'

'Oh, that was easy enough. The Congo Free

State is King Leopold's personal property, and that means his word is law. If he doesn't object to the natives being slaughtered – and he doesn't, as long as it brings in the profits – there isn't really much anybody else can do about it.'

'If he *is* the same Bickersdale – and that seems very likely – then he's an even nastier piece of work than I took him to be when I met him,' Blackstone said thoughtfully.

'Give me another day and I can probably find out a lot more about him for you,' Patterson said.

'Thanks. If you can find the time, I'd appreciate that,' Blackstone said. 'How are things back in the Smoke?'

'The case I'm working on should be over in a day or two,' Patterson told him. The sergeant hesitated for a second, then said, 'I think I'm going to have to bend the rules if I want to see justice done.'

'Bend them?'

'Well, more like break them, actually.'

'And why are you telling me this?'

'I'm not quite sure,' Patterson confessed. 'Maybe I hoped that if I told you, you'd try to talk me out of it.'

'But do you really *want* me to try and talk you out of it?' Blackstone wondered.

'No,' Patterson replied. 'Now that it's coming up to the crunch, I don't think I do. It seems to me that if I back out now, I'll regret it for the rest of my life.'

'Then I've just one piece of advice for you,'

Blackstone said.

'And what's that?'

'Be careful – and don't get caught.'

'You're like a father to me,' Patterson said, and even though his voice did still sound crackly and metallic, Blackstone could tell he was smiling.

'A father would take you across his knees and give you a good tanning,' Blackstone said. 'But, strong as my knees are, they'd never be able to support a fat bugger like you.'

'You can be very hurtful, sir,' Patterson said, with mock-sorrow. 'See you back in London.'

An unexpected shudder ran right through Blackstone's whole body, as if a sudden dark shadow had fallen over him – or as if he had sensed someone walking over his grave.

'I said, I'll see you back in London, sir,' Archie Patterson repeated.

'Yes,' Blackstone agreed. 'I certainly hope you will.'

Nine

Mick Huggins had never been able to understand why – when he knew he could snap the man in two as easily as he could snap a twig – Mr Bickersdale managed to scare him quite so much. Even now, in the cabin of his own boat, where he should have felt in complete control of the situation, he was finding it hard to stand still under Bickersdale's penetrating gaze.

'What exactly did our friend, the revolting Horace, tell you?' the mine-owner asked.

'Beg pardon, Mr Bickersdale?'

'What did Horace Crimp tell you, once he'd sprung you from the police holding cells?'

'Oh, I see what you mean. He said I'd been a bloody idiot to get in a fight with that bobby.'

'And so you have. Anything else?'

'He said that there'd been talk of havin' me bumped off.' Huggins laughed uneasily. 'But he was only kiddin', wasn't he, Mr Bickersdale?'

'Was he?' Bickersdale asked. 'Do you remember what I told you about my time in the Congo Free State, Huggins?'

'Most of it.'

'Do you recall how I made sure that our native soldiers weren't wasting bullets?'

Huggins shuddered. 'Yes, I remember that bit, Mr Bickersdale.'

'And does it strike you that a man capable of issuing that kind of order is also the kind of man who would make jokes about having people killed?'

'No, Mr Bickersdale.'

The mine-owner nodded. 'Good. Then we understand each other.' He paused for a moment. 'Did Crimp also mention that you should do everything you could to remain inconspicuous?'

'Sorry?'

Bickersdale sighed heavily. 'Did he tell you

212

that you should keep your head down?'

'Yes, he did.'

'That's what I told him to tell you. That's what I wanted you to do. But now, it seems, the situation has changed.'

'Has it?'

'Oh, yes indeed. I had hoped that your friend Inspector Blackstone would help me to find something of mine that has gone missing. But he hasn't, which is *very* disappointing. And to make matters even worse, he appears to have become so suspicious of me that he actually paid me a visit this afternoon. You don't know *why* he did that, do you? You don't know what it was that put him on to me?'

'No, Mr Bickersdale, I don't. I swear I don't.'

'And I believe you, Huggins. But the point is not so much *how* he found me, as that he has. And we just can't afford to have him poking around – not with one shipment due to arrive in the next couple of days, and another shipment due out again almost immediately.'

'You're right, there, Mr Bickersdale,' Mick Huggins said.

'Of course I'm right,' the mine-owner agreed. 'If I could postpone the outward shipment, then I would, but our client is likely to turn very unpleasant if he doesn't get the goods when he's expecting them, don't you think?'

'I don't like foreigners, so I wouldn't know,' Huggins said. Then, catching the glint in Bickersdale's eye, he quickly added, 'but I'm sure you're as right about that, as you have been

213

about everythin' else.'

'So if the mountain won't go to Mohammed, then Mohammed must go to the mountain,' Bickersdale said. He paused again. 'You have no idea what I'm talking about, do you?'

'Course I do, Mr Bickersdale,' Huggins said, unconvincingly. 'It's as clear as daylight.'

'Let me put it another way that you might find easier to comprehend,' Bickersdale said. 'If we can't stop the shipment when Blackstone's here, then we'll have to stop Blackstone being here when there's a shipment.'

Huggins smiled, a process that involved revealing a row of crooked and broken teeth. 'You want me to nobble him?' he asked.

'That's about the long and short of it,' Bickersdale agreed.

'I'll fix him so he won't be able to walk for a month,' Huggins promised.

Bickersdale frowned. 'I'm afraid that simply won't do,' he said. 'If we hurt him, we'll only confirm his suspicions. I want the solution we employ to be more permanent.'

'You want me to kill him?'

'Exactly.'

Huggins smiled happily. 'Will a razor job suit you?' he asked. 'Sneak up behind him an' slit his throat?'

'No, a razor job will most certainly *not* suit me,' Bickersdale snapped. 'If I'd wanted him murdered, I'd have had him shot while he was up at the mine. But a murdered policeman – or even one who suddenly disappears – gets other

214

policemen asking questions I'd really rather not have them ask.'

'I thought you *wanted* him killed.'

'Oh, I do. But I want him to have a fatal accident, to which there will be no witnesses. And I want you to arrange that accident. You have no objections to that, I take it.'

Huggins's smile widened. Whatever he'd promised the solicitor, he'd been planning to do Blackstone over anyway – and the fact that he was doing it with his boss's approval was just the icing on the cake.

'I don't have no objections at all,' he said. 'How will we do it?'

'Blackstone has been showing an unhealthy interest in the salt works. If he had an opportunity to take a closer look at it, I'm sure he would. And I plan to create that opportunity for him.'

'An' then what happens?'

'Think about it, Huggins. What sort of accident could you have in a salt works?'

Mick Huggins frowned; then his grin returned, and he said, 'Oh, yeah!'

Bickersdale stood up, and walked to the door. 'Make yourself available in the morning. I'll get word to you when I need you.' He opened the hatch, looked around outside, then turned back to face Huggins again. 'Oh, by the way...'

'Yes, Mr Bickersdale?'

'That girl who disappeared yesterday...'

'What about her?'

'It turns out that she was raped, strangled and

215

then thrown into one of the flashes.'

'Yes, I heard that myself.'

'Was it you? Were you the one who did it?'

'Oh no, Mr Bickersdale; I swear it wasn't me.'

The mine-owner gave the boatman a smile that chilled his blood. 'Liar!' he said pleasantly.

The dinner, which the Chief Constable of Staffordshire had invited Superintendent Bullock to, was supposed to be no more than a pleasant social event, but Bullock had other ideas. He saw it as an ideal opportunity to attempt to outflank all the local opposition and wrest possession of Lucy Stanford's corpse from their hands.

Bullock launched his undeclared campaign with the arrival of the game soup. 'You might consider allowing Dr Carr to perform the autopsy,' he remarked casually. 'She's said to be quite brilliant at her job – and she does have Home Office approval.'

'This isn't any reflection on you personally, Bullock, but I'm sick and tired of the people in London thinking that they can run our affairs for us,' the Chief Constable replied, as he sucked the soup through his thick moustache. 'We're not exactly country yokels up here, you know. My own medical examiner – Charlie Waddle – is a perfectly sound sort of chap.'

The Scotland Yard man nodded, and bided his time. 'Perhaps Dr Carr and Dr Waddle could perform the autopsy together,' he suggested over the Beef Wellington.

'Charlie Waddle would never stand for that,'

the Chief Constable informed him. 'He's a firm believer in keeping women in their place, and – unless they're dead – that place certainly isn't in the police morgue.'

By the time they reached the nightcap stage, Bullock had decided he had no choice but to adopt desperation tactics. 'Dr Carr wants to get her hands on the girl's body very badly...' he said.

'I'm sure she does. But we can't always have—'

'...and I want to get *my* hands on *her* body very badly, too.'

The Chief Constable almost choked on his brandy. 'Fancy her, do you, old man?'

'It's a little more than that,' Bullock said, hating himself even as he lied. 'It's becoming a positive obsession with me. I just can't sleep at night for thinking about her.'

'Well, you old ram!' the Chief Constable said. 'And am I to suppose that if she doesn't get what she wants, she won't let you have what *you* want?'

'Yes, she's made that very clear.'

The Chief Constable tut-tutted. 'These modern women,' he said. 'They're little better than whores, when you think about it.'

'True,' Bullock agreed, and then, hating himself again, he added, 'But you must admit, she's a very *tasty* whore.'

The Chief Constable thought it over for a while. 'Don't like to see any colleague of mine going without his oats,' he said finally, 'especially when he feels that they're oats he'd particularly enjoy. I'll have a word with Charlie Waddle first thing in the morning. He won't like it, but since he's coming up for election as Grand Master of the Lodge – and since he's going to need my support to get it – he's not likely to kick up too much of a fuss, either.'

'Thank you,' Bullock said.

'I mean, it's not as if either Charlie or your Dr Carr is likely to learn anything from examining the body, now is it?'

'Quite,' Bullock agreed – and immediately sent word round to Ellie Carr's lodgings that she could begin her autopsy the first thing the next morning.

Jamie Green had taken refuge in an abandoned pottery on the edge of town, but he knew that he could not stay there for ever – because even if the police didn't find him, hunger would eventually drive him out into the open.

When they caught him, the police would be bound to blame him for what had happened to Lucy, he told himself, and in *so many* ways, they would be quite right to do so.

His darling girl would never have left her house if it hadn't been for him.

She would never have met the monster who had killed her if it hadn't been for him.

It *was* all his fault!

He heard a scuttling sound in the corner, and turned just in time to see a big rat disappear under a pile of rubble.

It would not be the only rat in this building, he thought. There were probably legions of them hiding in the brickwork. Perhaps, when he fell asleep, they would all come out of hiding and pounce on him. There would be hundreds of them, digging their needle-sharp little teeth into his body. He wouldn't be able to defend himself, and though he might roll around the floor, screaming in agony, they would hold on – ripping at his flesh, gnawing at his bones.

Yes, perhaps that was what would happen. Perhaps he would die in excruciating pain. And perhaps, after all that had gone before it – all he had *allowed* to go before it – that would be no more than a fitting end.

It was a little after midnight. Blackstone had been asleep for half an hour, and he was back in the cave in Afghanistan again.

No, not *in* the cave, but *outside* it – shielding his eyes from the blazing sun, trying to get his thoughts straight.

'He was out here waiting for me when I came out of the cave,' Tom Yardley says, pointing down at the dead Afghan. 'He got off the first shot, and I'd have been dead myself if his rifle hadn't jammed.'

Blackstone looks down at the man. There is something not quite right about that wound in the Pathan's chest, he tells himself, but somehow he can't put his finger on exactly what it is.

219

Blackstone awoke with a sudden start, his heart beating like a drum roll, his pulse throbbing at twice its normal rate.

Why, when he had not thought about that particular incident in his Afghanistan adventures for years, was he suddenly having this same dream about it over and over again?

He fumbled in the darkness for his cigarettes, and lit one up. The answer was obvious, he decided, as he inhaled the acrid smoke. He had not thought of *Tom Yardley* for years, either, but it was only natural that Tom's letter – and his own presence in the village where Tom had met his sudden and convenient death – should bring those days back to him.

And yet, now that he thought about it, he wasn't actually having the *same* dream at all.

What was happening was that each time the dream intruded, it was getting shorter, so that now it didn't feature the *inside* of the cave at all. It was almost as if there was some part of his sleeping mind that was honing the dream down – focusing it on what really mattered.

But that made no sense at all. Why should it need to be honed down? What was the point of focusing on *any* of it? Afghanistan was long in the past. It could have no possible bearing on what was happening at that moment.

Blackstone stubbed his cigarette in the ashtray and fell immediately asleep again.

Friday: The horror! The horror!

One

Thick black smoke poured out of a hundred or more tall brick chimneys. The winding gear at a dozen rock-salt mines creaked and protested as it lowered men down to the drift or brought the results of their labours up to the surface. On the canal, the narrowboats, pulled by stolid horses and loaded down with salt, were just setting out for their next destinations. In the railway marshalling yard, salt trucks were being coupled to engines bound for Liverpool and Manchester, London and Glasgow. It was eight o'clock in the morning, and another working day was already well under way.

Blackstone was crouched down in the confined space between two large industrial ash cans and the wall of the Jubilee Salt Works' boiler room. He had taken up this position over an hour earlier.

This was not the ideal hiding place, he thought. In fact, if he was honest with himself, he'd have to admit that it was a bloody *awful* hiding place – a hiding place in which anyone really looking would have spotted him straight away.

But nobody *was* looking. And why would they

223

be? Why would it even *occur* to a passer-by that any man would endure such obvious discomfort, merely for the opportunity of getting a clear view of the Number One Pan?

There was a part of him that kept repeating that this was all a complete waste of time. But there was another part, a stronger one, that was continually reminding him that though this surveillance operation – like many others he had taken part in – would probably get him nowhere, there was always just a chance that it might!

Entering the Stafford Police Morgue felt not unlike walking into enemy territory, and Ellie Carr and Jed Trent were treated with icy disdain by everyone from the uniformed officer who admitted them through the front door to the clerk who showed them up to Dr Waddle's office.

The doctor himself was even less welcoming. 'I'm allowing this in order to oblige the Chief Constable, who happens to be a good friend of mine,' he told Ellie, 'but that doesn't mean I think it's right.'

'If you'd like to be present during the autopsy—' Ellie suggested.

'If that's what I wanted, then I *would* be – with or without your permission,' Waddle interrupted her. 'But I believe in solid, well-tested procedures, and I've no wish to be associated – in any way – with the latest fashionable ideas that you people from London have come up with. Now, if you don't mind, I'll introduce you to the corpse, then get off to my game of golf.'

He led them down to the morgue. When they reached the doorway, Ellie stopped and looked around her.

If Noah's Ark had had its own morgue, it would have looked just like this one, she thought.

The dead girl was lying on a marble slab, covered by a white sheet.

'I've had her stripped and washed,' Waddle said.

'You've had her *what*?' Ellie demanded, outraged.

'I didn't want a young lady like you to have to handle a dirty corpse, so I had her cleaned up. But it wasn't easy, as you'll understand when you see the cadaver yourself, so I hope you appreciate the effort we've made.'

Before Ellie had the chance to question both Waddle's intelligence and his parentage, Jed Trent stepped between the two doctors. 'Thank you, sir,' he said. 'I'd get to that golf course of yours as soon as you can, if I was you. Looks like it might rain later.'

Waddle nodded, turned on his heel, and left the morgue.

Ellie Carr, frozen to the spot, was clenching and unclenching her hands angrily. 'He's had her *washed*!' she said. 'The stupid bastard's gone and had her washed!'

'He might not have done too much harm,' Trent said soothingly.

'On the other hand – and this is much more

likely – he could well have destroyed vital evidence!' Ellie countered.

'Let's have a look at the body,' Trent suggested, taking the corners of the sheet between his thumbs and forefingers and stripping it away.

The girl's body was in an even more horrific state than they'd anticipated. The deep cuts covered her entire frame, and none was more than two inches from the next. Several of Lucy's ribs were exposed, and her intestines were spilling out of her stomach like a long, malignant worm.

'Why did he do it to her, for God's sake?' Jed Trent wondered. 'If he wanted to hurt her parents, surely slashing her face and cutting off her hands and feet would have been enough?'

'And if he'd done it for his sadistic pleasure, the cuts would have been much more frenzied and haphazard in their nature,' Ellie said, taking a surgical gown from the nearest peg and slipping it on. 'But this is all so ... so *controlled*.'

'What you said last night is starting to make a lot of sense,' Trent told her. 'He didn't do this to send us a message; he did it to *hide* something from us. But I'm buggered if I know what it is.'

'I'm buggered if I know either,' Ellie agreed. She reached across to the instrument tray for a scalpel. 'Let's just hope the corpse can tell its own story.'

Lawrence Bickersdale strode into the yard of the Jubilee Salt Works with more of the air of a man

226

who owned the place outright than the demeanour of a mere shareholder. He stopped in front of the Number One Pan to light a cheroot, then pushed the double doors open and disappeared into the steam.

Blackstone, now in his second hour of crouching behind the ash cans, found it hard to believe his luck. He'd been hoping he would see something suspicious – a package being passed, money changing hands – but he'd never imagined that Bickersdale would be so reckless as to expose himself at the centre of his operation.

It was ten minutes before the mine-owner emerged from the pan again, and when he did, he looked inordinately pleased with himself. Standing in front of the pan, he lit a second cheroot from the stub of his first, and set off in the direction of the salt works' office.

Blackstone shifted position a little, in an effort to ease the cramp in his leg. There could have been only one reason for Bickersdale's visit to the pan: the man had some more jewels he wanted to move, and was going ahead with it, despite the presence of a Scotland Yard detective in the village!

His arrogance was almost incredible, Blackstone thought.

He seemed to think he could be as blatant in his illicit dealings in England as he had probably been in the Congo Free State. Well, he'd soon learn he was wrong about that.

Jamie Green was awoken by a gentle prodding

in his side, and when he opened his eyes, he saw that a uniformed policeman was standing over him.

So the rats had not eaten him after all, he thought. Instead, they had decided to condemn him to another day of living hell.

'What's your name, son?' the policeman asked.

'James Green.'

'We've been looking for a *Jamie* Green all night.'

'And now you've found him.'

'But are you the *right* Jamie Green? The one who we've been looking for had ideas above his station – thought he could mix with the local gentry as if he was one of them himself. Is that you?'

'I never wanted to mix with the gentry,' Jamie said tiredly. 'I just wanted to be with my Lucy.'

'Lucy? Is that the dead girl?'

'Yes, it's the dead girl. The beautiful, wonderful, dead girl.'

The constable nodded. 'I'm going to ask you to stand up now, Jamie,' he said. 'I want you to do it very slowly.'

'All right.'

'And once you *are* standing, I'd like you to put your hands behind your back so I can handcuff you. Do you understand what I'm saying?'

'I understand.'

'Good. Start now. And remember what I said about doing everything slowly. I don't want any trouble.'

'And you won't get any,' Jamie promised him. 'Not from me.'

Joshua Watkins, the manager of the Jubilee Salt Works, normally expected even shareholders in the company to knock before they entered his office, but having taken one look at the furious expression that filled Lawrence Bickersdale's face, he decided that now was not the time to object to the fact that this particular shareholder had simply burst in.

'Is something the matter, Mr Bickersdale?' he asked.

'You could say that,' Bickersdale replied. 'I've just paid a visit to Number One Pan.'

'Why?'

'Why? Because I own a part of this company, and I can go and inspect my investment any time I damn well please!'

'You misunderstand me,' Watkins said hurriedly. 'What I meant to ask was, did you find something going on there that wasn't to your liking?'

'I found that you've so little understanding of how to run a salt works that they've employed a bunch of thieves, if that's what you mean,' Bickersdale snapped back.

'I beg your pardon?'

'And well you might. When I entered the pan, I was wearing the diamond tie-pin that my dear grandfather left me in his will, and when I left the pan I didn't have it any longer.'

'Are you sure that you actually put it on this

229

morning?'

'Yes.'

'And that one of the men took it?'

'There was simply no other way it could have gone missing.'

'Well, this is distressing,' Watkins admitted. 'And you may rest assured that I'll question all the men as soon as they've finished their work.'

'You'll question all the men *now*!' Bickersdale said.

'You want me to go down to the pan myself, and—'

'I want you to summon them to this office immediately, so that we can *both* question them.'

Watkins glanced up at the clock on the wall. 'But the salt must almost be coming to the boil by now.'

'It is.'

'And if I take the men away from the pan, then the batch could well be ruined.'

'It probably will be,' Bickersdale agreed. 'But I don't care. I value that tie-pin more than I value anything else in the world, and I want it back now. So either you summon the men immediately, or I will call the police. And if there's one thing you can be certain of, it is that a full-scale police search will damage production a great deal more than leaving a pan unattended for a few minutes.'

The manager sighed. 'I'll have the men sent for right away,' he said defeatedly.

A ghost of a smile flickered on Bickersdale's

lips for a moment, and then was gone.

What a fool Blackstone was, he thought. Did the inspector really think that after the conversation they'd had the previous day he would be allowed to roam around Marston as he pleased? Could he possibly believe that the man he was spying on – the man he was determined to destroy – would have missed spotting him crouched behind the ash cans? And didn't it occur to him – even for a second – that he might soon be walking into a trap?

The man was an amateur. A bungler. He wouldn't have survived for an hour in the Congo Free State. And, as a matter of fact, he wasn't due to survive for another hour in Marston, either.

Superintendent Bullock was not at all surprised when Jamie Green turned out to be a strikingly handsome boy, because Mrs Stanford had already told him that was the case. What *did* surprise him was just how young Jamie looked, for though he said that he was seventeen, he could easily have been taken for at least two years younger.

'Why did you run away, Jamie?' the superintendent asked.

'I got scared,' the boy replied. 'I thought you'd be certain to blame Lucy's death on me. But running away was the act of a coward! And a fool!'

'Or a guilty man,' Bullock pointed out.

'If I'd only stopped to think for a minute, I'd

231

have seen that it doesn't matter what you believe,' Jamie continued, and it was clear that he either hadn't heard what Bullock said or didn't care. 'It doesn't matter if I'm tried for murder and hanged – because now that Lucy's dead, I don't want to go on living anyway.'

There was an intensity and tragedy to his voice, and though Bullock wasn't sure that he *wanted* to believe him, he discovered that he already *did*.

'You must have really loved the girl,' the superintendent heard himself say.

A tear trickled down Jamie's cheek. 'I did love her,' he said. 'And she loved me.'

'But you must surely have known that you couldn't possibly have had a future together. You're just a groom. You could never have kept Lucy in the style to which she was accustomed.'

'She didn't care about living in style. All she wanted was to be with me for ever.'

'But didn't you realize that her parents would never accept it, however much their daughter wanted them to?'

'*I* did. *I* wanted us to run away together straight away. But Lucy thought she could talk them round. If she'd ... If she'd listened to me, she wouldn't be dead now. *Why* didn't I try harder to persuade her?'

'You can't blame yourself,' Bullock said.

'But I do,' the boy told him.

'How often have you seen her since you gave up your job in London and came back here?'

'Most days. She would manage to find some

excuse to slip away, so that we could we have a few precious minutes together.' Jamie paused. 'Did her mother and father know I'd come back?'

'Her mother did. She saw you from her carriage window, when she was driving through the town. But her father had no idea you'd returned.'

'Then Lucy must have been wrong.'

'About what?'

'For the last two or three days she thought that there was somebody watching her.'

'Did she have any idea who it might have been?'

'She thought it might have been a private detective, hired by her father. But if her father didn't know, it couldn't have been that.'

'Perhaps her mother...'

'*Mrs* Stanford would never have had her watched.'

'Did Lucy happen to catch sight of this person she thought was watching her?'

Jamie shook his head. 'No, she didn't *see* anybody. It was just a feeling that she had, and she must have been wrong.' A look of sudden horror appeared on the boy's face. 'Unless...' he gasped.

'Unless what?'

'Unless the man who was watching her was her killer! Do you think that's possible?'

Bullock nodded gravely. 'Yes,' he said. 'I think that's *more* than possible.'

* * *

The man walking towards the Number One Pan was wearing a suit that had been the latest fashion among the gentry four or five years earlier, and had a bowler hat – rather than a flat cap – perched on his head. When he reached the pan, he opened the door and stepped inside.

A foreman, doing his routine daily rounds, Blackstone assumed, from his hiding place behind the ash cans.

It took less than a minute for the inspector's assumption to be proved false. The foreman emerged again, and he was not alone. Following at his heel were the wallers and lump-men who had been working on Number One Pan. They looked ill at ease, but not guilty – as if they were about to be accused of something they hadn't done but thought it likely they would be convicted anyway.

The procession made its way towards the manager's office. The pan they had been working on – the pan that Bickersdale had visited only a few minutes earlier – was now completely deserted.

This was the kind of lucky break he had been hoping for, but never expected to get, Blackstone told himself, as he broke cover and walked quickly towards the double doors of Number One Pan.

Mick Huggins was hiding behind a wall of salt blocks in the store room just beyond the Number One Pan, and when he heard the doors to the pan swing open, he began to suspect that the moment for which he had been waiting for over two hours had finally arrived.

Huggins shifted position. Earlier he had shaved the corner off one of the blocks of salt and, looking through the gap he had created, he could see a tall, thin figure shrouded by steam.

So Blackstone really had come! Just as Mr Bickersdale had always maintained that he would!

Huggins shook his head in silent admiration of his boss. Bickersdale was the smartest man he had ever met, he thought, and this racket was the smartest one he had ever heard of. Nobody but Mr Bickersdale could have come up with the idea. Nobody but he could have supervised it with such ruthless efficiency. He didn't think twice about killing when he felt that killing was required. The man had ice in his veins and Huggins had come to regard him as an almost godlike figure.

The tall thin man shrouded in the steam looked briefly at the pan itself, then turned his attention to the salt moulds that had just been filled. Soon he would widen his search. Soon he would come into the salt store, with not the slightest idea of what was waiting for him there.

Mick Huggins smiled. He remembered how exuberant he'd felt after raping the young girl he had met quite by chance, and how he'd thought that beating up a hapless stranger in the Hanging Tree would be a perfect way to round off a very pleasurable morning.

It had been a mistake to pick Blackstone as his

235

target. Blackstone had spoiled it all by fighting back, and now he had to pay the price.

But this encounter would be different from the last one. This time, when he struck, Blackstone would not even see it coming – would know nothing at all until he started to feel a pain worse than anything he could ever have possibly imagined.

Two

Blackstone stood next to the steaming brine pan. His eyes were closed and his mind was firmly fixed on reconstructing the sequence of events that had probably occurred in the pan some fifteen minutes before he had entered it himself:

Bickersdale arrives with a packet of stolen jewels – possibly already wrapped in oil-cloth – in his jacket pocket.

He probably invents some reason for being there, but he has no real need to, because he is a shareholder, and he can go where he likes.

He finds an excuse to detach one of the men – his *man on the inside – from the rest of the workers, and when he is sure they are not being observed, he slips the package to him.*

And what does the man do with it?

Slips it straight into a mould of hardening salt?

No! The risk is too great. Bickersdale's unexpected visit will have set the other workers on edge, and nervous men notice things. Far better then to wait until later, when all the other men have relaxed again, or else are distracted by something else.

So what is Bickersdale's man to do with the contraband until the right opportunity arises?

He will have to hide it. And where else would he hide it but in the salt store next to the pan – a store which is already crammed full with thousands of blocks of salt, and where, unless you were actually looking for it, a small package will go unnoticed?

Blackstone opened his eyes again, smiled triumphantly to himself, and headed in the direction of the salt store.

He should have stopped and asked himself why it had all been *so* easy ... should have wondered why Bickersdale had delivered the jewels himself, when he could just as easily have sent one of his underlings to do it ... should have questioned the fact that the men had left the pan just at the right moment for him, even though the brine needed their attention.

He *should* have asked all this, but he was so pleased to have got a lucky break that he didn't.

And when the blow fell, he never even saw it coming.

* * *

The phone that had been sitting silently at the corner of Archie Patterson's desk suddenly began to ring, and Patterson felt his heart miss a beat, because this was the special phone – the one that connected him with the madam of the brothel, and *only* with the madam of the brothel.

'Yes?' he said, answering the phone in a slightly effeminate squeak, very different from his normal rich, nasal tone.

'I have a message for that fat friend of yours, the one who dotes on his sister,' said a harsh female voice on the other end of the line.

'What is it?'

'You're to tell him that the dress he ordered for his darling sister has finally arrived, and that he should pick it up some time today.'

'Good. I'm sure he'll be very pleased.'

'I'll bet he will!' The madam laughed, lasciviously. 'I'll bet he's just *bursting* to see it – if you know what I mean!'

'No,' Patterson said, 'I'm afraid I *don't* know what you mean.'

'Well, ain't you the little innocent?' the madam said scornfully. 'Anyway, make sure you tell him that dresses like this one are very much in demand, and if he *doesn't* pick it up today, I'll sell it to somebody else, and he'll lose his deposit. Have you got that?'

'I've got it.'

'That's what he's hoping – to get it!' the madam cackled, and then the line went dead.

Patterson hung up the phone. So she'd procured the girl for him, just as she'd promised.

238

Then it was about time that he paid Gabriel Moore another visit.

Blackstone's head was pounding like a bass drum, but he knew he couldn't afford to waste any time thinking about that now, because there were other, more urgent matters he had to worry about. He was sure he was moving, but equally sure that he was not doing it of his own volition.

His trunk was pressed up against something hard and muscular, but his head seemed to be upside down and lolling from side to side. His legs, too, seemed to be floating – and there was a hand holding those legs in place that did not belong to him.

'It's a pity you're asleep, you bastard,' he heard a rough voice say from somewhere close to his ear. 'I'd have been happier to have you awake when you took your hot bath – so you could have appreciated it more.'

He was being carried, he told himself. He was on somebody's shoulders and he was being *carried*.

He was glad he'd worked that out, but now he found himself wondering why the air was so steamy. What were you doing just before you blacked out? he asked himself. Concentrate! Try to remember!

He'd been in the Number One Pan – *that* was where the steam was coming from! – and he'd been about to enter the salt store. And then what had happened?

'A *lovely* hot bath!' crooned the voice.

Blackstone opened his eyes and – because his head was still hanging down – found himself looking at the floor of the salt pan. And beyond that, he saw the edge of the pan itself.

The man who was carrying him came to a halt. And suddenly Blackstone was being lifted clear of the shoulders and held high in the air.

'You're heavier than you look, copper,' Mick Huggins said. 'Still, I reckon I can hurl you to near the middle of the pan.'

He let his arms slope backwards slightly, to give his throw more momentum. As he tensed himself, Blackstone came to life, twisting violently and propelling himself away from the pan. Blackstone hit the wall with a sickening thud, then slid down on to the floor. He was completely winded, and for the next few seconds he knew that he would be out of action, however much he fought against it.

If Mick Huggins came at him again, he realized, he was finished. But Huggins was having problems of his own. The force that Blackstone had used to throw himself clear had knocked the narrowboat man completely off balance, and he stood teetering at the edge of the pan. For a moment it looked as if he might be able to right himself; then he stumbled and fell head first into the bubbling brine.

Blackstone struggled to his feet and hobbled over to the pan. Huggins had somehow managed to turn himself over so that he was on his back, but the excruciating pain had quickly overcome him, and now he could do no more than scream in agony.

Blackstone reached into the pan, grabbed hold of Huggins's jacket, and pulled him towards the edge.

Huggins didn't try to fight him, but he wasn't helping either. He probably didn't even know where he was. The pain was all he could think about. The pain was all that existed in the whole world.

Now that Huggins was close to the side, Blackstone could get a double-handed grip on the jacket. Spots of brine splashed on to his hands as he pulled. It hurt like hell, but it was nothing to what Huggins must be feeling.

He heaved the man who had just tried to kill him out of the pan and lowered him to the floor.

Huggins was in a frightful state. There was not an inch of his visible skin which was not blistered, and though his eyes were open, they were sightless. Yet from somewhere deep inside himself he was still finding the strength to continue to roar in agony.

Three

Even for a hardened ex-copper like Jed Trent, observing the autopsy on Lucy Stanford had been a strain – so much of a strain, in fact, that halfway through the procedure he had been overtaken by an irresistible urge to head for the nearest pub and swallow a couple of large brandies. When he returned to the police morgue, Ellie Carr had completed her work but was still standing next to the marble slab, staring down at the corpse.

'Any luck?' Trent asked.

Ellie looked up at him. 'Luck?' she repeated, and he could see from the expression on her face that she was both mystified and troubled.

'What I meant to say was, have you found anything that might get us closer to catching the bastard who did this?' Trent amplified.

'I don't know,' Ellie admitted. 'But I've certainly discovered a couple of things which are rather puzzling.'

'Like what?'

'Well, for a start, there's the state of her skin. It's obviously been very well cared for recently, but, even so, it still feels rougher than I'd have expected it to, given her privileged background.'

This was no time for humour – Jed Trent

understood that – but he still couldn't stop himself from chuckling.

'Have I said something funny?' Ellie asked sharply.

'It's not so much what you said as the assumptions that lie behind it,' Trent told her. 'To be honest, I think you've been reading too many of those romantic novels, Dr Carr.'

'I beg your pardon?'

'You know the sorts of books I mean – the ones in which the heroes – who are nearly always lords – have strong, manly jaws. And the heroines – who are never anything but ladies – have skin as soft as silk, and as fresh as the morning dew. Don't pretend you've no idea what I'm talking about, Dr Carr. You're a woman, and *all* women read that sort of tosh from time to time.'

'As a matter of fact, *this* woman doesn't,' Ellie said, sounding prim – and perhaps a little guilty. 'I'm far too busy, and I confine my reading to serious medical textbooks.'

'Of course you do,' Trent said, disbelievingly. 'But the point is that, however the aristocracy are described in flowery books like that, *you've* no reason to assume that they're any different from the rest of us. They have bad teeth and bunions, just like we do.'

'But not quite as often, and usually not quite as extreme,' Ellie said thoughtfully. 'Besides, why – after she's neglected it for so long – *should* she suddenly start taking better care of her skin?'

Jed chuckled again, even though he had the grace to look shame-faced immediately the chuckle had subsided. 'You need to spend less time with dead people and more time with live ones,' he said. 'If you got out more, you would not be so mystified by something that seems perfectly normal to me.'

'Would you care to explain?'

'Willingly. She probably started taking more pride in her appearance for the same reason that most women do.'

'Because she'd read too much romantic tosh?'

'No! Because she'd found the real thing. Because she'd got herself a man – this Jamie Green bloke.'

'You may possibly be right,' Ellie said, though she did not sound entirely convinced. She paused for a moment. 'The other thing that's got me perplexed is the contents of her stomach.'

'Oh?'

'The last thing Lucy ate was a piece of bread coated in lard. Now that's what I would have been given as a kid, but surely it's not something that would normally have appeared on the Stanfords' dining table.'

'Maybe it wouldn't,' Trent agreed. 'But put yourself in Lucy's place. She's slipping out to meet Jamie, and she knows she'll be gone for a quite a while. Isn't it possible that she had a quiet word with the cook and got her to make something up for her, in case she felt peckish?'

'Would the cook have given her *bread and lard*?'

'Why not? It's cheap, it's quick and it's nourishing. It's the sort of thing the cook would make for herself, if she was feeling peckish.'

'Even so...'

'Besides, maybe that's what Lucy asked her for.'

'Why should she have done that?'

'Because she knew that if she was going to run away with Jamie, that's the kind of food she was going to have learn to get used to, sooner or later.'

'You've got an answer for everything,' Ellie said.

'Of course I have,' Jed Trent agreed, slightly complacently. 'That's why you like having me around.' His face grew more serious again. 'Was the poor little kid interfered with before she was killed?'

'No, at least she was spared *that* humiliation,' Ellie said. 'At least she died a virgin.'

The doctor had covered Mick Huggins's skin with a soothing yellow lotion, and now Huggins lay on a hospital bed, his eyes gazing sightlessly at the ceiling, his blistered mouth occasionally uttering sounds that might possibly have been words.

Standing at the other end of the room, Blackstone and Drayman looked first at him and then at each other.

'Considering that he intended you to meet the same fate as befell him, I don't think *I'd* have bothered to pull him out of the pan at all,'

Drayman said.

'Maybe I wouldn't have myself, if there'd been time to think about it,' Blackstone replied, looking down at the blisters that were clearly in evidence on his own hands.

But he knew, deep down within himself , that it wasn't true – that if he found himself in the same situation again, he wouldn't act any differently.

'Anyway,' he continued, 'looking at it from another angle, I think I owe Mick Huggins a debt of gratitude.'

'You owe him a *what*!'

'A debt of gratitude. He'll have been told to make my death look like an accident. So if he'd followed his instructions, he'd have dumped me in the brine at the edge of the pan. If he'd done that, there'd have been nothing I could do to save myself, any more than there was anything he could do to save *himself* when he fell in. But instead of obeying orders, he decided it would be more fun to see just how far he could throw me – and that was what gave me the opportunity to escape.'

'You lost me,' Inspector Drayman said. 'What's all this talk about instructions and orders? As I understand it, Huggins was simply getting his revenge for what you'd done to him in the Hanging Tree.'

'Oh, that's how you read things, is it?' Blackstone asked. 'Then consider this: Huggins could never have attacked me if there'd been anyone else there in the pan. Agreed?'

'I suppose so.'

'But there wasn't anyone there, because all the workers had abandoned the pan, *right in the middle of the extraction process*. Now why do you think they did that?'

'I don't really know.'

'I do. I've just had a chat with Mr Watkins, the works manager, and *he* says that the reason the men were pulled off the pan was because Bickersdale insisted on it.'

Drayman looked up at the ceiling. 'Bickersdale again,' he said. 'I've told you before: you're becoming obsessed with the man.'

'He was worried that I was getting far too close to his jewellery-smuggling racket, so he set a trap for me,' Blackstone said firmly. 'And, like an idiot, I fell right into it.'

'I'm still far from convinced there *is* any racket.'

'If there wasn't, why would he have wanted me dead?'

'You're like a dog chasing its own tail,' Drayman said wearily. 'Bickersdale's a smuggler, so he tried to have you killed.'

'That's right.'

'And the fact that he tried to have you killed *proves* he's a smuggler. If you're wrong about either of those things, your whole theory collapses.'

They had reached an impasse. They both knew it, but might have gone on arguing anyway, had not Mick Huggins chosen that moment to moan something that sounded as if it just might be actual words.

'What was that he said?' Drayman asked.

'I think it was, "the girl",' Blackstone replied.

The two detectives moved closer to the bed.

'Boss wouldn't let me have her,' Huggins mumbled. 'Said it would damage the goods.'

'Can you hear me, Mick?' Blackstone asked. 'What are you trying to tell us?'

But it was obvious that Huggins *couldn't* hear him, and wasn't trying to *tell* them anything.

'Couldn't have her. Spoil the goods. Didn't care,' Huggins ranted. 'Plenty more fish in the sea. Found a girl on the road to Northwich. Had *her* instead.'

'Are you talking about Margie Thomas?' Drayman asked.

'Lovely she was,' Huggins rambled. 'Screamed like anythin'. Threw her in the flash when I'd finished with her.' He may have been smiling as he spoke, but given the state his face was in, it was hard to say for sure.

The two detectives waited for him to say more, but Huggins had finished. There was a rattle in his throat, and when Blackstone felt for a pulse, there was none to found.

'Well, there it is,' Blackstone said to Drayman. 'A death-bed confession. Though I doubt he *knew* he was confessing – or even where he was. But he still said it clearly enough. He raped the girl, then killed her, then threw her into the flash. You can close the case with a clear conscience.'

'What about the rest of the stuff he said?' Drayman asked. 'The boss wouldn't let him have the girl, because it would be damaging the goods. What do you think that means?'

'The boss who he talked about has to be Bickersdale,' Blackstone replied. 'He's the one who put up Huggins's bail, so it couldn't be anybody else.'

'And what about the girl? Who is *she*? and where does she fit in?'

'I don't know,' Blackstone said, sounding troubled.

Four

Superintendent Bullock looked across the interview table at Jamie Green.

The boy was all hunched up and looked completely exhausted. And who wouldn't be, in his situation? Bullock wondered.

'I just want to ask you a few more questions, and then you can rest,' he said gently. 'Is that all right?'

Jamie nodded lethargically. 'I suppose so.'

'What made Lucy decide to leave the house on the night she disappeared? Did she do it because she'd arranged to meet you?'

249

'Yes.'

'And where had you planned to meet?'

'There's a copse of trees about a mile from her home. There are no houses near it. It's very secluded.' There was a sudden sob in his throat. 'Secluded! That's one of the words Lucy taught me. But she won't be teaching me anything else, will she?'

'Lucy never reached the copse, did she?' Bullock asked.

'No.'

'Weren't you running a bit of a risk, arranging to meet like that?'

'Of course we were running a risk,' the boy said, suddenly coming angrily back to life. 'And because of it, Lucy's dead!'

'I didn't mean that,' Bullock said soothingly. 'I know what happened was terrible, but I didn't mean that at all.'

'Then what *did* you mean?'

'I meant, weren't you running the risk of her parents discovering that she'd sneaked out? They'd have been absolutely furious if they had, wouldn't they? They'd have made sure she never had the chance again. She'd have become a virtual prisoner in her own home.'

'Why does it matter what *might* have happened, now that she's dead?' Jamie asked anguishedly.

'It matters because I want to catch her killer, and to do that I'm going to have to learn as much as I possibly can about what happened on that night,' Bullock told him. 'So help me,

Jamie. Answer my questions, even if they don't seem to make a lot of sense to you. Will you do that?'

'All right,' Jamie agreed.

'Did you consider the risk of her parents finding out?'

'Of course we did,' Jamie admitted. 'But we both decided that it was a risk well worth running.'

'You see, that's what I still don't quite understand,' Bullock said. 'You told me you somehow or other managed to see each other for a few minutes every day, didn't you?'

'Yes.'

'So why did you *need* to meet at night? Why jeopardize what you already had?'

Jamie stared down at the table, and said nothing.

'What was so important about meeting that night?' Bullock persisted.

'I don't want to talk about it.'

'You have to.'

'I can't!'

'When we started this interview, there was only one thing I was sure of,' Bullock said, with a hint of sadness creeping into his tone. 'And that one thing was that you cared deeply for Lucy. Well, I was wrong about that, wasn't I? I was way off the mark.'

'I'd have died for her!' Jamie said.

'But you didn't die, did you?' Bullock asked harshly. 'She was the one who died. And now you won't even give me the information that will help me to catch her killer.'

Jamie swallowed hard. 'If I do tell you why we did it, how do I know you'll understand?'

'You don't,' Bullock admitted. 'But you have my word that I'll try to – and that's as much as any man can offer.'

Jamie swallowed again. 'I loved Lucy for herself,' he said shakily. 'For her beautiful nature. For her soul.'

'I *do* understand that.'

'But I ... I ... also loved *being* with her.'

'What does that mean?'

'Don't you know?'

'Yes, I think I do. But you're still going to have to spell it out a little more precisely for me.'

'If I tell you – if I put it into words – all it will do is cheapen Lucy's memory. And I couldn't stand that.'

'Say it!' Bullock urged. 'Admit that you made love to her.'

'No, I ... I can't.'

'I promise you, it won't cheapen her in my eyes at all, because I know that you were the man who she adored, and that you treated her with all the respect she deserved.'

'We made love,' Jamie said.

'When was the first time?'

'It ... It was in the Carlisles' stables, while I was still working as a groom there.'

'Then you were sent away to London?'

'Yes.'

'And since you've been back in Staffordshire,

you haven't had the opportunity?'

'No.'

'So that's why you arranged to meet that night?'

'Not being able to make love was killing us both. We were burning up. That's why we took the risk: because we couldn't stand it any longer!' Jamie buried his head in his hands. 'And just look what happened!'

'Jamie...' Bullock said softly.

'My Lucy's dead! Because we couldn't control our instincts! Because God decided to punish us for not waiting!' Jamie sobbed. 'Well, you asked for the truth, and you've got it. Are you happy?'

'Of course I'm not happy,' Bullock said. 'I could almost weep for you – you poor little bugger!'

Walter Clegg was standing outside the hospital when the two detectives emerged, and from the look that came to his face when he saw them, it was obvious it was no chance meeting.

'You've had another letter,' he said excitedly, holding out an envelope. 'I think it might be from the same man.'

The envelope itself was certainly similar to the last one, Blackstone noted, and once again his name was written on the front of it in block capitals.

He slit the envelope open, and took out the sheet of paper.

THE BLUEBELL IS TAKING ON SALT AT BICKERSDALES MINE AT TWO O'CLOCK THIS AFTERNOON. WHY DON'T YOU SEE WHAT ELSE ITS CARRYING?

'Was I right?' Walter Clegg asked. *'Is* it from the same feller as wrote to you the last time?'

'It seems to be,' Blackstone admitted.

'An' what does it say?'

'I thought we had an agreement that we'd keep you out of this,' Blackstone said.

'I never agreed – or if I did, it was only because I didn't see I had any choice in the matter,' Walter Clegg said hotly. 'But I've been thinking about it, Mr Blackstone. Tom Yardley was my mate – the best friend I ever had – an' if that letter is anythin' to do with him, I've got a *right* to know what's in it!'

Blackstone shook his head. 'I'm sorry, Walter, but you haven't. This is official police business. I can't tell anybody about it – not even you.'

Clegg did not look in the least mollified. 'People have been shittin' on me all my life, an' you're no better than the rest of them,' he said bitterly. 'I invited you into my home, an' let you sleep under my own roof. I thought that I could trust you. I thought that I could *rely* on you. But I was wrong, wasn't I?'

And without waiting for Blackstone to reply, he turned and walked quickly away.

Blackstone watched him for moment, then shrugged his shoulders regretfully and handed

254

the note over to Inspector Drayman.

'Ah, more fuel for the fire of your obsession!' Drayman said.

'It may be *my* obsession, but I appear not to be the only one to hold it,' Blackstone pointed out. '*I* didn't write the note, you know.'

Drayman sighed. 'Just what is it that you want me to do?'

'I want you to get a warrant sworn out that will allow you to search the *Bluebell*,' Blackstone told him.

'Sam...'

'You owe me, you know, Inspector. I've just solved the Margie Thomas case for you.'

'I wouldn't say you exactly solved it. You got into a pub brawl, and because of that—'

'Thanks to me, you'll be able to sleep at night again.'

'You have a point,' Drayman conceded. 'But what if I do get the warrant sworn out, and all we find on the boat is salt?'

'Then I'll willingly admit that I've been as obsessed as you always thought I was.'

'And you'll never mention smuggling again?'

'And I'll never mention smuggling again. Is that a fair deal?'

'No,' Drayman said, 'but it's about as good a deal as I'm ever likely to get from you.'

Ellie Carr was sitting at a corner table in the King Charles's Arms, listening to Superintendent Bullock telling her that he was in the process of ordering Jamie Green's release.

'You're going to let him go?' she asked. 'Just like that? Do you think that's wise?'

Bullock sighed inwardly. For months the newspapers had been demanding to know why he hadn't made an arrest yet, and his own superiors were finally beginning to join in the chorus. And now this chit of a girl – who might know a great deal about doctoring, but had no idea of detective work – had decided that she would have a pop at him too.

'Speaking as a policeman with a great deal of experience, I can see no reason not to release Jamie,' he said airily. 'I've had a chat with the lad, and I don't really think he had anything to do with the girl's murder.'

Ellie hadn't thought he had either; she'd said as much to Jed Trent. But somehow, Bullock's easy sweeping aside of the possibility raised her sceptically scientific hackles.

'Might I inquire as to what it is that's made you so certain he's innocent?' she asked, with an edge to her voice that would have alerted both Trent and Blackstone to the fact that they were treading on dangerous ground but seemed to go right over Bullock's head.

'Well, for a start, there's the fact that he didn't know any of the other victims.'

'But in order to murder Lucy, did he *have to* know any of the others? There have been full reports of all the other murders in the papers. If Jamie had read them, he could easily have decided that, by making Lucy's death similar to all the others, he would neatly deflect suspicion away from himself.'

Bloody amateurs! Bullock thought. The world was full of bloody amateurs, and they *all* thought they knew how to do his job better than he did himself.

He laughed, covering the irritation he was feeling with a coating of condescension. 'Don't you think you might just be a tiny bit out of your depth, Dr Carr?' he asked.

Sam Blackstone would never have said that to her, Ellie Carr thought, with growing anger. 'In what way am I out of my depth?' she asked.

'In your assumption – which you no doubt share with *most* of the uninformed members of the general public – that I've released *all* the details of the murders to the newspapers. There are a few vital ones that I held back, just in case a situation like this one should arise. There are details Jamie simply *couldn't* have known, however much he'd read. And I can assure you that Lucy's death isn't just *similar* to all the others – it's a carbon copy.'

Any minute now he's going to pat me on the head and tell me what a bright – if mistaken – little girl I am, Ellie thought.

She was being unreasonable, she realized. Bullock was a decent and conscientious policeman, who had probably had to work extremely hard in order to secure permission for her to examine Lucy's body. If he was now not handling her quite as well as he might have, it was only because he was emotionally and physically exhausted, and she would be wise to let matters

257

rest there.

'Of course, I should have realized you'd keep some details back,' she said, declaring a unilateral cease-fire.

'Besides, even without that, I trust my own judgement – just as I'd trust yours if you were a little older and a little more experienced in the ways of the world,' Superintendent Bullock continued.

'And just what does your older and more experienced judgement tell you about Jamie?' Ellie asked, rapidly lowering her mental flag of truce.

'It tells me that he really loved the girl. And even if I'm wrong on that point – and I don't think I am – it tells me he wouldn't have had the stomach for cutting her up like that.'

'It all depends on exactly what point of desperation she drove him to,' Ellie said, full guns blazing again. 'What my younger and less experienced observations have taught me is that love can often quite quickly turn to hatred, and hatred manifests itself in very violent acts.'

Bullock chuckled again at her naivety. 'And just what could Lucy have done to turn Jamie's love into hatred?' he wondered.

'She could have denied him what he wanted most in the world,' Ellie said. 'And he might well have decided that if he couldn't have it, then no one else could. And what's the best way to ensure that? By destroying her!'

'I take it that we're talking about sexual relations here,' Bullock said, still greatly amused.

'That's right,' Ellie agreed.

'Then there's one fatal flaw to your argument. Lucy *didn't* deny Jamie what he wanted!'

'Are you saying that she slept with him?'

'Several times, according to Jamie. Though he says they hadn't done it since he got back from London.'

'She *slept* with him!'

'Why do you seem so shocked, Dr Carr? It's not *that* unusual for such things to happen, you know. However much the churches might preach against it, and however often parents warn their daughters that it could ruin their lives for them, there's still an awful lot of people in this world who simply can't resist sampling the forbidden fruit.'

'Oh my God,' Ellie Carr said softly to herself.

Five

Jamie Green had no idea what was happening to him. An hour earlier he'd been told he'd be released as soon as the paperwork had been completed. Now he was back in the interview room, which probably meant that he was about to be subjected to another round of questioning.

He wondered what had changed, then decided he didn't really care what the answer was – didn't really care about *anything*.

The door opened, and a woman walked into the room.

'You must be Jamie,' she said, smiling warmly.

'Yes.'

'I'm Dr Carr, but you can call me Ellie.'

'I don't need a doctor,' Jamie said sullenly.

'Of course you don't,' Ellie agreed, sitting down in the chair opposite his. 'But you could probably use a friendly ear.'

'What?'

'Someone to talk to. Someone to tell how you're feeling. It must have been very hard to lose the girl you loved.'

'It was hard,' Jamie Green agreed, as tears began to stream down his cheeks again. 'Not *was*! *Is*! I don't think I'll ever get over it.'

'I don't think you will, either,' Ellie said sympathetically. 'But it won't *always* be as bad as it is now. You'll still carry the pain, but at least time will dull it a little.' She paused for a moment. 'I need to ask you some questions about what you and Lucy did together.'

'What do you mean?'

'Superintendent Bullock tells me that you made love to her – on more than one occasion.'

'He should never have told you that!' Jamie said, as anger replaced sorrow on his face. 'He had no right to.'

Ellie reached across the table and placed her hand on top of Jamie's. The boy looked down at the two hands as if he did not quite understand what was going on, but he made no attempt to break free.

'Superintendent Bullock *had to* tell me, because I'm helping him to search for Lucy's killer,' Ellie said softly. 'And why shouldn't he have told me? I am a doctor, after all.'

'I know, but—'

'And I'm also a *woman*. I know the sort of temptation Lucy must have been under, because I've been under it myself.'

'But you didn't give way to it, did you?' Jamie asked. 'You were strong enough to resist! And that makes you feel as if you're so much better than us.'

'You're wrong,' Ellie told him. 'I did give way.'

'And were you the same age as Lucy?'

'No, as a matter of fact, I was in my early twenties.'

'Well, then...'

'But age doesn't really matter in these cases, Jamie. All that's important is how you feel.'

'Was he older than you – this man you gave in to?'

'Yes. He was a senior doctor at the teaching hospital, and I was one of his students.'

He had told her he loved her, as she knew she loved him. He had promised her that they would marry, and that they would do their research together. But he was already married and had no intention of sharing whatever glory his research might bring him with anyone else.

She was grateful, in a way, that it had happened, because it had taught her a valuable lesson

261

early on. Now, when she slept with a man, it was solely for her own pleasure. And if she loved anything at all, it was her work.

'How did you feel once you'd done it?' Jamie asked.

She was tempted to tell him the truth, but she knew that the question was not about her at all – that he was asking her how she, as a woman, thought Lucy would have felt.

'I was happier than I'd ever been before,' she lied. 'I was proud of having given myself to the man I loved.'

Jamie smiled gratefully. 'So you *do* understand,' he said.

Ellie nodded. 'Before you slept with Lucy, were you a virgin yourself?' she asked.

'Yes. And I'm not ashamed of it!'

'There's no reason why you should be.' But that might explain the discrepancy between his statement and the autopsy findings, Ellie thought.

'Given your own inexperience, it's entirely possible that you didn't make love to Lucy after all,' she continued.

'I'm no liar!'

'I'm sure you're not. I know you *believe* you did it, but you may not have entirely succeeded.'

'It was just like it should have been,' Jamie said defiantly.

'Why don't you describe the first time to me?'

'Because I don't want to.'

'I can understand that. You're afraid that after you've described it, I won't believe you.'

'I don't care whether you believe me or not.'

'Or perhaps it's not that at all. Perhaps you're afraid that once you've heard yourself describe what went on, you won't believe it either.'

'Why are you doing this?' Jamie asked, anguishedly.

'It doesn't really matter what actually happened, Jamie,' Ellie told him. 'You *wanted* to do it – and Lucy wanted to do it *with you* – so even if you didn't get it quite right, that doesn't make you any less of a man.'

'You'll keep on at me until you find out what you want to know, won't you?' Jamie asked.

'Yes,' Ellie agreed. 'I'm afraid I have to.'

'The first time we made love was in the stables. It ... It was very hard to enter her at first...'

'Go on.'

'...and it seemed to be hurting her so much that I wanted to stop. But she told me to go on. So I did.'

'Did she say she'd enjoyed it?'

'Yes, she said she had – but I don't think she was telling the truth.'

'Why would she have lied?'

'For me! She wanted me to think I'd made her happy.'

'What about the second time?'

'The second time it was a lot easier to get inside her, and once I was there, she moaned like I'd never heard a woman moan before.'

'Let's get back to the first time,' Ellie suggested. 'Was there any blood?'

'I'd rather not say.'

'But I need to know. And I think you need to know too.'

'Know what?'

'Whether you really did it properly. Because you're still not *quite* sure, are you?'

'I was until you walked into the room!' Jamie said angrily. 'I was before you started asking me all these questions.'

'Was there blood?' Ellie asked.

'Yes, there was a lot of blood. I thought we must have done something wrong. I wanted to take her to the doctor right away. But Lucy said I mustn't worry. She said it was *supposed* to be like that.'

'Well, well, well, what a surprise!' the madam of the house in Waterloo Road said, looking up from her chaise longue at the chubby young man who was standing, somewhat nervously, in front of her.

'Surprise?'

'I wasn't expecting you to call round until some time this evening, yet it's only just past noon, and here you are already.'

Patterson shifted his weight awkwardly from one foot to the other.

'You didn't say I should come in the *evening*,' he pointed out. 'You just said it should be some time today.'

'That's true enough, but the fact that you're here *so* early shows just how eager you are, now doesn't it?'

264

Patterson shrugged, as if he were pretending that he didn't really care one way or the other. 'You told me you had the girl and, since I happened to be in the area, I thought I might as well come to see her,' he said unconvincingly.

'You thought you'd come to "see" her, did you?' the madam repeated, with amused contempt. 'Well, before you "see" her, I'll need to see the rest of the money. And I'm afraid the price has gone up.'

'But we had a deal,' Patterson protested.

'You're right, we did,' the madam agreed. 'But that deal was based on the understanding that I'd be providing a different class of girl from the one I've actually been able to lay my hands on. I promised you a tradesman's daughter, didn't I?'

'Yes.'

'Well, this girl's much better than that.'

'How is she better?'

'She's the daughter of a solicitor's clerk. The poor man's fallen on hard times, due to drink, but he took excellent care of his family before that. The girl's been *very well* brought up. She'll never have dreamed she'd ever end up in a place like this.' The madam leered. 'I expect she'll find what's about to happen to her a great humiliation – and *very* frightening.'

'How do I know you're not lying about the girl?' Patterson demanded.

'Now I could take offence at that question,' the madam told him, 'but since I know you didn't really mean to be rude, I won't.'

265

'I'll still need an answer,' Patterson said firmly.

'All right. You can believe me because I'm an honest business woman, and I don't lie.'

'That's not—'

'You can also believe me because, when you meet the girl, it'll be obvious what sort of background she comes from. And if that's not enough for you, you can ask the girl yourself, just before you start "seeing" her.'

Patterson licked his lips. 'How much extra will the new girl cost me?' he asked.

'Another fifty pounds.'

'That seems ... er ... reasonable.'

'Have you got the money on you at the moment, or will you need to go to the bank for it?'

'I've got the money on me,' Patterson said, reaching into his pocket and producing a thick wad of bank notes.

Now it was the madam who was licking her lips. 'That'll be seventy-five pounds,' she said. 'The girl costs a hundred, but I've remembered that you gave me twenty-five pounds as a deposit when you were here the other night. See how honest I am?'

'Yes,' Patterson replied. 'You're very honest. You're a real credit to your profession.'

Superintendent Bullock was sitting at the desk in the office that the local police had assigned him. In front of him lay Ellie Carr's report of the autopsy she'd performed on Lucy Stanford,

266

which he had intended to read earlier but still hadn't quite got round to.

The office door opened, and Ellie Carr herself walked in. She looked rather shaken, Bullock noted. Now why was that? Possibly it was because she'd just learned that conducting an interrogation was a harder slog than it might at first appear. Or perhaps it was because – during the course of the interrogation – she'd learned that she didn't know quite as much about police work as she'd thought she did.

'I've spoken to the boy,' Ellie said, 'and I believe he did exactly what he says he did.'

Bullock knew that now was not the right time to take a dig at her, but he found himself unable to resist the temptation. 'So what price now your theory that Jamie might have killed Lucy because she wouldn't let him have his wicked way with her?' he said jovially.

'Have you read my autopsy report?' Ellie asked coldly.

'No, not yet,' Bullock admitted.

'I thought not. Because if you had, you'd know that the girl I examined was a virgin.'

'Come, come, Dr Carr; since we now both know that she can't have been, it's obvious you must have made a mistake.'

'I don't make mistakes,' Ellie said.

'Everybody makes mistakes.'

'Not over matters as simple as that.'

'But if you're right...'

'And I can assure you I am.'

'...then, logically, there's only one conclusion

267

we can reach.'

'Exactly' Ellie agreed. 'And that conclusion is that the girl I've just done the autopsy on *wasn't* Lucy Stanford.'

Six

There were two men standing at the crown of the humpbacked bridge. One of them, Blackstone, was looking up the canal towards the Melbourne Mine. The other, Drayman, was pacing nervously back and forth.

'Is there still no sign of the *Bluebell*?' Drayman asked, for the fourth or fifth time.

'No,' Blackstone replied. 'But I'd be surprised if there had been yet. According to the letter, it's not even due for at least another hour.'

'You talk about that letter as if it were Holy Writ!' Drayman said. 'But it's not, is it? It's an anonymous note, which could have been scrawled by just about anybody.'

Blackstone shook his head. 'Not just about anybody. Whoever wrote it has to be very close to Bickersdale.'

'I should never have agreed to any of this, Sam,' Drayman said, as he continued to pace. 'When it ends in a fiasco – as it's almost bound to – we're going to look complete bloody fools. But that won't matter to you, because you'll be long gone. I'm the one who has to continue to live here.'

'It's almost over,' Blackstone told him. 'Don't lose your nerve now.'

'The more I think about it, the more your theory fails to add up,' Drayman continued, as if Blackstone had never spoken. 'You first started to believe that Lawrence Bickersdale had to be a jewel-smuggler when you saw how salt blocks were made. Isn't that right?'

'No, I started to believe it when I read the letter that Tom Yardley had sent me.'

'But it was seeing the salt blocks that convinced you he'd been telling the truth?'

'It certain explained why Bickersdale had chosen Marston as the centre of his operation.'

'But, according to the anonymous letter you put so much faith in, the contraband's being loaded up at the Melbourne Mine,' Inspector Drayman pointed out.

'I know.'

'And they don't *make* blocks of salt at the Melbourne Mine! They make them at the Jubilee Salt Works!'

'I know that, too.'

'So if Bickersdale really was involved in smuggling, then the trail would start from the salt *works*, not the salt *mine*.'

That flaw in the argument had been worrying Blackstone, too, though, given the fragile state of Inspector Drayman's nerves, he thought it best not to show his concern.

'Perhaps this particular piece of jewellery that

they're shifting is too big to go in a block of salt,' he suggested.

'Too big! And just what kind of jewellery is too big to go in a block of salt?' Drayman asked derisively 'Perhaps it's the Queen's coronation crown he's fencing, though I can't say that I remember reading any reports of it actually being stolen.'

'Maybe it's bars of gold he's smuggling.'

'You're clutching at straws,' Drayman said. 'Face it, Sam: your entire theory is built upon a foundation stone of salt blocks, and if you once remove them, the whole structure comes tumbling down. Which is why I'm afraid that if we *do* stop that boat, we'll find nothing on it. Which is why I think that by the end of the day we'll both have very red faces.'

He was wrong, Blackstone thought. He *had to be* wrong. Because Tom Yardley would never have written that letter if he hadn't been seriously worried. Because Tom would never have been murdered – and Mick Huggins would never have dared to try and kill a police inspector from Scotland Yard – if there'd been nothing to hide. Because the anonymous letter-writer had been spot on with his first piece of information, so why should he be wrong with the second? But, most important of all, Blackstone knew that Drayman was wrong because his *gut* told him he was.

A uniformed constable came running up the bridge, waving an envelope in his hand. At the crown he came to a halt, caught his breath, then said, 'Telegram for you, Inspector Blackstone. It's marked "Urgent".'

Blackstone took the telegram from him, slit open the envelope, and saw that the message was from Ellie Carr. 'LATEST VICTIM OF KILLER DEFINITELY NOT LUCY STANFORD, DESPITE FACT FOUND WEARING LUCY'S CLOTHES,' Ellie had written: 'BULLOCK BAFFLED. ME BAFFLED. ANY IDEAS? IF SO, PLEASE SEND SOONEST.'

Despite the seriousness of the telegram's contents, Blackstone found that he was smiling. The telegram sounded so much like the way Ellie spoke that she could almost have been there, he thought – and then he realized that he really wished she was.

The girl was waiting for Patterson in a room on the second floor of the house in Waterloo Road. She was sitting on a chair, in the corner, as if she felt that being close to two walls gave her some kind of protection. She was small and very pale, and the elaborate lace chemise in which they'd dressed her seemed hideously inappropriate for a child like her.

'Are you the one?' she asked Patterson, with fear in her eyes and a tremble in her voice.

'The one what?' the sergeant asked.

'The one who they told me downstairs was coming to make me into a woman?'

Patterson felt sick to his stomach. 'I'm not going to do anything at all to you,' he promised. 'I won't even touch you. All I want to do is ask you a few questions. Would that be all right?'

The girl, still plainly terrified, just nodded.

Patterson squatted down, so that his face was level with hers, and then smiled as reassuringly as he was able.

'Where do you live?' he asked softly.

'Here. They told me downstairs that from now on, I live here.'

'Where did you live *before* they brought you here?'

'In a cheap boarding house. Down by the docks.'

'On your own?'

'No. With my father.'

'And before even that?'

A smile – infinitely sad and infinitely wistful – came over the girl's face. 'We had a nice house in Holloway,' she said. 'It had a lovely garden for me to play in.'

'And what happened? Why did you move?'

'Mother died, and Father started drinking. When he lost his job, we had to leave the house.'

'Does he still drink?'

'Worse than ever. That's why he said I should come and live with the lady. He said she'd take good care of me.'

'Do you think it was because she could look after you that he agreed to let the lady take you away?'

The girl shook her head, and a small tear trickled down her cheek.

'Then why *did* he agree?' Patterson asked.

'I think it was because the lady gave him a ten-pound note.'

'Where's this lady now?'

'Downstairs.'

He'd heard as much as he needed to, Patterson decided – or, at any rate, as much as he could *take*.

He walked over to the window, drew back the curtain and looked down into the road. He saw a street-cleaner standing there, though the man was making no effort to sweep the street and seemed much more interested in watching the house.

Patterson waved to him. The man nodded, and moved his cart along.

Another two minutes passed before there was a sound of pounding feet in the street and, looking out of the window again, the sergeant could see half a dozen uniformed policemen running towards the house.

Patterson opened the bedroom door, and stepped out into the corridor.

'Where are you going?' the girl asked, alarmed by the thought that this man – who had been so nice – was now about to abandon her.

'Don't worry, I'll be back in a minute,' Patterson assured her, 'but I really do need to find you something a bit more decent to wear.'

Seven

From a distance the approaching narrowboat looked like nothing so much as a long green ridge tent, miraculously floating on the water.

'That's it,' Drayman said almost mournfully, lowering his field glasses and turning to Blackstone. 'That's the *Bluebell*.'

Blackstone nodded. 'So I see.'

'There's still time to decide you've made a mistake.'

'I've made no mistake,' Blackstone replied. And he believed what he was saying.

It was unlikely that the *Bluebell* was carrying jewels, he admitted, since – as Drayman had so clearly pointed out – it had loaded up at the mine rather than the salt works. And though he himself had mentioned the possibility of gold bars, he'd done it mainly to pacify the local inspector and did not give much credence to that theory either – because gold didn't grow on trees and there hadn't been a major bullion robbery in England for years.

But Bickersdale had to be up to *something*, or he'd never have had Tom killed and ordered an attempt on Blackstone's own life. And if that 'something' didn't involve the use of narrow-

boats, then why had he put Huggins in charge o.
one?

He turned his thoughts back to Ellie's telegram. He'd been amused by the style in which
she'd written it, and intrigued by the discoveries
she'd made. But it had also disturbed him
greatly. Reading it, a bell had rung in the back of
his mind, and his mental warning light had
flashed – almost as if the telegram was not about
what was happening in Staffordshire at all, but
was much more a warning to him personally. He
didn't understand why this should be the case,
since Ellie was assisting in an investigation to
track down a vicious killer, while he was
attempting to arrest a smuggler. Yet the uneasy
feeling it had given him refused to go away.

'Five minutes left,' Inspector Drayman said.

'Don't worry, we'll get a result,' Blackstone
told him. 'When this is all over, you'll be a
hero.'

'When this is all over, I'll be standing in the
corner with a dunce's cap on my head,' Drayman replied. 'And if I know my chief constable,
he'll probably leave me there for years.'

'Bridget Latouche, I am arresting you...' Patterson began. He paused. 'Is that your real name –
Bridget Latouche?'

'Go to hell,' the madam replied, with blazing
hatred in her eyes.

'If you refuse to supply me with any other
name, then I must assume it *is* your real one, and
that assumption will make the caution I am

'bout to deliver valid in the eyes of the law,' Patterson said evenly.

'Do you know who my attorney is?' the madam snarled. 'Henry Knox-Partington! He eats coppers for breakfast – even fat coppers like you! He'll have me sprung from that nick of yours before you've had time to take a shit and wipe your arse.'

'Bridget Latouche, I am arresting you on the charge of procuring a girl below the age of consent for illicit purposes,' Patterson said. 'You do not have to say anything, but anything you do say may be taken down and used in evidence against you.'

'Then take this down,' the madam said. 'You are pathetic, Archibald. You're fat, and you're ugly – and the only woman who'll ever look at you is one you've paid for. Nobody will ever love you.'

Patterson smiled. 'That's where you're wrong, Miss Latouche,' he said, thinking of Rose. And it was because of thoughts of Rose, he realized, that he had had such feelings of anger ever since this investigation began. Because if things had gone a little bit differently for her – if her mother had died or her father had turned to drink – she could well have ended up in a house like this one.

Blackstone and Drayman stood at the head of the dog-legged path that led from the bridge to the canal side.

'I'll go down first,' Blackstone said. 'If there's

any shooting, there's no point in us both being in the line of fire.'

'But why *should* there be any shooting?' Drayman asked.

'Because we're dealing with dangerous criminals here.'

'I think it's far more likely that we're dealing with an honest narrowboat man going about his legitimate business.'

There was no point in arguing the toss about it now, Blackstone thought. Within half an hour, one of them would have turned out to be a fool, and he was betting – against the odds – that it would be Inspector Drayman.

Blackstone walked down the path. The horse and boat were almost level with him. He stepped forward, and when he took hold of the horse's bridle, the animal stopped moving immediately.

'What the hell's goin' on?' demanded the man at the tiller, at the far end of the boat. 'Let go of me horse, before I'm forced to get off this boat an' kick yer bleedin' head in.'

He was a big, ugly bastard, Blackstone noted. And though he probably *wasn't* Mick Huggins's brother, he easily could have been.

Inspector Drayman appeared from out of the shadows. 'Police,' he said to the narrowboat man. 'What's your name?'

'Peck. George Peck.'

Drayman held up the warrant for him to examine. 'This gives us the right to search your boat, Mr Peck.'

'I ain't done nothin'!' the narrowboat man

277

protested.

'And I'm not *accusing* you of doing anything,' Drayman said levelly. 'All I want to do is search your boat.'

'It'll be a waste of time. There's nothin' in my cabin that hasn't been bought an' paid for.'

Drayman gave Blackstone a worried look – a look which clearly said that if the narrowboat man was guilty of anything, he certainly wasn't showing any signs of it on his face.

'How about in the cargo section?' Blackstone asked.

Peck laughed. 'Oh, you'll find somethin' in there, all right,' he said. 'Finest Cheshire salt. Tons of the stuff.'

The two uniformed constables appeared at the bottom of the dog-legged path. Each of them held a large griddle in his hand.

'You're never goin' to sift through all my salt, are you?' Peck asked Drayman.

'Every grain of it, if we have to,' Blackstone said quickly, before Drayman had a chance to reply.

'But it'll hold me up too long,' the narrowboat man protested. 'I'll never get to Liverpool on time.'

'My heart bleeds for you,' Blackstone said. He turned to the constables. 'Remove the cover from the cargo hold.'

It was neither a simple nor a speedy process. First the tarpaulin that covered the entire frame had to be untied and rolled back. Then the individual side cloths, which underlay it, had to be

278

unfastened too. And all the time this was going on, Inspector Drayman stood watching from the towpath – and visibly worrying.

When the cover had been finally stripped away, it was to reveal – just as Peck had promised it would – several tons of finest Cheshire salt.

'Where did this come from?' Blackstone asked.

'The Melbourne Mine,' Peck told him.

'I've been there and seen the mine for myself,' Blackstone said. 'I doubt they mine this much salt in a year.'

Peck shrugged. 'I wouldn't know about that. I work for Postlethwaite Carriers. I don't have nothin' to do with the mine at all.'

He was lying, Blackstone thought. The boat might be registered to a man called Postlethwaite, but Peck was one of Bickersdale's thugs.

'Start the search,' he told the two constables.

The constables stepped on to the boat at its forward end and looked dubiously down at the cargo.

Drayman was looking dubious, too, Blackstone noted. It would be a truly mammoth task to sift all that salt, and the only way to stop the local inspector from ordering his men to abandon the job halfway through was to distract him with something else.

'Shall we search the cabin, Inspector?' he suggested.

'What would be the point of that?' Drayman

asked, lethargically, but he followed Blackstone to the after end of the boat anyway.

George Peck had remained at the tiller throughout the whole proceeding, but now he stepped down on to the towpath and gestured towards the cabin door. 'Be my guests,' he said expansively, 'but I've already told you, you won't find nothin' wrong.'

It was just a single step from the afterdeck into the cabin. A cast-iron stove filled most of the area closest to the door. Beyond that were cupboards and a let-down table. At the far end of the cabin there was a bed. Looking around, Blackstone found himself wondering how whole families ever managed to live in such a tiny space.

There was the sound of a gentle thud.

'What was that?' Blackstone asked.

'It's nothing,' Drayman said dismissively. 'When there's a breeze, as there is now, the water in the canal ripples, and when it ripples, it bangs against the sides of the boat. You'd know that, if you lived around here.'

And your point is that I don't live around here, isn't it? Blackstone thought. Your point is that I'm a know-it-all from the capital, who's come up here and got everything wrong.

A second thud followed, louder this time.

'If it's water, why does it seem to be coming only from the afterdeck?' Blackstone wondered.

Drayman glanced through the open door. 'Don't know,' he said. 'Maybe there's an in-visible man out there, performing a clog dance.'

There were three more thuds in rapid succession.

'It's coming from *below* the deck!' Blackstone said.

He stepped out of the cabin, on to the deck itself.

'Did you hear that?' he asked George Peck, who was still standing on the towpath.

'Hear what?' Peck asked.

He was trying to sound casual, Blackstone thought, but for the first time since they'd stopped the boat he was beginning to *look* concerned.

Blackstone stamped his foot on the deck, and heard a hollow sound. 'What's under here?'

'A locker. For ropes an' stuff.'

'I think you're lying,' Blackstone said.

He was almost *sure* the man was lying. More than that, he had begun to understand why Ellie's telegram had affected him as it had – and now he thought he knew exactly what lay beneath the deck cover.

Drayman had ridiculed his jewel-smuggling theory, and Drayman had been right. But only partly! There *was* smuggling going on – but it had nothing to do with rubies and diamonds.

'I want you to open this locker for me,' he told Peck.

Peck turned away – as if he was doing no more than expressing his contempt for Blackstone – then suddenly made his break for freedom up the dog-legged path.

'Stop him!' Blackstone shouted to the con-

281

stables on the forward end of the boat.

Peck was moving fast, but without due care. Halfway up the dog-legged path he missed his footing and fell sprawling forward. He rolled over, and was back on his feet in seconds, but seconds was all it had taken the uniformed constables to reach him.

Peck threw a violent punch at the nearest constable. It connected with his jaw, and he went down, leaving the second constable ample space to swing his truncheon and catch the narrowboat man a cracking blow on the side of the head.

For an instant, it looked as if Peck might be able to withstand the assault, then his legs buckled beneath him and he fell to the ground.

Blackstone turned to Drayman. 'Doesn't look much like an innocent man to me,' he said.

They unscrewed the deck cover, lifted it clear and got their first sight of the girl. She was wearing a dress that looked as if it had been made of rough sacking. Her hands and feet were tightly bound and she wore a gag across her mouth. Her torso had been strapped to the floor, but her head was free enough to allow for a little movement, and it must have been that with which she had beaten out her desperate message.

Blackstone unstrapped the girl, and lifted her gently out of the locker.

'We're policemen,' he cooed reassuringly. 'We've come to rescue you. You're quite safe now.'

He carried her into the cabin, laid her on the bed, then knelt beside her. 'Safe, very safe,' he said softly, as he began to untie her. 'As safe as houses. As safe as if you were in your own bed. Do you understand? Nod your head a little, if you do.'

The girl nodded.

Blackstone freed her from the last of her bonds. 'I want you to move your hands and feet, just to get your circulation working properly,' he said. 'But nothing too violent. Just very, very gentle movements.'

The girl wriggled her ankles and wrists obediently, and Blackstone began to remove her gag. 'Don't try to speak immediately,' he advised her. 'Wait until I tell you to. And when you do, if you find it hurts too much, stop immediately.

She was a pretty girl of eleven or twelve, he noted. Her skin was very pale, which was only to be expected after all the terror and exhaustion she'd had to endure in captivity. But even allowing for that, he could see that at least a part of that paleness was her natural colouring.

'I'm going to ask you your name now,' he said. 'Try to say it, but if you can't quite manage – if your throat feels too tight – then don't worry about it. There'll be plenty of time for talking later.'

The gist of Ellie's telegram ran through his head again: *Latest victim definitely not Lucy Stanford, despite fact found wearing Lucy's clothes. Any ideas?*

He hadn't had any ideas earlier, but he had a very clear one now. And he was not the least surprised when the girl gasped, 'I'm ... I'm Emma Walsingholme.'

Eight

The man who had been ordered to stand guard outside the Melbourne Mine that afternoon answered to the name of Arthur Fisher, though he had had countless other aliases in the past.

At first, while it was still pleasantly warm, Fisher had not minded being outside, but now, as the air seemed to grow hotter and hotter, he began to wish that he was inside with the rest of the lads.

He looked longingly across at the dormitory block, and wondered if he could risk abandoning his post for just a few short minutes. Yet even as the thought was forming in his mind, he was reminding himself that Mr Bickersdale had decreed a guard must be posted at all times – and Mr Bickersdale was not a man you crossed if you had any ambitions to go on living.

Fisher's head slumped forward, and he could feel his eyelids starting to droop. He was falling asleep on the job, his drowsy brain told him, and that would never do.

'Put your hands in the air!' said a harsh,

authoritative voice from somewhere to his left. 'And keep them there!'

Fisher's head snapped back and his eyes opened fully. He was suddenly wide awake again.

The first thing his reawakened self saw was the three uniformed police constables – and the two men who were not in uniform – moving rapidly towards the dormitory block.

The second thing he saw was yet another constable, who was standing a few yards away from him and pointing a rifle directly at his torso.

'I said, put your hands in the air!' the constable repeated.

Fisher glanced sideways at his double-barrelled shotgun, which was leaning against the wall.

'Don't even think about it!' the constable warned him.

He had a choice of either going for the gun or going for the constable, Fisher decided quickly. He settled on the gun.

'Bloody idiot!' the constable said, almost to himself, and as Fisher made a grab for his shotgun, he fired the rifle.

The bullet hit Fisher in the chest, and soon found its way to his heart. There was no need for a second shot.

The five men in the dormitory were in an excellent mood. The latest consignment of goods had been dispatched, and the next was not due to be collected for another few days. They had time on their hands and could do with it what they liked. And what they had *chosen* to do was sit around the table and get drunk

They were already halfway down their second bottle of cheap brandy when they heard the rifle shot.

'Wha' – Wha' was that?' one of them slurred, but before any of the others had time to answer, the door crashed open and the room was suddenly filled with armed policemen.

'I'd advise you not to resist!' Blackstone shouted – though he was rather hoping that they would.

The men at the table looked up at the three rifles and two pistols that were pointing in their direction, then one of him raised his hands in the air. And the rest were quick to follow.

They found Hubert Robertson, crouched down behind his desk, with his eyes closed and his fingers in his ears.

'Oh-my-God!' the clerk was mumbling, as two of the constables took hold of him and wrenched him to his feet.

'Where's your boss?' Blackstone demanded.

'Oh-my-God, oh-my-God, oh-my-God!' Robertson moaned.

The flat of Blackstone's hand caught him squarely in the face, making his head rock, and his thick-lensed glasses fall to the floor.

'Where's Bickersdale?' the inspector repeated.

'He's ... he's down the mine.'

'Alone?'

'Yes. Apart from ... apart from...'

286

'Apart from the girls?' Blackstone suggested.

'Apart from the girls,' Robertson agreed.

Drayman looked down the deep shaft in the winding shed. Somewhere below, in the darkness, was the cage. And somewhere beyond the cage – hundreds of feet underground – was Bickersdale.

'What do we do now?' he asked. 'Wait for the bastard to come back to the surface again?'

'No, that's too risky,' Blackstone said. 'He's got the girls down there, and God knows what he could do to them if he starts to suspect that something's gone wrong.'

'So we're going down?'

'So *I'm* going down.'

'And *I'm* coming with you.'

'If Bickersdale *is* already suspicious, he'll be waiting for the cage, and anybody in it will be a sitting target,' Blackstone pointed out.

'There's no disputing that,' Drayman agreed.

'So there's no point in putting both of us in the line of fire. Besides, I work better alone.'

'No doubt you do,' Drayman said. 'But this is my patch and my responsibility.'

'Even so...'

'Either we go down together...'

'I've told you, I'll be better...'

'...or I'll get my lads to arrest you, and *I'll* go down alone. Which of those two things is it to be?'

'We go down together,' Blackstone said, giving in to the inevitable.

The cage clanked and jerked down to the bottom of the mine. It hit the floor with a soft thud and then was still.

Blackstone and Drayman knew that if Bickersdale was expecting them, now was the time they would find out about it. But when three or four seconds had passed – and they were still alive – it seemed that he wasn't.

They stepped out of the cage.

Ahead of them lay the vast crystal rock cavern, supported by its massive salt pillars. It was in just such a place as this one that Tom Yardley had met his death at Lawrence Bickersdale's hands, Blackstone thought – and wondered if he would be any luckier himself.

'We'll split up,' he whispered to Drayman. 'You move along the wall to the left, I'll move along the right wall. If you happen to come across Bickersdale, shoot the bastard – and don't stop firing at him until you've emptied your gun.'

'Understood,' Drayman said.

The gallery wall was cold to the touch, and the oil lamps – which were fixed to the wall – cast eerie shadows as he passed them. It was like being back in that Afghan cave, Blackstone thought with a shudder.

He stopped for a moment and listened for the sound of Drayman's footfalls, but the gallery was as silent as a tomb.

Sticking as close to the rock face as he could, he wasn't even aware of the door until he felt his hand brush against it. It was made of solid oak, but there was a small grill inset to allow for ventilation. Beyond it, Blackstone saw – peering through the grill – was a small room that had been carved out of the rock. There was not much light in the cell, but he thought he could see a figure lying on a bed – and guessed that it was a girl.

He moved out into the open, knowing it was a risk to expose himself like that, but knowing also that only a fool fights a battle without first getting a clear picture of the terrain.

From his new position, he could see six more doors, behind which probably lay six more cells – but there was still no sign of Bickersdale.

He did not see the oil canister lying on the ground until it was too late – until he had caught it with his foot and sent it toppling over. It clanged loudly as its side hit the floor, the sound of the clang echoing around the vast cavern – and with that echo disappeared all chance of catching Bickersdale by surprise.

Blackstone took cover behind the nearest of the huge salt pillars. Now all he could do was wait.

He did not have to wait long. The door of one of the middle cells creaked cautiously open. Blackstone stuck his head around the pillar for the briefest of moments – but in that moment he saw two people step out into the gallery.

The first of them was a girl. She could not have been more than fourteen or fifteen, and she looked terrified.

The second was Bickersdale. He had crouched

down slightly, so that he could use the girl as a shield – and he had a gun pointed at her head.

'Is that you, Inspector Blackstone?' Bickersdale called out, and his words bounced around and around the vast gallery: ' ... 'spector Blackstone ... 'spector Blackstone ... 'spector Blackstone.'

'Yes, it's me,' Blackstone confirmed, from behind the cover of his pillar and, like Bickersdale's words, his own quickly reverberated back at him: ' ... me ... me ... me.'

'I can't see you,' Bickersdale told him.

'I know you can't,' Blackstone agreed. And because of the echo, you can't even use my voice to get a fix on my position, he thought.

'Step out into the open, where I can take a look at you,' Bickersdale commanded.

'Not until you've let the girl go,' Blackstone told him.

'Do you think I'm that much of a fool?' Bickersdale asked. He fell silent for a few seconds; then he said, 'Where are my manners? You haven't been properly introduced, have you? Why don't you tell Inspector Blackstone who you are, my dear?'

'I'm Lucy,' the girl croaked.

'Lucy who?' Bickersdale said snappishly. 'Tell the inspector what your surname is.'

'Stanford. I'm Lucy Stanford.'

'Lucy has been something of a disappointment to me,' Bickersdale said. 'She was not at all what she was supposed to be, were you, Lucy?'

'You mean she wasn't a virgin?' Blackstone asked.

'That's precisely what I mean. She's been damaged goods right from the start, and so of extremely limited value. And if you force me to, I'll kill her without a second's hesitation.'

'Why not just give yourself up now?' Blackstone suggested.

'Whatever for?'

'Because you're finished. There's only one way out of this mine, and that's under the control of four armed police officers.'

'You're quite wrong about that,' Bickersdale said. 'There's a second way out,' – he laughed bitterly – 'as I've recently discovered to my cost.'

'Even if you get clear of the mine, you'll never get clear of the area,' Blackstone argued.

'The odds are against it,' Bickersdale agreed, 'but I've beaten the odds before. And just to increase my chances, I'd like to make certain you no longer pose a threat – which is why I really *would* appreciate it if you stepped out from whatever pillar you're hiding behind.'

'If I do that, you'll kill me,' Blackstone said.

'Not necessarily. I may just decide to incapacitate you by shooting you in the leg,' Bickersdale countered.

'You'll kill me,' Blackstone repeated.

'Yes, that's probably true,' Bickersdale agreed easily. 'But if you *don't* come out, I certainly *will* kill the girl. So why don't you throw down your gun and let me see you?'

'You're bluffing,' Blackstone told him.

'About killing the girl?'

'Yes.'

'What makes you think that?'

'You know that once you've killed her, there'll be nothing stopping me from killing you.'

'Perhaps. But if the choice is between being shot now or hanged later, I'd rather be shot now.' For a few more seconds Bickersdale was silent again; then he said, 'I'm getting bored with playing this game, Inspector Blackstone, so this is how it will end. I'll count to three, and if I don't see you by the time I finish counting, I'll shoot the girl.'

'Listen...' Blackstone said desperately.

'One...' Bickersdale began, '...two...'

Blackstone tossed his gun away, and once it had hit the floor he stepped well clear of the pillar.

The moment he'd done it, Bickersdale flung the girl to the ground and aimed his pistol directly at the inspector.

'That soft heart of yours will be the death of you,' Bickersdale said, and laughed. He was still laughing when the bullet from Inspector Drayman's gun struck his forehead as a prelude to ploughing into his brain.

There were four girls imprisoned in the mine. Two of them had previously been inmates of the workhouse – and so were missed by nobody. Two came from much more comfortable homes – and were believed to be dead.

All the girls were in a state of shock, but by the time they were back on the surface, wrapped in blankets and sipping hot sweet tea, they were at least *starting* to believe that their ordeal was over.

'You saved my life,' Blackstone said, as he and Drayman watched the girls being taken away in an ambulance wagon.

'It was foolish of me to aim for the head,' Drayman said. 'I might so easily have missed. I should have gone for his mid-section.'

'Well, you'll know better next time,' Blackstone said.

Inspector Drayman shuddered. 'I'm rather hoping that there won't *be* a next time.'

'And with any luck, there won't be.'

'You've killed a man, haven't you?' Drayman asked.

'Yes,' Blackstone agreed. More men than he cared to remember, he thought. Pathan warriors ... Ghazi warriors ... Russian Cossacks ... armed robbers ... would-be assassins...

'I don't mind admitting, the whole experience has shaken me up quite a bit,' Drayman said. 'It's not just the nausea – though that's bad enough – it's that I feel as if I'll never be quite the same man again. It's as though, by taking another man's life, I've lost something of my own. Did it feel like that to you, the first time you killed someone?'

'Yes,' Blackstone said.

'So it's normal?'

'I don't know whether it's normal or not, but I

think it's how all decent, ordinary men *should* feel.'

'That feeling must go away in time, mustn't it?' Drayman asked hopefully.

'Not so as you'd notice,' Blackstone said.

Nine

Hubert Robertson was sitting in the chair that had once been for the exclusive use of his late – and very unlamented – employer. He was handcuffed to the arm of it, but even if he hadn't been, he looked too terrified to move. In fact, Blackstone thought, glaring down on the clerk, he looked terrified enough to soil himself.

'I'm ... I'm innocent of any of this,' Robertson jabbered. 'I'm just a clerk. I kept the books and wrote the letters. I ... I had nothing at all to do with what was going on down in the mine.'

'Just a clerk,' Blackstone repeated, contemptuously. 'A clerk who saw everything that was happening – because he couldn't have missed it, even if he'd tried – and yet still did nothing about it.'

'I didn't *dare* do anything about it,' Robertson moaned. 'Mr Bickersdale was a very frightening man. I'm still afraid of him, even though you say he's dead. You've no idea what horrors he was capable of.'

'Can you imagine being so frightened of anybody that you'd completely abandon any idea of normal human decency?' Blackstone asked Drayman sceptically.

'Indeed I can't,' Drayman answered.

'It's easy for you to say that!' Robertson whined. 'Because you don't *know*! You just don't *know*!'

'What don't we know?' Blackstone asked.

Robertson gulped in air. 'Bickersdale used to tell me about the days when he was a soldier of fortune in the Congo Free State,' he said shakily. 'He ran his own private little army. He was the only white man in it. He ... He told me that he didn't want his nigger soldiers wasting ammunition, so he counted the number of bullets he issued them with before he sent them off on a raid. And when they came back ... Oh God!...

'When they came back *what*?'

'They'd ... They'd have to prove to him that they'd used the ammunition properly, by bringing him a human hand for every bullet they'd fired. And if they didn't, then he'd have *their* hands cut off instead.'

'That's just a *story*,' Blackstone said dismissively. 'Something he told you just to frighten you.'

'It was *true*,' Robertson protested. 'It *had* to be true. And even if it wasn't, I saw what happened to Clem Davis.'

'Who's he?'

'He was one of Mr Bickersdale's narrowboat men. Mr Bickersdale accused him of stealing

295

the petty cash from the office and got the other men to tie him up. Then he went to work on him. With a knife! He didn't make any of the cuts deep enough so that Davis would bleed to death right away, and when he'd finished slashing away at him, he just left him where he was.'

'For how long?'

'For how long do you think? Until he died! The other men wanted to help Davis, but Mr Bickersdale had ordered them not to, and they were too scared to disobey him. It ... It took the poor swine two days to die, and for most of that time he was begging us to do something for him – even if it was only to put him out of his misery.' Robertson gulped in more air. 'And the truly awful thing is that Davis hadn't even done it.'

'Hadn't done what?'

'Stolen the money.'

'Then who had?'

'Nobody had! All the time he was being tortured, Davis was screaming that he was innocent. The other men thought he must be lying, but later – when he was dead – Mr Bickersdale told me that what he'd been saying was quite true. No money ever *had* gone missing.'

'So Bickersdale had made a mistake?'

'No! It was a demonstration! Mr Bickersdale wanted to show the men what would happen if anyone ever *did* steal from him. *Now* do you see why I didn't dare say anything? The man was a complete monster. You *do* believe me, don't you!'

Blackstone nodded. 'Yes, I think I probably do.' He lit up two cigarettes, and handed one of them to Robertson. 'Why don't you tell me how it all began?' he suggested.

It began, the terrified clerk told Blackstone and Drayman, when Bickersdale had been forced to accept that he'd been duped into buying the Melbourne Mine, and that all it would do would be to cost him money.

For days Bickersdale had been in a black fury, and then a change had come over him. He'd sat down – very calmly – and started to think of ways in which he could not only regain the small fortune he'd lost, but make it grow into an even bigger one. And that was when the idea had come to him.

'He'd travelled all over the world, and met a great many men with more money than they knew what to do with,' Robertson said. 'And he'd seen for himself just how much some of those men were willing to pay for a virgin.'

'But not all virgins are worth exactly the same amount, are they?' Blackstone asked.

'No. Like any other commodity, the better the quality, the greater the cost,' Robertson agreed. Then he saw the look of anger growing in Blackstone's eyes, and quickly added, 'I'm talking in commercial terms, of course – the way Mr Bickersdale would have talked. I'd never have thought that way myself.'

'I'm sure you wouldn't,' Blackstone growled.

'You have to understand that while Turkish virgins are not quite ten a penny, there are still

297

plenty of them around, and each one is only worth a few pounds to a rich Ottoman merchant. But any girl with a paler skin can command much more. And a girl who's actually been brought up to be a lady is worth a great deal.'

'How much?' Blackstone asked.

'I don't know.'

'How much!'

'I ... I believe that Mr Bickersdale charged nearly a thousand guineas for one particular girl.'

Even though the very thought of it made Blackstone want to heave, there was a colder, more analytical part of his brain that could understand how the buyer's mind might work. Men like them would enjoy the sense of power they obtained from deflowering virgins – and the more the girls hated it, the greater would be the men's satisfaction. And that, of course, was why girls from a genteel background were so highly valued.

A poor girl would undoubtedly find the whole experience horrendous, but she would have grown up knowing that life is *never* fair and can often be extremely unpleasant. But a young lady, who had been brought up to believe that she was one of the chosen ones – that she would always be protected from the uglier side of life – would find it almost unbearable.

'At first, Mr Bickersdale took young girls from the orphanage and trained them to pretend they were young ladies,' Robertson continued. 'But that turned out to be very unsatisfactory.'

Yes, it would have, Blackstone thought. In just a few short weeks, it would be impossible to cram eleven or twelve years of breeding and assumptions into anyone, and the girls trained in this way would never have been able to sustain the illusion.

So Bickersdale had soon come to realize that, in order to be successful, he would have to be able to offer the real thing.

'Why did he go to all the trouble of faking the deaths of the young ladies he kidnapped?' Blackstone asked, though he'd already worked out the only possible answer for himself.

'Mr Bickersdale thought that if a girl of good breeding went missing, the police would never give up searching for her until they'd finally found her,' Robertson said.

And he'd been right about that. The fathers of the missing girls would use their influence on men with even *more* influence – and, working under such pressure, the police would make a much greater effort than they'd ever have done if it had been a girl of a lower class who'd been abducted.

A reward – large enough to turn half the population of the country into police agents – would be posted. The girl's picture would appear everywhere. Extra officers would be drafted in to search all ports and railway stations. And that would only be the beginning.

'But if the police believed she'd been murdered, they wouldn't be looking for *her* at all,' Blackstone said. 'They'd only be looking for her killer – and, unlike the girls, they'd have no idea what *he* looked like.'

'Yes, that's right,' Robertson agreed.

'So Bickersdale took these poor bloody girls out of the workhouse, and passed them off as the girls he'd kidnapped.'

'Yes.'

In order for the trick to work , he'd had their faces hacked at beyond recognition, and their hands – made rough by scrubbing and cleaning – cut off. He had had their feet amputated, too, because, even at that young age, those feet would already have been deformed through wearing boots that didn't quite fit. The girls' clothes had played an important part in this illusion. What grieving parents, seeing a horribly mutilated body wearing their daughter's dress, *wouldn't* assume it was their child?

Bickersdale, always the planner, had not stopped even there. Though he had seen to it that their skin was softened by the application of lotions for several weeks before they were murdered, there was always a chance that a doctor or an undertaker might take a closer look at that skin than the distraught mother and father had, and notice it was still a little rough. But such an examination was less likely when his men had finished slashing at the bodies, for not only were there no large areas of skin *left* to examine, but the horrendous effects of their work would turn all but the strongest stomach. And that particular plan had worked perfectly. Not one of the surgeons or morticians who had seen the first nine

bodies had made any comment on the skin –
though Blackstone was prepared to wager that
when he spoke to Ellie, she would have something to say about the skin of the tenth victim.

'The young ladies were all brought here by
narrowboat, were they?' he asked.

'Yes.'

That, in itself, had been a brilliant idea, Blackstone was forced to admit. Because there was a
natural association, in most people's minds –
and most *people* included most *policemen* –
between crime and speed. Who would ever have
suspected that the criminals would make their
getaway using a mode of transport that was no
faster than the horse – pulling a large weight
behind it – could walk?

But there was one even greater advantage
Bickersdale had gained from using the narrowboat to do his dirty work – and that had been
anonymity.

The police investigating the murders had been
able to find no witnesses who reported seeing
strangers in the area, but the narrowboats, while
not being local, were not completely alien,
either. They were just part of the scenery –
something to be taken for granted and not even
commented on. And though Blackstone didn't
have the details of all the kidnappings in his
head, he was prepared to bet that none of them
had taken place too far away from a canal.

He picked up a piece of paper that had been
lying in front of him, and slid it across the desk
to the clerk.

'This is a list of the members of the gang we already have in custody,' he said. 'Are there any names missing?'

Robertson scanned the list. 'No.'

'You're sure about that?'

'Well, there is one name missing – but he's dead.'

'And what name is that?' Blackstone asked.

'Tom Yardley's name,' Robertson told him.

Ten

Henry Knox-Partington had the reputation of being one of smartest lawyers in London, and it was said that, whilst he would never actually step across the line into *provable* illegality, he would certainly do everything else he possibly could to get his clients off the hook.

At that moment Knox-Partington was sitting in the police interview room, with his client, Miss Latouche, beside him. He seemed calm, confident, and in no hurry to start the proceedings at all. And why should he have been in a hurry, when, every few minutes, the mental meter in his head clicked up another guinea in fees?

Opposite the madam and her attorney sat Sergeant Patterson and Inspector Maddox. Maddox had been in an excellent mood ever since he had received warmest congratulations from the Home Office on the arrest, and even the arrival of a dangerous shark like Knox-Partington seemed to have done nothing to dampen his good humour.

'My client, Miss Latouche, wishes to begin by making a statement,' the attorney said. 'Once she has completed it, she will be more than willing to answer any questions you might care to put to her. Do you have any objections to that procedure, Inspector?'

'None at all,' Maddox said affably. 'Let her say whatever she likes. It doesn't really matter, because – when push comes to shove – we've got her bang to rights.'

The solicitor raised a quizzical eyebrow. 'Bang to rights?' he repeated. 'We'll see about that.'

'We certainly shall!'

Knox-Partington turned to face his client. 'Please start when you're ready, Miss Latouche.'

The madam picked up the type-written sheet of legal paper that lay in front of her. 'A few days ago I was approached in my home by a Detective Sergeant Archibald Patterson of the Metropolitan Police,' she read.

'But you didn't know he was a police sergeant at the time – or you'd never have let him through the door,' Maddox said sneeringly.

'That is totally untrue,' the madam said. 'Sergeant Patterson identified himself to me immediately.'

'I most certainly did not!' Patterson protested.

'If you are not prepared to let Miss Latouche

303

finish her statement without further interruption, then this interview will be over,' Knox-Partington said.

Maddox chuckled. 'Fine! Let her get on with it.'

'Sergeant Patterson informed me that there was some concern being voiced in the upper ranks of the Metropolitan Police about very young girls being sold into prostitution,' the madam continued.

'I never—' Patterson began.

'I'm warning you, I'm perfectly willing to instruct my client to say no more,' Knox-Partington said.

'He further informed me that the Metropolitan Police were intent on stopping this disgusting trade, and asked if I would be willing to give them my co-operation,' the madam said. 'Being of like mind with them on this matter, I readily agreed. Sergeant Patterson then asked me if I would attempt to buy an under-age virgin, whilst making it clear to the person from whom I was purchasing the poor unfortunate girl what a terrible fate awaited her. He said that once I had made the purchase, the evil man who had sold her to me would be immediately arrested, and so the world would be made at least a little safer for innocent young women.'

'This is pure fiction,' Patterson said.

'Oh, for heaven's sake, let her have her say,' Maddox told him. 'When all's said and done, it's no more than her swansong.'

'I told the sergeant that, as a law-abiding

woman of good character, I had absolutely no idea where one might buy a virgin,' the madam said, 'but he replied that presented no real problem, because he was more than willing to point me in the right direction. I purchased the girl as he had instructed me to, and asked him to collect her from my home at once.'

'Why did you do that, Miss Latouche?' Knox-Partington asked. 'What was your hurry?'

The madam sniffed. 'I found it terribly distressing – more distressing than you can possibly imagine – to have the poor girl under my roof. I wished her to be removed to some refuge which the police could provide, so that I could put the whole unpleasant and disturbing business behind me.'

'I see. Kindly proceed.'

'Sergeant Patterson duly arrived, but instead of removing the girl, as I'd fully expected him to, he said he wished to talk to her privately. Though uneasy about that, I agreed.'

'Why?'

'Because I was brought up to respect the wishes and requests of the forces of law and order.'

'Of course you were.'

'I can hardly find the words to express the shock and horror that I felt when several policemen arrived at my door and informed me that I was under arrest.'

'Have you quite finished?' Maddox asked.

'I've quite finished,' the madam confirmed.

'Then I simply have to say that, though I've

heard some amazing cock-and-bull stories in my time with the Metropolitan Police, that one tops the lot. You found it all terribly distressing, you say. You were shocked and horrified! You're not a nun, madam! You run a brothel, for God's sake!'

'I provide board and accommodation for a number of young ladies,' the madam said primly.

'And all of these young ladies of yours are as pure as the driven snow, I suppose!'

'I must admit, that some of them have been known to entertain their gentlemen callers in their rooms. I have asked them to cease the practice, but you know how wilful the young can be.'

'When this case comes to court, we'll produce at least half a dozen witnesses who'll swear under oath that they handed over money to Miss Latouche in order to pay for sex with those girls,' Maddox told the solicitor.

Knox-Partington smiled. 'I doubt very much whether you'll be able to produce a *single* witness who'd be prepared to admit that he went to Miss Latouche's house for immoral purposes,' he said. 'The gentlemen callers at Waterloo Street have their *own* reputations to consider.'

'Are you sure – are you absolutely convinced – that there won't be at least one brave soul who is prepared to put his sense of duty above his own personal considerations?' Maddox asked.

'Yes,' Knox-Partington said firmly. 'But even if I'm wrong on that, what of it?'

'What of it!'

'Miss Latouche would then probably be convicted of keeping a disorderly house...'

'Exactly!'

'...and would no doubt be fined, as a result. But she has not been charged with that particular offence at the moment. What she *has* been charged with is procuring the services of an under-age girl for immoral purposes. And that is a charge we strenuously deny.'

'Sergeant Patterson will give evidence,' Maddox said.

'And Miss Latouche will take the stand – dressed modestly and without a hint of paint on her face – and will strenuously deny what he has said. So it will simply be a case of her word against his. If you had *two* police witnesses, of course, it would be an entirely different matter. But you haven't.'

'How would it ever be possible for us to have two witnesses to such a thing?' Maddox asked reasonably. 'Miss Latouche would never have agreed to talk so openly with two men as she was with one.'

'Whatever procedures you choose to adopt when conducting your investigations – and whatever restraints are inherent in those procedures – is a matter for you alone,' Knox-Partington said airily. 'My only concern is – and must be – whether or not you have sufficient evidence against my client. And in this case, you clearly do not.'

'When my sergeant first saw the girl, she was

307

wearing no more than a chemise,' Maddox said. 'That surely is clear proof of the purpose for which Miss Latouche intended to use her?'

'The girl was wearing a chemise when – on police instructions – Miss Latouche purchased her,' the attorney said smoothly. 'Miss Latouche tried to persuade the girl to put on something more becoming instead, but she refused.'

'She won't say that in court.'

'That's possibly true. But, unfortunately, she is far too young to be a credible witness.'

Maddox smiled, and Patterson realized that his new boss had been really enjoying this verbal fencing with the lawyer. In fact, he had be positively *revelling* in it – playing with Knox-Partington in much the same way as a powerful cat might play with a helpless mouse.

'What about the money?' Maddox asked gleefully. 'You hadn't thought about that, had you?'

For the first time, Henry Knox-Partington began to look vaguely uncomfortable. 'The money?' he repeated.

'When we raided your client's house, we found over two hundred pounds in cash...'

'And since when has that been a crime?'

'...some of which had been handed to her by Sergeant Patterson, only minutes before the raid. Now if Miss Latouche's story is true, why would Sergeant Patterson have given her money?'

'There is a perfectly simple and straight-forward explanation for that,' Knox-Partington said, though it was clear from the expression on his face that if such an explanation *did* exist, he was still desperately searching for it. 'Of course!' he continued. 'The money was to cover the expense of purchasing the girl, which purchase, I must remind you once again, Miss Latouche only became involved in at the specific request of the police.'

'If that argument is to hold up, then the amount of money that Sergeant Patterson gave Miss Latouche should no more than equal the amount that it cost her to procure the girl, shouldn't it?' the police cat asked, dealing the legal mouse another powerful blow with its front paw.

Knox-Partington took out a silk handkerchief and mopped his brow.

'Well?' Maddox asked.

'It should ... er ... be more or less the same,' the attorney admitted. 'Though, of course, we must also take into account the other expenses Miss Latouche will have incurred during the course of the operation.'

'Such as?'

'Such as cab fares.'

'Sergeant Patterson paid your client twenty-five pounds on his first visit, and seventy-five on his second,' Maddox said relentlessly. 'When we arrest the man who sold the girl to Miss Latouche, will he confirm that the fee she paid him was a hundred pounds, less the cost of the cab fares?'

'I fail to see why you're pursuing this particular argument at all,' Knox-Partington said, getting his second wind. 'We once more find ourselves in a "he said, she said" situation. Sergeant Patterson says he gave my client a hundred pounds, whilst Miss Latouche maintains that she only took *ten* pounds, because I now recall that she paid her cab fares herself.' He turned to his client. 'Isn't that right, Miss Latouche?'

'That's right,' the madam agreed. 'I paid for the cabs out of my own pocket. It just didn't seem right to charge the police for them, when they were working so hard to stamp out this venal trade in young girls.'

'A nice try,' Maddox said, almost admiringly. 'But, of course, that argument would collapse completely if we could *prove* that one hundred pounds of the money we found in Miss Latouche's house during the raid was, in fact, provided by the Metropolitan Police.'

Knox-Partington gulped. 'But you *can't* prove it,' he said, somewhat weakly.

'As a matter of fact, we can,' said Maddox, who seemed to have grown tired of playing with the attorney and was about to deliver the *coup de grâce*. 'The serial numbers of the banknotes that were paid over to Miss Latouche are to be found in a sealed envelope, which is currently residing in the safe in the Assistant Commissioner's Office.' He turned to Patterson. 'Isn't that right, Sergeant?'

Patterson made no reply.

'I said, isn't that right, Sergeant?' Maddox repeated.

'Not exactly, sir,' Patterson said.

'What do you mean? Not exactly?'

'Writing down the serial numbers is the one detail that I appear to have overlooked,' Patterson confessed.

Eleven

Blackstone paced up and down the yard in front of the Melbourne Mine office, his mind in a turmoil.

There's one name missing – but he's dead, Hubert Robertson had said, when shown a list of the gang members taken into custody.

And what name's that? Blackstone had asked, never dreaming that the answer would have the devastating effect on him that it actually had.

Tom Yardley's name, Robertson had replied.

Tom Yardley's name!

Tom had been his comrade. Tom had saved his life in Afghanistan. It was almost inconceivable that the man who had first alerted to him to what was going on in this village could actually have been a part of it himself.

Furious at allowing himself to have been knocked off balance for even a second, Blackstone marched back into the office.

Robertson was shrunk down in his chair, as if already anticipating the returning man's anger.

Blackstone glared down at him for perhaps half a minute, then said, 'I don't know what you hope to gain by trying to blacken the name of a dead hero, but it won't do you any good at all.'

'But I'm only telling the truth,' Robertson whined. 'Yardley *was* part of the gang.'

Blackstone had made a promise to himself he would remain calm once he was back in the office, but now he grabbed Robertson by his lapels, and pulled him clear of his seat.

'I could kill you easily,' he growled. 'I could snap your neck, and you'd be dead.'

He felt a hand gripping his shoulder tightly, and heard Inspector Drayman say, 'That's enough, Sam!'

Yes, Blackstone thought, it was enough. It was *more* than enough. He was a police officer, and there was no excuse for him behaving as he was.

He released his grip on Robertson, and the clerk flopped back awkwardly into his chair.

'Convince me that what you're saying is true,' he said, much calmer now. 'Give me one good reason why Bickersdale would have wanted Tom as a member of his gang.'

'Once he'd come up with the idea of using the Melbourne Mine as a base for his new operation, he moved all the men who'd been working here to his other mine,' Robertson said, with a tremble in his voice.

Blackstone nodded. 'Yes, he would have had to do that, wouldn't he? He couldn't possibly put his vile plans into effect while there were still ordinary, decent working men around.'

'But that left him with a problem,' Robertson said. 'Once his miners had gone, he had no idea what was being said about him in the village.'

'And why should he even have cared what was being said?'

'Why do you think? Because if the villagers were getting suspicious, he wanted to know about it. He didn't want to wake up one morning and find himself surrounded by policemen. If anything was going to go wrong, he needed time to cut and run.'

'So why didn't he send one of his gang down to the pub to hear what was being said?'

'Because that wouldn't have worked. People in Marston would never speak openly – in front of outsiders – about what they were thinking. They needed to be in the company of somebody they knew – somebody they trusted. *Somebody born in the village.* And that person was Yardley.'

'Then you're claiming that Tom Yardley was no more than Bickersdale's nark?' Blackstone asked. 'In that case, he wasn't really one of the gang at all, and probably had no more idea of what was going on up here than anybody else in the village?'

'He knew,' Robertson said.

'How can you be so sure?'

'You've seen the cells that Mr Bickersdale kept the girls locked up in, haven't you?'

'Yes?'

'They're carved out of solid crystal rock. That's a skilled job. The cut-throats Mr Bickersdale brought in from the outside were only *pretending* to be miners. They would have had no idea of where to even begin.'

'Tom did that?'

'Yes, he did.'

The cells are, in many ways, things of beauty. When the light from the oil lamp catches them right, they glisten, and the shadows melt into the crystal to create strange and wonderful patterns.

Bickersdale never notices this. All that matters to him is that they are carved out of solid crystal rock, and that the only way in or out of them is through doors so sturdy that even the strongest man could not break them down.

But there is one cave with a door that is even sturdier – and this cave, the men have been told, they must never go near.

They know what it contains. It is here that Bickersdale stores the money he has made from the white-slave trade, and rumour has it that it amounts to more than six thousand pounds.

It torments the men that they cannot break down the door and take the money. But hard and ruthless as they are themselves, they are still afraid of Bickersdale. They remember what he did to Davis – how much the man screamed, and how long it took him to finally die.

Besides, it would be impossible to escape with the money once they had it. The only way in and out of the mine is in the cage, and every time that cage goes up or down, Bickersdale is

*standing there – a pistol in his hand – watching
it.*

*So while they might dream of the money –
might lick their lips at even the thought of it – it
is as safe at the bottom of the mine as if it were
in the vault at the Bank of England.*

Or so they think.

And so Bickersdale himself thinks.

But there is one man who has other ideas.

'Are you actually saying Tom Yardley stole
Bickersdale's money?' Blackstone demanded.

'Yes, he did.'

'But how is that possible?' Blackstone asked.
'How *could* he have done it, when there was
only one way in and out?'

But even as he was speaking he was remem-
bering what he and Bickersdale had said to one
another at the bottom of the mine.

*There's only one way out, and that's under the
control of four armed police officers*, he'd told
Bickersdale.

You're quite wrong about that, the other man
had replied. *There's a second way out – as I've
recently discovered to my cost.*

'There wasn't only one way.' Robertson said.
'Not for an experienced miner like Tom Yardley.'

*It is a little after eight o'clock in the morning
when Bickersdale goes down into the mine. The
pockets of his frock coat are weighed down with
the gold coins they contain. He walks along the*

315

passageway to his strongroom, takes out his key, and inserts it into the lock.

He knows that his men believe he has six thousand pounds stashed away here, but they are wrong. The figure is closer to ten, and today he will be adding another thousand.

He opens the door and senses immediately that something is wrong. The air in the room is colder than it normally is, and he can feel a draught where there should not be one.

He advances into the cave, holding his oil lamp in front of him. The first thing he sees is that his iron chest is open and the money gone. The second thing is that there is a hole in the base of the back wall.

He gets down on his hands and knees and crawls along the low tunnel. When he has gone no more than a hundred yards, the tunnel opens up into a higher, wider passageway. He understands immediately that this passageway belongs not to his own mine but to the abandoned one that lies beyond it.

He is not sure whether to go to the left or the right, but finally chooses the right. He follows the passageway for another hundred yards, until a second one intersects it. He is forced to accept that he is in a maze – in a honeycomb of tunnels that connects both to mines that have long ceased to function and mines that are still being worked. He knows that if he carries on much longer he will lose his sense of direction and might be wandering about for days.

He retraces his steps carefully and, as he does

so, he is thinking. The men who work for him are thugs and murderers. Though they might pretend to be miners, they would be as lost down here as he is himself. But there is one man who wouldn't be – one man brought up in the village who could find his way around below ground as easily as he could above.

And that man is Tom Yardley.

'So then he had Tom killed, did he?' Blackstone asked.

'No,' Robertson said.

'You're lying to me again!'

'I swear I'm not.'

'If Tom had really done what you say he did, Bickersdale would never have let him get away with it.'

'You're right,' Robertson agreed. 'But he wouldn't have had him killed like that, either.'

'Why not?'

'Because he didn't know what Yardley had done with the money! Bickersdale's plan was to have his men grab Yardley when he was leaving the mine and bring him up here. If Yardley had told Bickersdale where the money was right away, he'd would have been killed right away. If he hadn't, he'd have been tortured until he did tell, and then he'd have been killed. But Yardley never did leave the mine. Before he ever came back to the surface, he blew himself up.'

Blackstone shook his head, slowly and mournfully, from side to side. 'I don't think so,' he said. 'I don't think that's what happened at all.'

317

Twelve

There were two of them – Blackstone and the drift manager – in the cage that was descending to the bottom of the Victoria Mine.

'I don't know what you expect to find down here,' the drift manager told Blackstone. 'After the explosion we searched the gallery thoroughly, just to make sure we hadn't missed anything. So I can assure you that all Tom Yardley's body parts – however small and however bloody – were buried with him.'

'It must have been a messy job,' Blackstone said.

The drift manager shuddered. 'I like to think I'm not a squeamish man myself, but I couldn't eat for a day after. All that raw meat! All that splintered bone! It was terrible.'

The cage bumped against the floor and they stepped out of it.

This was the second time in just a few hours he'd been in a cavern like this one, Blackstone thought, looking around at the flickering oil lights and huge salt pillars. He could only hope that this time there was no blood-letting.

The drift manager led him along the gallery to the rock face. 'There's not much to see,' he said.

'After we ... After we cleared away Tom's remains, we cleared the salt as well. We couldn't waste it. The work of the mine has to go on, you know, in spite of personal tragedy.'

'I can quite understand that,' Blackstone agreed, lifting his oil lamp and studying the rock face.

There was no longer any evidence at all of the huge explosion, he thought, but then there wouldn't have been. The excavation of the drift had probably advanced several inches – or several feet, for all he knew – since then.

He followed the wall along, and when he had almost reached the corner he saw the tunnel. 'Where does that lead?' he asked the drift manager.

The other man shrugged. 'I don't know. It's been there for as long as I've been working here. There are dozens and dozens of tunnels under this village, you know. Some of them lead to other mines, which was why they were excavated in the first place. But others just peter out, so you've no idea what their original purpose was. To tell you the truth, it doesn't really interest me. When I go back up in that cage, I like to leave all thoughts of this bloody mine behind me.'

'I imagine you do,' Blackstone said.

He walked over to the tunnel, and held his oil lamp up. The lamp illuminated the first few yards, but further away the walls became fainter and fainter, until there was only darkness.

'I'd like to explore this tunnel,' he said.

The drift manager showed no enthusiasm at all for the idea.

'I didn't mind bringing you down here,' he said, 'but like I told you, the sooner I'm out of this mine, the happier I am.'

'I don't want you to come with me,' Blackstone said. 'You can go home if you like, as long as there's some way for me to get out of here once I've finished what I have to do.'

'Oh, there's no problem about that,' the drift manager replied. 'There's a rope next the shaft. Pull on it, and it rings a bell top-side. Then they'll know that you want to be brought up.' He paused. 'But it's not a good idea to go exploring on your own. That tunnel could come to a dead end in a hundred yards, or it might run for miles and connect with half a dozen other tunnels. You could get hopelessly lost.'

Blackstone pulled something out of his pocket. 'Not if I fix one end of this to my starting point and trail it behind me as I go,' he said.

The drift manager looked at what he was holding in his hand. 'A ball of string!' he said in amazement. 'Whatever made you think to bring a ball of string with you? Did somebody tell you about this tunnel?'

'No,' Blackstone said. 'But I was almost certain that it would have to be here.'

The tunnel forked less than fifty yards from its opening. Blackstone took the left fork, for no other reason than that it seemed a little wider than the right.

If he found nothing along it, he told himself, he would return to the junction and explore in the opposite direction. And if that didn't work, he would search for other branch tunnels off the main ones.

He was well aware it might take him a long time, but he was quite prepared for that, because he was convinced that in the end – by patiently eliminating all other possibilities – he would blunder across what he was looking for.

It simply *had to be* down there.

The moment he saw the bedding, he knew he had made a lucky choice first time out. It wasn't much – a couple of rough blankets and a pillow – but it was enough to tell him that someone had been camping out here.

There was other evidence, too – a spirit stove, a kettle, a saucepan, a cup, a drum of water and several cans of tinned food. And there was a newspaper, which was already several days old.

Blackstone picked the newspaper up, and was not surprised to find that one article in it had been ringed in red pencil.

'Another horrendous murder!' the headline read:

The body of a young girl, Emma Walsingholme, was discovered in a drainage ditch in Staffordshire yesterday. The murder appears to be the work of the Northern Slasher, and brings the number of his victims up to nine.

Scotland Yard has informed us that due to

the temporary indisposition of Superintendent Bullock, who has investigated the previous killings, the inquiry in this case will be led by Detective Inspector Samuel Blackstone.

Blackstone flung the newspaper to the floor in disgust. It not only represented the last piece of the puzzle, it also answered several questions that had been troubling him for some time – and *should have* been troubling him for even longer.

There was a sound of footsteps some distance away. Blackstone snuffed out his oil lamp, and waited. A light appeared out of nowhere, as whoever was carrying it turned a corner.

Blackstone did not move, and the light came closer and closer.

'Where've you been?' Blackstone called out.

'To the latrine, I suppose. That's your army training for you. They always taught us never to shit close to where we were camped, didn't they?'

The light stopped, and hovered in the air like an indecisive firefly; then a voice said, 'Sergeant Blackstone?'

'That's right,' Blackstone agreed. 'Why don't you come a bit closer; then we can talk like civilized men?'

For a moment the light did not move, then Tom Yardley began to walk towards him.

Blackstone bent down, relit his own oil lamp, and picked up the newspaper again.

'It must have been this article that gave you

322

the idea,' he said, waving the newspaper at Yardley.

'What idea was that, Sarge?'

'How *did* you manage to fake your own death, Tom?' Blackstone asked, ignoring the question. 'What other poor bugger had to die so that you could go on living?'

'I'd never kill anybody, Sarge. You know that. Not a white man, anyway.' Yardley chuckled. 'Remember how we fixed them nigger warriors in that cave back in Afghanistan? How I had to finish them off, because you'd gone and got yourself knocked out?'

'I certainly remember some of that,' Blackstone said. 'But I'd rather talk about the question of your "death". If you didn't kill anyone, where *did* you get the body from?'

'Dug him up from the graveyard,' Tom Yardley said. 'It wasn't difficult. He'd only been dead for two days, and the earth hadn't properly set.'

'You despoiled a grave!'

'I didn't like doing it, Sarge. It didn't seem right at first, an' I almost couldn't go through with it.'

Liar! Blackstone thought. 'But in the end, you managed to talk yourself into it,' he said aloud.

'That's right,' Tom Yardley agreed. 'I told myself that he was already dead, so whatever I did wouldn't hurt him. An' havin' known the man as he'd been in life, I didn't really think he was the sort of feller who would have begrudged me the opportunity to survive.'

'And once you had the stiff, the rest of your disappearing trick was easy, wasn't it?'

'Pretty easy, yes.'

Yardley packs the rock face with explosive – far too much explosive.

'I'm setting the fuse now, so take cover,' he says.

His crew disappear behind the closest pillars, as they normally do.

'Not there,' Yardley shouts. 'This is a bloody big charge I'm usin'. I want you at the very end of the gallery.'

Tom is the blaster. He knows what he's doing. The crew obey his instructions without question.

Yardley waits until they can no longer see him, then moves quickly to the tunnel. The corpse he has left there has been dead for two days. It has started to stink, and under the overalls he has dressed it in the maggots are probably already at work.

But neither of those things will matter. The overpowering stench of the cordite will easily cover the smell. And the force of the explosion will disintegrate the worms.

He carries the corpse to the rock face. This is the tricky part, because if any of his team chooses that moment to look around the pillar, the game is up. But none of them do – and why should they?

He lights two fuses – one running to the explosives on the rock face, the other to the explosives he has packed in the corpse's overalls – and

returns to the mouth of the tunnel.
'I'm going to light the fuse now,' he calls out,
then ducks into the tunnel. And because he has
timed it so perfectly, the explosion comes no
more than a second later.
When the air finally clears, all his men can
find is a few body parts that could easily have
once belonged to Tom Yardley – but didn't.

'Clever, wasn't I?' Tom Yardley said.
'I wouldn't go that far,' Blackstone told him.
'It was certainly a very *effective* plan – but it
wasn't very original. At best, it was no more
than a variation on a theme by Bickersdale.'
'You always were a bit poetic, Sarge,' Tom
Yardley said, sounding perhaps a little hurt.
'Bickersdale never tried to keep it secret from
his men that he'd got a fortune at the bottom of
his mine, did he?' Blackstone asked.
'He did not. He taunted us with it – the
bastard! I think part of the pleasure he got from
the money was knowing that we wanted it, but
daren't do anything about it.'
'You knew how to steal it, but not how to *get
away* with stealing it. You could have run, I suppose, but if you'd taken your family with you,
you'd have been easy enough to find. And you
didn't want to leave your family behind, now
did you, Tom?'
'I couldn't have done that,' Tom Yardley
agreed. 'I've got three beautiful little girls, an' I
love them to pieces.' He reached into his overall
pocket. 'I've got some pictures of them, if you'd
325

like to...'

'It's a pity you didn't think about *other* little girls and *other* fathers,' Blackstone interrupted.

'Oh, come on, Sarge, be reasonable,' Yardley said dismissively. 'They were nothin' to do with me.'

'Your "death" solved the immediate problem of Bickersdale looking for you, but there was still the problem of how you were going to be reunited with your wife and kids,' Blackstone said. 'Even though you were presumed dead, your family would have had to stay in the village, because Bickersdale would have been watching them all the time – in case they knew where you'd hidden the money. And if they'd moved, he would immediately have smelled a rat.'

'I wanted both my kids *and* the money,' Yardley admitted. 'That's not unreasonable, is it?'

'The more you thought about it, the more you realized that the only safe thing to do was get Bickersdale and his men out of the way altogether. And when you saw that article in the newspaper – the one about your old sergeant investigating the very crime that had its origins in this village – you could see just how to do it.'

'I thought it would be good for your career if you cracked this case, Sarge.' Yardley said.

'There was one grain of truth in the letter that you sent to me,' Blackstone said, ignoring the comment. 'You really *didn't* trust the local police. Because with that amount of money involved, how could you be entirely sure that

326

Bickersdale *hadn't* got them in his pocket? But you *could* trust good old Sergeant Blackstone. You knew that he was honest, and that once he'd got his teeth into something like this he wouldn't rest until he had a result.'

'Like when we were in Afghanistan together and—'

'You thought I'd be able to work out what was going on here for myself, but just in case I couldn't, you decided to give me a few pointers. But the first one – in the letter you wrote to me while I was in Staffordshire – sent me off on completely the wrong track.'

'Did it?' Yardley asked, surprised. 'Why was that? I thought I'd made it clear enough what I was on about by mentioning Fuzzy Dustman.'

'Faisal Dostam was a diamond-smuggler.'

'Was he?' Tom Yardley asked. 'I didn't know that.' He laughed. 'Well, I never! What a big difference there is between what gets discussed in the sergeants' mess an' what the ordinary soldiers talk about between themselves.'

'What do you mean?'

'There was you, thinkin' of Fuzzy as a jewel-smuggler, while to us lads in the barracks he was the feller who you went to if you wanted a whore.' He smiled fondly at the memory. 'An' what lovely girls he had workin' for him. Some of them couldn't have been more than twelve or thirteen, but they knew more tricks than any other prostitute I've ever been with.'

'You disgust me,' Blackstone said.

Tom Yardley seemed puzzled by the remark.

'Come on, Sarge, everybody's entitled to a little bit of fun now an' again,' he said.

'And after the letter that you signed there were the two anonymous notes you sent me,' Blackstone said, getting back to the point. 'Who delivered those notes to Walter Clegg's house, by the way? Was it Walter himself?'

'You certainly seem to think it was,' Yardley said evasively.

'Oh, I do,' Blackstone agreed. 'He might give the appearance of being an insignificant little nobody, but he played me like a violin. It was Walter who put the idea into my head that you'd been murdered. And it was Walter who first suggested that since Bickersdale's mine wasn't making any money, he must be involved with something else. He's been feeding me information all along – leading me by the nose until I'd done exactly what you wanted me to do.'

'How *did* you piece it all together?' Tom Yardley asked. 'I don't mean the Bickersdale part – I mean about me.'

'I was wondering when you'd ask that,' Blackstone told him. 'I knew from quite early on that it was someone connected with the gang who was sending me the anonymous letters.'

'How?'

'Because of the information they contained. The only people who knew that Huggins worked for Bickersdale were the members of the gang. And they were also the only ones who knew that the *Bluebell* would be used to transport the girl. So when I made the arrest, I was expecting one of the gang to be missing. And one of them was. You!'

'But you thought I was dead.'

'I thought that Bickersdale had had you *killed*. But once Robertson persuaded me that he hadn't, I started to ask myself how an explosives expert like you could have *accidentally* blown himself up. And, of course, he couldn't. Besides, dead men don't write anonymous letters.'

'You've been as smart as I expected you to be, Sarge,' Tom Yardley said. 'So what happens now?'

'Now, I arrest you.'

'But you can't do that,' Tom Yardley said, horrified. 'They'll hang me, if you do!'

'Very probably,' Blackstone agreed.

'Listen, Sarge, there's plenty of Bickersdale's money to go round,' Yardley said. 'We could both live like kings.'

'You think I'd take that money, knowing how it was earned?' Blackstone asked angrily. 'I don't want anything to do with it, you bastard!'

'No, of course you don't,' Yardley said hastily. 'I should never have insulted you by offering it.' A sly grin spread across his face. 'Anyway, if I'd thought about it, I'd have realized that it wasn't even necessary to try and bribe you, wouldn't I?'

'Would you?'

'Definitely. You won't turn me in. You could never bring yourself to do it, because you're under an obligation to me. And I know you: you take your obligations very seriously.'

'What particular obligation are you talking about, Private Yardley?' Blackstone wondered.

'Why, the obligation that comes from me havin' saved your bloody life, of course.'

The Pathan warrior is lying on the ground under the harsh Afghan sun. There's something not quite right about the bullet wound in his chest, but Blackstone can't work out what it is.

'Now the time's come for you to save mine,' Yardley continued. 'But it won't be a risk for you, like it was for me. You don't have to put yourself in the firin' line. All you have to do is step to one side while I make my escape. An' then we'll be even.'

Blackstone put both his hands into his pockets, and when he withdrew them again, each one was holding a pistol.

'This is Inspector Drayman's gun,' he said, holding the barrel of one of the pistols in his left hand, and offering the butt to Yardley. 'It's already killed one man today. Take it from me.'

'What's ... What's this about, Sarge?' Yardley wondered.

'Take it, Private Yardley!' Blackstone said. 'That's an order.'

Mystified, Tom Yardley took the gun.

'Now step back,' Blackstone told him, and when Yardley had retreated a few yards, he said, 'That's far enough.'

Yardley looked down at the gun in his hand. 'What's this for?' he asked. 'Why would I need

330

a pistol?'

'To protect yourself.'

'Who from?'

'From me. I'm going to arrest you. Your one chance of escaping is to shoot me.'

'But you've got a gun as well,' Yardley pointed out.

'That's true.'

'An' if I try to shoot you, you'll shoot at me.'

'True again,' Blackstone agreed. 'And I may even kill you. But consider the alternative.'

'The alternative?'

'You'll be sitting in your cell, one cold morning, and they'll come for you. They'll strap your hands behind your back, place a hood over your head and lead you through to the room next door.'

'Please, Sarge...' Yardley said.

'You'll be aware of something slipping over your head, and when you feel the touch of it on your throat, you'll realize it's a noose. You'll only have a few seconds to wait before they pull the lever, but it will seem like an eternity to you.'

'Why are you doing this?' Yardley moaned.

'Then you'll drop!' Blackstone said. 'The prison authorities like to claim that death is instant – but it isn't! It can take up to half an hour for you to die. Since you'll be unconscious, you're not *supposed* to feel a thing while you're slowly expiring, but we can't really be sure whether that's true or not, can we? Because the only person who really knows is in no position to tell us.'

'I don't want to shoot you, Sarge,' Yardley said. 'We're old comrades-in-arms.'

'So you have a simple choice,' Blackstone said, ignoring him. 'The *possibility* of a bullet now against the *certainty* of the rope later. I know which one I'd choose.'

Yardley looked down at his pistol again. The longer it was in his hand, the heavier it seemed to be weighing on him.

'And since you say I'm so much in your debt, I'll give you a more than sporting chance,' Blackstone said. 'I'll promise not to fire until you have.'

Yardley opened his hand, and the pistol clattered to the floor.

'I'm frightened,' he sobbed, hugging himself. 'I'm so very, very frightened.'

They stood side by side, next to the winding shed, and watched the police van coming ever closer. They could almost have been mistaken for friends, had it not been for the fact that one of them was wearing handcuffs.

The hysteria that had gripped Tom Yardley in the mine had drained away, and been replaced by a mood of passive despair. He had not spoken for some time, and it was only when the uniformed constables climbed down from the van and began to walk towards them that he said, 'It wasn't really loaded, was it?'

'What wasn't loaded?'

'The pistol you gave me down the mine. There

weren't real bullets in it, were there?'

The constables drew level with them. 'Has he been properly cautioned, sir?' one of them asked Blackstone.

The inspector nodded. 'Yes, he has.'

'Then we'll take him into custody, if you've no objections.'

'No objections at all.'

The constables each took one of their prisoner's arms and started to lead him away. When they gone no more than a few feet, Yardley came to a halt and looked over his shoulder. 'It *wasn't* loaded,' he screamed. 'Was it?'

'Come on, you, we don't want any trouble,' one of the constables said severely.

'Wait!' Blackstone said. 'I think there's something your prisoner needs to see.'

He took Inspector Drayman's pistol out of his pocket, released the safety catch and looked around for a suitable target. His eye fell on a tree just beyond the boundary of the mine. He sighted the gun, and pulled the trigger. There was an explosion and then the sound of a bullet thudded into the thick bark.

'I ... I really *could* have killed you,' Yardley said.

'Yes,' Blackstone agreed. 'You really could.'

'Then I don't understand how you could ever have thought of giving me the gun.'

'No,' Blackstone said, almost sadly. 'And being the man you are, you never will.'

Thirteen

The police property department in New Scotland Yard was a fairly large room, divided into two unequal parts by a waist-high counter and a meshed steel grill that ran from the counter to the ceiling.

The area behind the steel grill was the property sergeant's domain. In it there were a series of shelves on which evidence was stored for as long as it might be deemed necessary. Thus it was that bloody axes shared shelf space with bad cheques, and burglars' tools sat cheek by jowl with the jewellery those same tools had been used to steal.

The area in front of the grill – which could be accessed from the corridor – was smaller and much narrower. Here police officers waited while the sergeant produced the evidence that the prosecution service needed to make its case, and members of the public waited for property that had previously been impounded but could now be released.

It was to the property room that Patterson went after his debacle with the brothel madam and her solicitor, and there, too, that the madam made an appearance herself, some thirty minutes later.

Patterson was standing at the far end of the room when Miss Latouche entered the office, but – since corpulent policemen in fairly small spaces are very difficult to miss – she noticed him immediately. For a second it looked as if she were about to speak to him; then she tossed her head back disdainfully and turned towards the counter.

'Can I help you, madam?' the sergeant asked.

'You can give me what's rightfully mine, if that's what you mean,' the woman snapped at him.

'I'm sorry, madam?'

'You can hand me back the money which should never have been taken from me in the first place.'

Patterson said nothing. He'd guessed from the start that this woman would be greedy – that she'd not only want the money she'd had in her possession before he'd paid her the seventy-five pounds but would claim the police 'bait' money as her own as well.

She probably considered it no more than taking her rightful revenge on the police for what they'd tried to do to her, he thought – and he wouldn't be in the least bit surprised if, once she'd got the money in her hands, she didn't wave it at him contemptuously.

The duty sergeant grimaced at the way the woman had spoken to him, then said, in a very reasonable tone, 'Of course, madam. Right away. Could I just see your receipt first, please?'

'Bloody bureaucracy!' Miss Latouche said,

335

but even as she was complaining she was reaching into her purse for the document.

She laid the receipt on the counter, and the sergeant read it.

'Two hundred pounds!' he said. 'That's a great deal of money, madam.'

'Perhaps it is – to you!' The madam turned her head towards Patterson. 'But we're not all coppers, struggling to make ends meet, you know. Some of us are used to the better things in life. Some of us don't need to put cardboard in boots when they develop holes. Some of us don't even bother to take them to the cobbler's – we simply throw the boots away and buy new ones.'

The attack was being aimed mainly at him, Patterson realized, but if the madam also managed to offend the property sergeant in the process – as she clearly was doing – then she was not overly concerned.

'A little courtesy costs us nothing, madam,' the property sergeant said reprovingly.

'Now that – at least – even *coppers* can afford,' the madam said tartly. 'But we're not here to discuss good manners. You've still got my money – and I want it back.'

The duty sergeant turned and walked over to the shelves. Though he must have known exactly where the money was, he made a great show of checking several shelves before eventually returning to the counter with a metal box.

He opened the box, took out a thick envelope, and slid it – and the receipt – under the grill.

'If you wouldn't mind signing the back of the receipt, madam,' he said, indicating the pen and inkwell to her left.

'Certainly I'll sign it,' Miss Latouche said. 'As soon as I'm sure the money's all there.'

'I can assure you, madam—'

'I'd much rather assure myself.'

The madam opened the envelope and made a great show of counting out the white bank notes. When she laid them down on the counter again, Patterson stepped forward and swept them up.

'Here, what's going on?' the madam demanded.

Patterson fanned the notes out, like a magician performing a card trick.

'I'll need you to confirm for me that this is, in fact, your money, madam,' he said.

Miss Latouche gave him a look that was an uneasy mixture of hatred and triumph.

'Of course it's my money, Fat Boy.'

'In that case, I'd like to examine it more closely before it's handed over to its rightful owner.'

'Well, you can't!' Miss Latouche protested.

'I wasn't talking to you, madam,' Patterson said mildly. 'The remark was addressed to the property sergeant.'

'Then *you* tell him he can't,' the madam said to the man behind the grill.

The sergeant smiled.

'I'm afraid he can, madam,' he said, with not the slightest trace of regret in his voice. 'If you'd signed when I asked you to, the money would now be considered to have been returned to you. Since you didn't, it's still police evidence, and if Mr Patterson wishes to examine it, there's nothing I can do to stop him.'

The madam stamped her foot angrily. 'This is an outrage!'

'It's the law, madam,' the sergeant said.

Patterson peeled one of the notes off and held it up to the light. He placed that on the counter, took a second, and repeated the process.

'What in God's name are you doing?' the brothel-keeper demanded, as he reached for a third.

'I should have thought that was obvious,' Patterson replied. 'I'm examining the bank notes.'

'What's wrong with them?'

'There's nothing at all wrong with the ones I've examined so far.' Patterson paused for a moment. 'Ah, this *is* interesting!'

'What's interesting?'

'I've just noticed that the next few notes all appear to have exactly the same serial number.'

'But that's impossible!'

'Not if they're forgeries, it isn't.'

Patterson held one of the bank notes up to the light, and examined the watermark.

Gabriel Moore had been right when he'd said he was well past his best work, the sergeant thought. This was nothing like the high standard of counterfeiting he could have produced in his heyday.

'Would you mind telling me how you came

338

into possession of this forged bank note, madam?' he asked.

'Well, obviously, if it is forged then I'm an innocent victim of a forgery ring,' the madam said. 'Some member of the counterfeit gang passed the note off on me, and I never even noticed.'

'I suppose that could be possible,' Patterson agreed. 'If we arrested everybody who was in possession of a forged bank note, the gaols would be full to bursting.'

'Well, exactly,' the madam agreed.

'But when someone has more than one of the notes in his or her possession – and I believe you have seven of them – then that's stretching credulity just a little too far, don't you think? Anyone who had *seven* of them must be a member of the gang whose job it is to slip the notes into general circulation.'

'That's outrageous!' Miss Latouche said.

'And I must inform you now, madam, that the law takes a very dim view of such activities. Indeed, in sentencing terms, it tends to come down harder – much harder – on counterfeiters and their associates than it does on criminals whom I personally would consider to be guilty of much worse offences – those who deal in child prostitution, for example.'

'Are you saying that ... that...'

'I'm saying that, if convicted – and based on this evidence you're almost certain to be – you face the prospect of several years' hard labour.'

'You've planted that money on me!' the

madam screamed.

'How could I have done that?' Patterson wondered. 'These are the very same banknotes that my colleagues seized when they raided your house, and since then they have been here in the property room. I myself haven't touched them at all until a few moments ago, as the sergeant here will verify. Won't you, Sergeant?'

'Indeed I will,' the property sergeant agreed.

'You know very well what I mean!' the madam said. 'I'm not saying you switched the money *now*.'

'Then what are you saying?'

'That these notes you say are forged – the seven ten-pound notes – are the very ones you gave me when you came to my house.'

'I think you must be mistaken, madam,' Patterson said. 'The only money I gave you was a single ten-pound note.'

'That's not true!'

'And if you've forgotten that, madam – as you certainly appear to have done – then you need only read your own sworn statement to remind yourself.'

'You're fitting me up,' the madam said, with growing horror. 'You've had this planned all along.'

'You're certainly entitled to believe that, if you choose to,' Patterson said evenly. 'But once again, I must remind you that your sworn statement would seem to contradict your current claim.'

'Why are you doing this horrible thing to me?'

the woman asked, in tears now.

'I'm not doing *anything*, madam,' Patterson said. 'Or, at least,' he added with a smile, 'nothing that you can actually *prove*. But if you were to spread the word among your friends who share the gutter with you that you *believe* I've fitted you up – and that I'd be likely to do the same to them if they dabbled in child prostitution again – then there's certainly nothing I could do to stop you.'

Epilogue

London, Saturday

It was Saturday night, and the saloon bar of the Goldsmith's Arms was full of people who had worked hard all week and were now intent on having a damned good time. Blackstone looked around at them: at the flower girls who, having paid their weekly visit to the public washhouse, had completed their toilet for the next seven days; at the coster-mongers, who dreamed of one day owning their own barrows, but were resigned to continue renting until, some time in their thirties, they went to the great street market in the sky; at the dockers, who formed long queues at the dock gates before dawn, in the hope that a ship was due to land that day, and there would be work for them; at the car-men, who transported any-thing and everything all over London, and wor-ried that one day soon the internal combustion engine would replace their horses and carts; at the petty thieves and con artists, who picked pockets or talked the unsuspecting public into handing over a few pence; at the ex-boxers, who had fought in the Whitechapel Wonderland on their way up, and under railway arches on their way down...

'You seem happy enough to be back, sir,' Patterson said.

'I am,' Blackstone agreed.

And he really was, he thought. This was his city and, for all their faults and weaknesses, these were his people. And, though he had no idea when his death was to come, he hoped that when it did, he would be in London.

At the far end of the bar, a cabbie and car-man were involved in a loud discussion which threatened to eventually turn into a fight, but for the moment was no more than hot air.

'Know any good charities, sir?' Patterson wondered.

'I can think of any number of them. Why do you ask?'

'I've got a bit of spare money to get rid of. Seventy quid, as a matter of fact. And I thought I'd give it to something worthwhile.'

'You've got seventy pounds?' Blackstone asked, astonished. 'Where the hell did that come from?'

'Operational expenses.'

'Then if you haven't spent it, you'll have to give it back.'

'I can't exactly do that,' Patterson said. 'Not without admitting that the money I paid over to Miss Latouche was...' He paused. 'I don't really think you want to know the details, sir.'

'No, I suspect I don't,' Blackstone agreed. 'Let's change the subject. Quickly!'

'This case of yours can't have been easy on you,' Patterson said. 'I know we're supposed to enforce the law without fear or favour, but handing over the man who once saved your life...'

'You've never actually served in the army, have you, Archie?' Blackstone interrupted.

'Is that another way of saying you don't want to talk about what happened in Cheshire?' Patterson asked.

'Not at all,' Blackstone assured him. 'But before I *can* talk about it, I need to explain a few things to you.'

'Fair enough,' Patterson agreed.

'There's all sorts of positions a rifleman can adopt when firing his weapon,' Blackstone said. 'The British soldier is usually standing or down on one knee, but when the Pathan warrior has a choice, he prefers to do it lying down.'

'I see,' Patterson said, though it was clear that he didn't.

'Now, according to Tom Yardley, the Pathan was waiting for him outside the cave, and would have killed him if his rifle hadn't jammed. But it did jam, and Yardley shot him instead.'

'Wait a minute,' said Patterson, who was beginning to catch on to Blackstone's way of thinking. 'I thought you told me earlier that the Pathan was shot in the chest.'

'I did.'

'But if he'd been lying down...'

'Here's what I think happened,' Blackstone said. 'It was the *Pathan* who was coming out of the cave, and *Yardley* who was waiting in

345

ambush outside.'

'But that must mean...'

'It must mean that none of Yardley's story was true. He didn't kill the Pathans in the cave, as he later claimed he did. They were killed by Corporal Jones and Private Wicker, before they bought it themselves. What Tom Yardley did was cut and run.'

'But he did go back into the cave, didn't he?' Patterson said.

'Yes, he did,' Blackstone agreed. He reached into his pocket, and took out his gold watch. 'And I think the *reason* he came back was for this.'

'When did you come up with this theory of yours?' Patterson asked.

'I think it had been germinating for a long time,' Blackstone said, 'but it wasn't until I was down the mine that it really became clear. You see, I couldn't believe that any man could be both a hero and also involved with a monster like Bickersdale. That's why it took me so long to accept that Tom was a member of the gang.'

'But once you knew he was in the gang, the idea that he was a hero began to slip away?'

'Exactly. I began re-examining the incident in the cave in a new light, and finally saw what must have happened.'

'But you couldn't be sure, even then,' Patterson guessed.

'No, I couldn't,' Blackstone agreed. 'Good men do sometimes turn bad. But I don't think I've seen a brave man turn into a coward.'

'And that's why you gave him the gun?'

'Yes. He knew he'd hang if he didn't fire it, but even then, he didn't dare take the risk. Because this wasn't an ambush, in which he had the advantage. This was one man against another, on equal terms. And he was too yellow to take the chance.'

'You were taking a bit of a chance yourself,' Patterson said. 'There was always the possibility that he'd manage to kill you.'

'Yes, there was, but I had to be sure I was right about him – and not just for my own sake.'

'Then who else...'

'I went to Cheshire to pay a debt of honour. And I have. But the debt wasn't to Tom Yardley, as I'd thought. It was to Corporal Jones and Private Wicker, who might still be alive if he hadn't let them down.'

The argument between the cabbie and the carman had moved up a notch. Now the two men stood a clear three feet apart, and all the other drinkers had formed a wide circle around them, like spectators at a cock fight.

'Has the landlord called the police?' Blackstone asked the waiter.

The waiter nodded. 'Five minutes' ago.'

The car-man said something in an undertone which made his friends laugh loudly, but turned the cabbie's face red with anger.

'Don't just stand there, takin' his abuse!' an aging prostitute screamed at the cabbie. 'Be a man!'

The cabbie put his hand into his pocket, and

347

when he pulled it out again, it was holding a cut-throat razor. As he made a move to open the blade, two of the car-man's cronies jumped him, which caused two of the cabbie's cronies to jump *them*, and soon a full-scale fight had broken out.

'It's none of our business, sir,' Patterson said.

'Quite right,' Blackstone agreed. 'Let's leave it to the uniforms.'

But both men were already rising to their feet, more than willing to throw themselves into the fray.

Author's Note

The town of Northwich and village of Marston are real places, and in 1901 looked much as I describe them. The mining, and the geological disasters which resulted from it, are accurately depicted. The characters, however, are entirely fictitious, and though I have allowed Tom Yardley to live in the house where I was brought up, he is no ancestor of mine.